CHARGED

THE GROUNDED TRILOGY BOOK TWO

G. P. CHING

Charged, The Grounded Trilogy Book Two

Published by Carpe Luna, Ltd., PO Box 5932, Bloomington, IL 61704

www.carpeluna.com

First Edition: December 2014

Cover art by Christa Holland

www.paperandsage.com

v2.5

ISBN: 978-1-940675-13-8

BOOKS BY G.P. CHING

The Soulkeepers Series

The Grounded Trilogy

Soulkeepers Reborn

PROLOGUE

Dr. Emile Konrad was fascinated by pain. The delicious exhilaration as sharp silver approached unmarked flesh was one no drug could emulate. Was it the patient's widened eyes that made him sigh in contentment? Or something more? Fear, perhaps. He prided himself on the horrors within his black bag, capable of eliciting a response by sight alone. An increase in respirations, pallor, a bounding pulse. One must be careful at this stage not to cause hyperventilation. Nothing was as disappointing as a plaything lost to unconsciousness.

The Green Republic wanted information and therefore it was only natural Konrad not gag his patient, but in truth the doctor wouldn't have it any other way. He needed to hear the results of his handiwork, to see the bunching muscles and breathless torque of his subject. It was a disappointment when the patient gave up the goods too quickly. To do so would deny him the ultimate high—the scream.

Unfortunately, this patient had the spineless and weedy quality of a traitor. He'd have to savor the moment. The man's mouth hung open for one... two... three seconds before the shrill screech pierced the room. The corners of Konrad's mouth pulled toward his ears, and he inhaled deeply, the scent of blood enhancing the thrill. What a rush.

"Where is the girl?"

"I t-told you, I d-don't know." The man writhed against his bonds in a vain attempt at comfort, but the steel examination table was unforgiving.

"Let us review," Konrad said. "We have established that you are a member of the Liberty Party. Through an act of treason, you attacked CGEF in an attempt to gain control of the energy hub and overthrow the Green Republic. You did this in collusion with Korwin Stuart and Lydia Lane, who are now missing. Given the considerable talents of these two, I find it difficult to believe that you are unaware of their whereabouts."

"She came from nowhere," the man babbled in a rush. "Maxwell raised Korwin in the manor. We all knew him. But Lydia *appeared* one day. I don't know where she's from or where they are now. Maybe she took him back to wherever she came from."

"Hmmm." Konrad contemplated the revelation, stroking one stubbled cheek. According to the probes hooked up to the man, he was telling the truth. At least his chemistry said he was, and Konrad's equipment was nearly impossible to fool. Lydia's identification claimed she was from Willow's Province, yet there was no record of her birth and only a minimal paper trail linking her to a Lakehurst address in the middle of nowhere. Green soldiers had searched every inch of Willow's Province as well as Stuart Manor without gaining a clue to their whereabouts. They'd released flasher drones over the Outlands and in the most remote regions of habitable land. Nothing.

He must find Lydia and Korwin. Operation Source

Code, his life's work and greatest accomplishment, was permanently halted until he did. The loss of the beta specimens was intolerable, as unacceptable as the loss of the Alpha Eight. The deaths of David and Natasha had been a particularly hard blow, their bodies found burned beyond recognition in the wreckage of Lydia and Korwin's escape.

No, he must not allow this loss. Dr. Konrad selected a new tool from his black bag, a twisted, clamping implement that glinted in the overhead light. He lowered his thin lips to the man's ear. "You don't know the whereabouts of Lydia and Korwin, but you must know where the Liberty Party is currently organizing. Where should I look for the one who would know?"

The man gulped air in panic, staring at the sharp implement in Konrad's hand as it hovered over his breastbone. "A-all of the information about the Liberty Party—all of the members' names and addresses, the organizational charts— all of it is in a vaulted basement in Stuart Manor. Maxwell called it the Compound. The place was rigged to lock down if the manor was infiltrated."

Well now, finally a useful tidbit, although Konrad wondered how David had missed this fact while undercover. Certainly, as the butler, he would have been privy to such knowledge. Yet, what the patient said explained a vexing anomaly. When the Green Republic had arrested Korwin and Maxwell and taken control of Stuart Manor, Konrad thought it odd that Maxwell, a well-known albeit retired scientist, had no office or laboratory. A man of his many scientific pursuits would be expected to have a modest workshop for tinkering. A hidden compound made sense of the omission.

"Very good," Konrad said. "Your honesty will be rewarded."

The man blew out a painful breath. "You'll let me go?"

Konrad lifted an eyebrow. "In one way or another." Dr. Emile Konrad was fascinated by pain, but he could be merciful when a patient earned his mercy. Reverently, he returned the tool in his hand to his black bag before reaching for an oxygen mask beside the examination table. He strapped the mask on the man's face and turned the dial on the attached canister. It did not contain oxygen. The foggy mustard-colored contents flowed into the tube with a hiss. Slowly, the patient calmed, then closed his eyes, and eventually stopped breathing altogether.

"As promised," Konrad told the dead man. "An easy exit, I am sure you would agree." He patted the man's shoulder, then stood and reached for his phone.

Protocol demanded he call Pierce directly with any new information. Stuart Manor was now evidence and property of the Green Republic. But Pierce would want to follow procedure. Pierce would request the proper channels be followed to investigate the possibility of a hidden chamber. The man was becoming a bottleneck, too powerful for the Republic's good.

No. This job called for a special set of skills. He needed someone who wasn't afraid to break a few rules to get the job done. Someone who was properly motivated to succeed.

The phone rang against his ear. Seven times. It always rang seven times. As expected, when the call connected, no greeting whatsoever was offered.

Konrad didn't hesitate to speak into the void. "I have a job for you."

ONE

LYDIA

I AM CLOSEST TO GOD WHEN I'M SINGING. SOMETIMES, when I'm at the Sunday Singing and all lined up with Mary and the other girls, a lightness bubbles within, a kind of hopefulness about the world. All I think about is the warmth and joy in that barn, between my friends and me, my community.

"Lydia," Mary whispers. "I think Nathaniel is going to ask to drive me home."

I grin. A ride home from the Sunday Singing is a gesture of romantic intention, the start of courtship in our Amish community. "Will you accept?"

"Most definitely."

Reflexively my eyes drift to Korwin. He sits across from me, as is tradition in Hemlock Hollow. Girls on one side, boys on the other.

"You'll let me drive you home again tonight?" he whispers with a grin, folding his hands on the long wooden table.

"Of course," I say. It's expected at this point. We date every Sunday night, although I think Korwin prefers the Sundays we don't have service, which in Hemlock Hollow is every other week. On those nights, he comes to see me after my father goes to bed, and it's just us, sitting on the porch swing, talking about everything under the sun and moon. That's easier than this, where people still notice he's different. He still forgets words to the songs the rest of us have been singing our entire lives and makes the occasional faux pas, like calling someone's mother Mrs. or saying someone looks gorgeous when our deepest desire is to be plain.

Still, I'm proud of how far he's come. At first, he could barely stay awake through the three-hour service on Sunday morning. Waiting to eat lunch until the second seating, while the older members ate first, was a foreign concept to him. But he's stuck with it, even when the other boys haven't exactly made it easy for him. There's still a lot of people taking sides, thinking Korwin stole me from Jeremiah or some equally silly false sense of loyalty. It's made it harder than necessary, but still he persists.

"How did things go this week?" I ask him.

"Good. Threshing. I think I'm used to it now. No more blisters." He flashes his palms. "Working on my Pennsylvania German with Nathaniel. He's very patient."

"What about your baptism? Has Deacon Lapp mentioned a date?"

He doesn't answer me. Nathaniel leads off a tune from his end of the table and the others join in. It's a sloppy start. Laughter breaks out as we all try to sing the first verse. Korwin tries his best to sing along, but he doesn't know this one. When I glance in his direction, he smiles weakly at me.

During the next break, I take up talking with Mary about the Samuels' sick cow and miss talking to Korwin, who is in conversation with Jacob Bender. The Benders have always been progressive, and I hope the polite friendship grows deeper, for Korwin's sake. I can't remain the only one in his corner. Not forever.

It's after midnight by the time we finish the singing, and I say my goodbyes as all of us herd out to the buggies. Mary waves to me as she climbs into Nathaniel's buggy, face beaming. Next to them, Jeremiah is alone in his. He meets my eyes through the glass front, his horse waiting restlessly. Even in the inadequate moonlight, I can make out the silvery scar that runs from the outside of his left eye to his jaw. My fault, as are the scars I've left on the inside. I flash him a half smile, and he nods before clucking the horse into motion.

"Everything okay?" Korwin asks.

I stir from my guilt-ridden reverie and hop into the seat next to him. "Yes. Sorry. I'm tired, I guess. Can hardly keep my eyes open."

His mouth tightens as if he wants to say something, but he holds his tongue. Instead, he slaps the reins. The Lapps' horse breaks into a trot.

"I know this is hard for you, but if you keep participating, it will get easier," I say to Korwin. "It's just a matter of time."

He raises his eyebrows. "I think it's getting better. Jacob's been going out of his way to include me in things... conversations with the others. He even invited me hunting next weekend."

"That's great news."

"I'm good at threshing. Lots of folks say I'm a hard worker. Most folks."

"You are a hard worker," I say.

"Just a matter of time," he says.

"So, when does Deacon Lapp say you can be baptized?" Abram Lapp had been kind enough to take Korwin in when he came to Hemlock Hollow after escaping the Green Republic. But Abram had never been particularly warm with his charity. Most of the other candidates for baptism have already set dates, but Korwin is still waiting for the deacon's blessing, as if Abram holds him to a higher standard.

Korwin takes a deep breath. "He won't give me an answer. Honestly, he seems skeptical that I'm going to stay."

I scoff. "It's been almost a year! You've done everything he's asked you to, haven't you?"

"I have." He glances in my direction. "Don't worry about it. Jacob told me tonight that Abram is ultraconservative. He thinks he's probably testing my faith. I won't give up. I'll stick with it for as long as it takes."

"Maybe I could have Dad talk to him?"

"It's fine, Lydia. I don't want to be a whiner."

"It's me who's whining." I laugh. "We can't be married until you're baptized. I'm not sure I can wait."

"You?" He groans and looks at me mischievously.

We've done nothing more than kiss since returning to Hemlock Hollow. Physical relationships before marriage are considered sinful here. But it's becoming increasingly difficult to follow the rules. The attraction I feel for Korwin is more than hormones and chemistry. Our electrokinetic physiology draws us to each other like magnets. The force of it is difficult to refuse.

"The fireflies are exceptionally active this year," I say, changing the subject. Out the window, I watch a dance of blinking lights swirl above a freshly threshed field.

"My father always called them lightning bugs." His voice is soft, almost reverent.

"You miss him."

"Of course I do."

I don't like to think about Korwin's father. Inevitably, when I do, it brings up memories of the English world and how the Green Republic murdered Maxwell Stuart. I wasn't myself there. Everything good and pure about me was changed, used, abused by their way of life. I thank God for getting me out of there alive.

"It's a mating ritual," I say to lighten the mood. "The male firefly lights up his backside to attract a female."

Korwin grins. "Smart bugs. Does it work on humans?" He turns toward me and an electric blue glow fills the cab, beaming from his face and exposed forearms.

"Stop," I stage whisper, slapping his shoulder. "Someone could see." I search out the window to make sure there is no one behind us.

"Relax. We've been alone on this road for miles." He's barely got the words out when the buggy stops abruptly.

"What's going on?"

"I don't know. Daisy just stopped." Korwin snaps the reins, but the Lapps' horse only stomps her feet. He raises the reins again, but I place my fingers on his wrist.

"Wait." I jump out and walk to the horse's side. "Easy," I say as I place a hand gently on her flank. She bobs her head and snorts. The dappled gray mare cocks one foot off the packed dirt road.

"What's wrong with her?" Korwin asks, joining me at her side.

"I'm not sure. Something's bothering her though. She's not putting weight on this foot." I run a hand down her leg, and she picks up her hoof for me. Silver glints in the moonlight. "Korwin, do you have a hoof pick?"

"Yeah. The Lapps keep one under the seat." He jogs to the cab and returns a moment later, pick in hand. I take it from him and gently wedge the tip under the item, careful not to scrape the frog, the soft vee-shaped segment of the hoof, too aggressively. The offending object pops out and lands between us.

FLASH. Light blinds me. Daisy screams and rears. I scramble out of the way, arms wide. "Whoa! Whoa, Daisy."

Before I've registered what's happened, Korwin curses. I smell burning chemicals. When my eyes adjust, he's holding a mangled and melted piece of machinery in his hand. The thing looks like a dead spider—a scorched plastic body and eight jointed metal legs melted and curled into the abdomen.

"What is that?" I ask.

"A flasher. Lydia, this is bad."

"Why? What's a flasher?"

"This is a sophisticated piece of spy equipment. It *was* a mobile camera and transmitter. When triggered, it takes a picture of its surroundings and transmits it back to whoever is doing the spying."

For a moment, my face can't decide how to react to this information. My eyes twitch, and my mouth opens and closes in confusion. "How did it get here?"

"I've heard of the Green Republic doing this in the deadzone. They drop these things from drones. The pictures they get back tell them about the activity in the area."

"I've never seen one of these in Hemlock Hollow," I say, shaking my head. "This is new."

"They're looking for us," Korwin whispers.

"Do you think it saw anything?" The way it flipped out of the horse's hoof, the flasher was traveling away from us when it went off. I pray it photographed the night sky or the open field.

"I don't know, but I tried to destroy it before it could

transmit anything. Hopefully, if it did catch anything, the photo didn't go anywhere."

I check the horse, who is still huffing and stomping her feet. "We're lucky Daisy didn't bolt." I rub slow circles on her flank. "Easy. Easy, girl."

"Maybe we should tell your father about this." He frowns at the thing in his hand.

I recoil and shake my head. "No."

"They're not going to give up. The Green Republic can't tolerate us being alive and missing. They'll assume we've joined up with the Liberty Party, which means we are public enemy number one."

"It's not our problem." I climb into the buggy.

Korwin balks. "Not our problem?" He stares at me for a moment and then climbs in beside me.

"God will take care of us. He always has. Let the Englishers run themselves into the ground looking for us. I don't care."

"There won't just be one flasher," Korwin insists. "Even now, they could be peppered across the countryside. What if the Kauffmans come across one while threshing? What if a child finds one? What if the Green Republic learns that Hemlock Hollow is a thriving, organized community rather than a cage for sick and wild scavengers?"

I shake my head. "You've got to trust in God. He won't let that happen. He'll protect us."

"Maybe we are supposed to protect ourselves. We know about this. We have the knowledge."

"What are you suggesting?"

"Maybe we should tell the bishop."

"Are you mad? We'd have to explain what we are and why they're after us. The *Ordnung* would shun us, Korwin."

"Shun us. What's shunning?"

"Kicked out of the *Ordnung*. Sent packing. This type of thing would be the worst type of vanity. Some would think it was sorcery. They don't understand beyond the basics of science. We can't do this to them."

"But what if there's more?"

"I seriously doubt they are going to waste this technology on us. For all we know, it might have walked from the Outlands."

"Highly unlikely, but possible," Korwin says. "I just think we should do something."

I turn in my seat and glare at Korwin. "What exactly would you propose?"

He sighs and prods Daisy into motion. We ride in silence, his eyes vacant with thought. "If we can't tell the bishop, and you don't want to tell your father—"

"It would be a sin to worry him about this."

"Then we have to handle this ourselves. There's only one thing we can do," he whispers.

"What?"

"We search for flashers in the most populated areas. If we see any more, we know how big of a threat this is. Then we can decide what to do."

I nod. "Fair enough. And if we don't find any, we forget this ever happened and go on with our lives."

"Fair enough." We've arrived at my house. He pulls into the driveway and parks the buggy.

"What should I do with this?" he asks, retrieving the burnt flasher from the bin in the dash.

"Bury it. We can't allow anyone in the *Ordnung* to see it."

He slips it into his pocket with a nod, a silent promise to do the deed later.

With a deep sigh, I place one hand on his, an act that makes a tingle of energy flow from my fingers. "Do you want to sit on the swing for a while?"

He smiles, blinking slowly as if he's enjoying our connection as much as I am. "Wouldn't miss it."

Without hesitation, I slide from the seat and run for the front porch, laughing. He chases me, catching me around the waist and scooping me into his arms in order to carry me up the three stairs to the porch swing. He's just set me on my own two feet when a sound from the darkness chills me to the bone.

A man's voice rasps, "Well, well, well. Aren't you the loving couple?"

TWO

"David?" I squint into the darkness.

"The one and only."

My lips part on a swift inhale. "We thought you were dead."

He steps out from under the mulberry tree in my front yard, into a swath of moonlight. He looks older than I remember. Thinner. "Faking death was an important part of my escape plan. Having met Dr. Konrad, I'm sure you understand."

"Natasha?"

"Did not fair as well." His face is momentarily grim.

"I'm sorry. I'd hoped you'd given her the solution in time."

"Too far gone," he says.

I nod once. Memories of my time with David flood my head. He'd been responsible for Maxwell's and Korwin's arrests, and under the guise of training me, beat me to a pulp. For that, I hate him. But the confusing part is he also made me strong. He made me capable of escaping and saving Korwin. If it weren't for David, I wouldn't have known where the Greens were keeping Korwin or how to escape. All the same, I feel little warmth when I look at him, even having believed him dead a moment ago. His physical presence makes me squirm with unease.

"What do you want?" Korwin asks.

"To speak with both of you. You need to know what's happening on the outside."

Just then, the door behind me opens and my father's face appears. He scans the dark horizon before fixating on David. "Voices carry. Get inside." He seems as unhappy to see David as I am.

I lead the way inside and light the gas lamp above the farmhouse table. It flares to life with a hiss. As my eyes adjust, I'm able to make out David's formfitting navy blue uniform, made from the kind of material that maintains body temperature in any weather.

"Are you still working for the Greens?" I ask, blunt and accusing.

David pulls out a chair and sits down without breaking eye contact with me. "No." He crosses his arms. "Are you?"

"Of course not!"

"But you did before. I trained you."

"I was cooperating to save the people I love."

He leans forward, elbows on the table. "Exactly. You and I have that in common."

My bottom hits the chair across from him, and I scowl to think that I am anything like David, although I can't deny it.

"Now that we've cleared that up," Korwin starts. "How did you find us?"

"Lydia is a bad liar, and I have good ears. The argument you had with Maxwell when he kidnapped Jeremiah? I was standing in the kitchen. Why would you think I wouldn't hear? Not to mention, Hannah and Caleb work for the Liberty Party now."

"Did you share that with the Greens?"

"No. Despite what you think, there were several things I did not share with the Greens."

"And lots of things you did or my father wouldn't have been captured and killed," Korwin snaps.

"I had to give them something or they'd suspect my loyalty. I did not foresee that the Greens would separate Korwin from his father. Even I didn't know where they were keeping him in CGEF." David stops his harried words abruptly and runs his tongue across his upper teeth. He closes his eyes as if he's in pain. "I don't owe you an explanation. I did what I had to do."

"Saving yourself came first, huh?" I say.

He opens his eyes and fixes me with a pointed stare. "Saving my wife came first. I failed at it, too, in case you forgot."

The memory of Natasha's wasted body comes back to me, and I turn my attention to my clasped hands.

"Let's cut to the chase, David. Why are you here?" Korwin says.

My father nods and taps the table in agreement.

"Things on the outside have gotten worse since Maxwell's death. We think one of the rebels captured during the insurgency talked. We're worried Konrad's learned of the Stuart compound."

"Konrad's alive?" The last I saw him, he was twitching on the concrete in front of CGEF.

"Alive and as evil as ever. If he succeeds in accessing Maxwell's research, we're all doomed. Not only is the compound home to a wealth of classified information about the Liberty Party and its supporters, but the scientific knowledge about you two could help Konrad resurrect his research without you. We can't let that happen."

"Impossible," Korwin says. "Even if he knew the compound was there, he'd never get inside. The place is a fortress, and we left it sealed, physically and biologically."

I glance at my father and then at Korwin. I've never asked him what happened the night Stuart Manor was taken by the Greens. I never wanted to know the painful details. Like everything else in the English world, I've tried to bury it, to cast aside the memories as ancient history. My time in the English world pushed me beyond the limits of propriety, but that's all behind me now. It happened, after all, before my baptism, when all my sins were washed away.

"How can you be certain the compound was sealed effectively?" David asks. "I'd heard the Greens overtook the manor in minutes."

Korwin rubs his chin. "Dad had a panic button. When they broke through the gate, he executed emergency protocol. He locked down all entrances and exits. The Greens might figure out the physical key—the code is complex but not unbreakable—but the biological key is my father's blood, and that doesn't exist anymore. He's dead, or did you miss that news flash?"

David shakes his head. "I didn't miss it. I'm sorry for your loss. I'd hoped to get Maxwell out of there."

"Yeah, I'm sure you're all broken up about it." The look Korwin gives David could sear flesh.

"So, then there's no way in," I say, breaking the tension. "The compound is safe. You have nothing to worry about."

"There are ways," David says.

"Why do you care?" my father asks.

David groans. "Because Maxwell Stuart's basement office housed the only copy of the Liberty Party's organizational charts and all of the data about you two. Everyone involved, all of our plans, all of the research and tissue samples. Konrad has been systematically torturing the men captured during our botched rebellion with one goal." David narrows his eyes at me. "Konrad will stop at nothing to get his hands on you two."

"How many has he killed so far?" Korwin asks softly.

"Around fifty."

Suddenly, I feel nauseous. My stomach twists, and I fold my arms around my middle. "That's awful. I don't understand. They hit us with a rocket. With all the rubble, I thought they presumed we were dead."

"They did, at first. But then they sifted through all of the rubble and didn't find you. Your DNA was not among the dead. Mine was, only because Natasha died in my arms, and I'd made careful preparations to ensure my DNA was with her."

My mouth drops open.

"Do you think they'd let you go so easily? You two were Konrad's most prized possessions—the hope to resurrect Operation Source Code. And you, Lydia, you are a one-woman army."

"What is that supposed to mean?"

"I programmed you myself. You are an expert in hand-to-hand combat, weapons, stealth operations. You know things about the Greens that could do some serious damage."

I shake my head. "No, I don't. Sure, I learned to fight. I shot a gun. But I hardly remember any of it."

"Oh, you'll remember when you need to remember." Guile oozes from his half-baked smile, and he crosses an ankle over his opposite knee in a way I find haughty.

"What did you do to her?" Korwin asks between clenched teeth.

"He injected me with something," I whisper.

Korwin glares at David. "Tell me it wasn't Nanomem."

David's jaw shifts, and he glances at the table.

"He told me it was a supplement mixed in with my painkiller that helped me remember our training." I glance between Korwin and David.

Korwin sighs. "Nanomem is a controversial technology."

"Technology? You told me it was a supplement, like vitamins." I look pointedly at David.

"I never said it was like vitamins."

"How does it work?" I ask Korwin.

"Nanomem is a serum containing biological memory via nanotechnology. The cells he injected into you attached to your nervous system, and the proteins inside those cells fed information directly into your head. It is fairly close to how someone might program a computer, but on a biological level."

My father's face screws up, and he taps the table with his open palm. "Are you saying that Englishers can put memories into our heads? I've never heard of such a thing."

David leans toward him. "Yes, that's exactly what I'm saying. Inside your nervous system, there are cells called neurons. When you experience something, you remember it because your body forms synapses or connections by creating special proteins associated with memory. Nanomem is a serum created by copying the memory proteins from one person and injecting them into another. Those false memories attach themselves and form new synapses in the person's brain. Phantom memories."

I take a deep breath. "I have someone else's memories inside my head?"

"Mine, to be exact," David says. "I needed a way to ensure what I knew made it out of CGEF. I might have died helping you escape. You were my hope for the rebellion. All my military experience is in your head."

A laugh parts my lips and I glance from David to Korwin and back, waiting for the punch line. "This must be a joke. I assure you, I do not have your memories inside my head. I think I would know."

In a blur, David seizes a long silvery object from his pocket and hurls it toward my face. I snatch it from the air and whip it back in his direction. It barely misses his head. Only after he catches it, and thumbs a button on the side, do I register that it is only a flashlight. The entire exchange occurs in two blinks of an eye, as if we'd practiced it all day.

I grip the sides of my chair as my limbs begin to shake. "What have you done to me?"

"I imagine you haven't had much use for what I've given you living here, but believe me, it will be there when you need it."

Korwin slides his chair back and rises to put an arm around my shoulders. My father has gone stone still, mouth an angry slash.

"You mentioned side effects," my father mumbles.

Korwin nods. "The serum is outlawed in the English world, which is why you've never heard of it. It was tested on university students a few years back, and there was a higher than average rate of psychosis among the test subjects. What David isn't telling you is the technology can't differentiate well between memories. Inevitably, other stuff comes through. Imagine taking a test in history and suddenly remembering being shot during the Great Rebellion or having a leg blown off by a landmine. That's the kind of stuff that was happening to people."

"You." I glare at David. "You are cruel. You knew this and injected me anyway?"

David stands and paces toward the sofa. "If I hadn't, you would have never been able to escape CGEF with your family in tow." He points accusingly at me. "I did you a favor. I saved your goddamned life."

My father is on his feet, staring at David in an oddly aggressive way. "You will not use the name of the Lord in vain in my house, David. I don't care who you are or who you've saved."

David's shoulders slump. "My apologies."

"Get to the point. Why are you here?"

"The Liberty Party needs your help," he says. "What remains of the leadership have organized a rebel base inside the reactor."

"The nuclear reactor?" Korwin asks. "What about the radiation?"

"The reactor was salvaged using a new technology after the meltdown. It's completely habitable now. Why do you think everyone in the preservation isn't glowing green?"

Korwin runs both hands through his hair.

"We can't reignite the rebellion without you." David hammers the table with the side of his hand. "The Green Republic has created a hostile environment, and the Liberty Party doesn't stand a chance without a secret weapon like the two of you. We need your help."

I shake my head. "It's not our problem."

"Are you serious? Don't you think they'll eventually look for you here? It's only a matter of time, Lydia, before there's no place else to look."

The memory of the blackened flasher rolls through my

mind, and I lower my eyes from David's. The Greens have already started looking here. I won't give him the satisfaction of sharing that particular detail. Besides, it's more than likely an isolated incident.

"I think you should leave," my father says.

Korwin stands, folding his arms across his chest. "We're not interested."

David doesn't move until I stand and frown in his direction. "Leave now. I don't want any part of your rebellion."

"You don't know what you're saying."

"Go," I say again, and this time I walk to the door and open it. In the wee hours of the morning, the sounds of crickets and cicadas float in on the night air.

David sighs and walks through the door. "I can't force you. Jonas says you had an *agreement*." He's talking about the deal we struck to take down the reactor in exchange for our freedom. I'm relieved Jonas is honoring it. He points to the reactor behind the wall in the distance. "You know where to find me if you change your mind."

"I won't change my mind," I say.

With a shake of his head, he slips down the porch steps and blends into the darkness.

THREE

"MAAM AND I PASSED BY YOUR PLACE LAST WEEK. THE celery in your garden is coming along nicely. Are you excited?" Mary whispers to me as our needles dive and pull through the layers of fabric stretched out before us. We sit next to each other on hard wooden chairs in the main room of Ruthie Mae's house amongst the chatter that always accompanies a quilting bee.

Celery is the quintessential ingredient in about a dozen wedding dishes. Every Amish mother knows to plant extra celery in her garden the May before her daughter's marriage. Our weddings are in November, after autumn harvest, so it's natural for the Samuels to take notice of my extra planting as a harbinger of things to come.

"I just hope it's warranted. Otherwise, creamed celery every night for dinner." I raise my eyebrows at her.

"Why wouldn't it be?" She laughs. "I thought Korwin already asked you and had your father's blessing."

"Deacon Lapp hasn't approved Korwin for baptism."

"Approved?" Mary asks, pausing her stitches. "He's been in the prebaptismal classes since May. He should be ready by August, yes?" Her words are too loud and the other women at the bee stop their sewing and stare in our direction.

Old Ruthie Mae Yoder, Jeremiah's paternal grandmother, raises her ancient, yellow-rimmed eyes from her work to lock with Mary's. "Got to be sure he's ready to commit," she says. "Needs proficiency in Pennsylvania German and to demonstrate an ongoing knowledge and respect for the *Ordnung*."

"Pennsylvania German?" Mary snorts. "These days, it's more important to speak like an Englisher than Amish."

I nudge her with my elbow. "His Amish is very good. Almost as good as mine," I say. "And he's demonstrated his commitment for almost a year."

"Outsiders always struggle to keep the rules," Ruthie Mae says. "Too easy for him to go back. Abram is right to wait." She lowers her eyes to her quilting and says in a bitter, biting voice, "Too many people changing minds these days."

I stare at her for a moment, sifting her words like grain through my fingers. Does she mean Hannah and Caleb? How they went on *rumspringa* and never came home? No. Korwin and I came back. We proved we wanted to be here. This is about something else. My body stiffens.

"Are you referring to Jeremiah and me?" I ask. My words are soft and respectful but have a slight edge.

She purses her lips. "That would be one example of the indecision of youth."

"Ruthie Mae, there was nothing to be indecisive about. Jeremiah never courted me."

"Seems you did enough together since the time you were small. Sometimes you've got to judge a thing by actions, not words."

My hands tremble. Ruthie Mae, as one of the eldest in our *Ordnung* and cousin to Abram Lapp, has the deacon's ear. She is also Jeremiah's grandmother. She could easily be the reason for the delay. Why hadn't I considered this before? "Actions? Jeremiah never offered me a ride home from the sing. Never kissed me."

"I recall you holding hands a number of times." Her foggy blues glare at me.

Shrugging, I try to hold back but can't. My next words come heated. "I recall many people holding hands without courting or marrying." I stop sewing. My last stitches are uneven, and I lay my needle down, folding my hands in my lap.

"Perhaps Jeremiah was waiting for the right time. A good man waits until a girl is ready to be a wife and mother."

That sets me off. How dare she suggest that I wasn't ready last year? If anyone wasn't ready, it was Jeremiah, who wanted to go on *rumspringa* before he settled down. I didn't even want to go. "God's ways are often unknown to us," I say. "But I thank Him for bringing Korwin and me together as Korwin is a blessing to this *Ordnung* and to me."

"Maybe. Won't hurt to wait another year to be certain though. God's ways as mysterious as they are. I suppose it was God's will that Jeremiah be born with the face of an angel, and also God's will that he be scarred by the devil. Mmmhmm, only time will heal old wounds."

Not only is she blaming me, the *devil*, for Jeremiah's scar, she's suggesting that I've wounded him and should not be allowed happiness while he suffers alone. My jaw unhinges to tell her there are plenty of girls in Hemlock Hollow who would be interested in Jeremiah, scar or no scar. But then, out of the corner of my eye, I catch electric blue worming under the skin of my thumb in my lap. The tingle is back. Sweat breaks out on my forehead from the effort to contain my power. I am dangerously close to breaking a glow in the dim room. I push my chair back and rush from the room.

"Lydia?" Mary calls.

I'm out the door in a flash, bent over and panting in the gravel driveway. The blessed sun shines down masking my glow, but I can tell it's there, just under the surface. Since our return to Hemlock Hollow, Korwin and I have practiced controlling our abilities. The first time we kissed, we almost blew up the basement garden of Stuart Manor. Now, we can kiss without raising our body temperature. This is the first time in months my electrokinesis has gotten away from me, but then I don't recall ever being so angry. A year? Another year? It may not be much to Ruthie Mae, but it's plenty to Korwin and me.

The door opens and Mary stumbles down the steps to where I'm bent over with my hands on my knees. "Are you okay?" she asks, rubbing my back.

"I think so," I say. The tingle retreats with each deep breath. "Ruthie Mae is being cruel. I can't believe she said that to me."

Mary removes her hand from my back and crosses her arms over her chest. "I love you, Lydia, but you must know she's not the only one."

I straighten and turn toward her. She takes a seat on the porch steps. "Still?" I ask.

"It's not just that everyone expected you to marry Jeremiah. Korwin is different."

"Of course he is. He grew up English. It's just going to take some time for him to adjust."

"He can't grow a beard," Mary blurts. "Nathaniel told everyone Korwin hasn't shaved since he got here."

"He-he has a medical condition," I sputter too quickly.

"But a beard means something here, Lydia. He's never going to look... married."

"It doesn't bother me," I scoff. "Our way of living and commitment will be proof enough of our marriage."

"Sometimes he tempts people."

"Tempts?" Her statement befuddles me. As far as I can tell, Korwin has bent over backward to follow the rules.

"He was dancing and whistling a worldly tune while he cleaned out the stable last week."

Ack. I shake my head. "I bet he stopped as soon as someone called attention to it. I'm sure it was subconscious. Obviously, he is no stranger to hard work."

"You have to remember, Lydia, he's a man. He could be called to lead once he's married. They won't baptize him if they don't think he could minister if it were God's will."

"He could do it. He's smart and kind. Besides, isn't that the point of believing in God's will? If God chooses him, He will make him ready."

She tips her head and hits me with the accusation I can tell is the best in her arsenal, the one she's been holding back for when I wouldn't listen to reason. "He struggles with vanity."

Now I'm offended. I pop one hip out and narrow my eyes at her. "Mary Samuels, there is nothing vain about Korwin."

Raising her chin, she refuses to back down. "He's been painting. Got Elizabeth to bring him back art supplies from the outside. He hides them in the Lapps' barn loft, but Nathaniel's seen what he's done."

"No."

"Nathaniel didn't say anything to his father, but he warned Korwin to stop. Told him he'd have to give it up once he's baptized."

"It's a minor offense," I say, although I have no idea if that's true. Painting itself isn't a problem. Our order paints their houses and barns. But painting something to hang on the wall would be considered inviting pride. We strive for humility, to be plain. Art could be a way to attract attention or compliments or as a source of self-satisfaction. "How many paintings? What of?"

"I don't know. I haven't seen them," Mary says.

I shift my hips and tilt my head.

"But Nathaniel told me on the ride home from the sing. He's trying to help Korwin. Said he wouldn't tell anyone if Korwin stopped and got rid of the paintings."

But he told you, I think. Gooseflesh breaks out across my arms despite the warm weather. People in Hemlock Hollow are experts at discussing others' sinfulness. I wonder how far the rumor has traveled and what damage it's done.

"I have to see." I grab my bicycle from where I've left it near the house and start riding toward the Lapps' barn, which is more than a mile away from Ruthie Mae's.

"I'll come with you," Mary says, mounting her own.

I nod once. We set off in silence, without saying goodbye to the others, although I know I'll hear about leaving the quilting bee early when the news gets back to my father. It would be a beautiful day for a ride, if not for the worry that Mary is telling the truth and the silence that stretches between us.

In the English world, Korwin painted as a hobby. He had a studio full of art, mostly colorful depictions of animals. I should have foreseen this. I should have warned him that he couldn't continue his hobby in Hemlock

Hollow. Although, the fact he hid it in the barn means on some level he understands the shame of it. I'm sure I can get him to stop, or redirect his talent to painting in an acceptable way—furniture and walls.

"Upstairs," Mary says.

I climb the ladder to the haymow. As soon as my vision tops the highest rung, I gasp.

"What's wrong?" Mary asks.

"We shouldn't have come here," I say. "Don't come up. I don't want you to see this."

Climbing onto the platform, I approach Korwin's makeshift art studio. It's worse than I'd expected.

Mary gasps when she sees. Obviously, my warning was in vain because she slides into the space next to me, jaw dropping.

Every portrait is of me. Me in his buggy, the light filtering in from behind my *kapp*. Me milking Hildegard, my cow. Me quilting. This is a big deal, an obvious and disturbing infraction. The second commandment repeats itself in my head. *Thou shalt not make to thyself a graven image, nor the likeness of anything that is in heaven or in the earth beneath.*

My gaze darts around the loft, landing on a bag in the corner. A brief inspection reveals Korwin's paint and supplies.

"Help me," I say, handing Mary a brush.

"What do you want me to do?"

"No one can see these. Paint over them. All of them. Make them as black as night."

She nods her agreement, and we get to work.

FOUR

"WHAT HAVE YOU DONE?"

Behind me, Korwin stares from the top of the ladder. I don't know how long he's been there, but Mary and I have finished and all six canvases are now slate black. I turn to face him and the hateful look he gives me makes me drop the paintbrush in my hand. My lips part but I don't know what to say.

"She's saving you," Mary answers for me. She raises her chin. "What you've done is sinful. This isn't allowed here."

"Sinful?"

"You've painted her image. Not only is this a source of pride for you, it tempts Lydia to vanity. I could hardly keep my eyes off of it. How is she supposed to? It's wrong and immodest." She sounds condescending, and I quickly try to ease the tension.

"It's not your fault, Korwin. I'm sure you didn't realize what you were doing was wrong, but this goes against the law of our *Ordnung*. It breaks the second commandment. You can't paint here. Even if it wasn't prideful, it's considered impractical and a waste of time."

Korwin's stony gaze peruses the canvas nearest me, the one that used to be of me in his buggy drinking hot chocolate. Truth be known, it was my favorite of them all, and the most tempting. I struggled to paint over it.

"I know it is against your rules," Korwin murmurs. "Nathaniel told me."

"Then why didn't you stop? Why didn't you destroy them?"

"Because it's a stupid rule, and it's wrong."

Mary gasps and all of the breath is squeezed from my lungs. In silence, I wait for him to take it back, to say he understands and will comply with the rules. But he doesn't.

Slowly, deliberately, I shake my head. "Korwin, no. You just don't understand. In time, you'll see this isn't important."

"It's important to me." His hazel eyes burn, and there isn't a hint of humor in his expression.

"They won't baptize you if you refuse to give it up."

He shifts his straw hat back on his head and rubs his eyes with his thumb and forefinger. "How is it different from quilting? Quilting is art."

Mary huffs. "They're not the same at all. A quilt isn't an image to idolize. It isn't a representation of a person or a distraction from God. It's something you use to stay warm. Quilting is work."

Korwin places his hands on his hips. "All I hear is that you have an acceptable way to be creative and I don't." He scowls. "Mary, if the quilts are just to keep you warm, why isn't the material all the same color? How come you girls sew them in pretty patterns?" He circles his finger as if tracing the rings on a double wedding ring quilt.

"The patterns are traditional. Each has a meaning and we finish the quilts as a community," I say.

"Right. It's okay because you all do it," Korwin says sarcastically. He rolls his eyes.

"When you came here, Korwin, you promised to follow our rules. We have rules for good reasons."

He crosses his arms and steps toward the canvas. "What if I want to remember you just as you are, today? I can't take your picture."

"Why do you need to remember me? I'm right here."

"Once I'm baptized and we're married, we'll be caught up in family and farm. It will never be like this again. I want a remembrance of this."

"It's not supposed to stay like this," I say softly. "Things change. People change. The only thing permanent is God. That is why we keep our focus on Him and practice piety and hard work. "

Mary backs me up. "Everyone falters. That's why we help each other to do the right thing."

Korwin's eyes shift toward her. "Am I supposed to say thank you?"

Even I can hear the venom in his words. "Korwin..."

He rolls his neck and gives me a hard look.

"You'll understand when you're one of us and have learned what we know. It won't be so hard once you finish classes and get baptized. It's just the way it is," I say.

"We'd better get back, Lydia," Mary says, frowning. "I think Korwin needs some time alone to think about his actions."

After one last disappointed glance toward Korwin, I follow Mary down the ladder.

"Get rid of them, Korwin," I whisper in my kindest voice, paused on the top rung. "It's a worldly trapping. Cast it aside."

I'm disheartened when he looks away from me, toward

the black canvases, with nothing even close to an acknowledgment.

* * *

THE REST OF THE WEEK GOES BY IN A RUSH, USHERED away on days spent managing the farm while Dad and the other men do the threshing and put up hay. Our garden is exceptionally fruitful for July and I've already started canning peas and green beans. Mary often helps me, and I return the favor, even though my help is hardly necessary given her large family.

After a day of canning at the Samuels' home, I detour to Bishop Kauffman's, the weight of Korwin's transgression weighing my shoulders. In my soul, I know if he is baptized his doubts about this life will melt away. Once we are together, he'll be too busy building a life with me to worry about painting. I blush as thoughts of being with Korwin come to me—to be able to kiss and touch without guilt or limits. November seems like an eternity to wait. I have to ensure it isn't longer.

"What brings you here, Lydia?" Bishop Kauffman says when I enter the barn where he does his woodworking. He does not stop sanding the top of a headboard he's working on, what will likely be a new bed for one of the couples getting married this November. A sudden longing fills me. I want the bed to be mine.

"Can we have a talk? About Korwin?"

"What type of talk?"

"An important one."

He stops sanding and turns his bearded face toward me. "Is this a confession? Private confessions should be made to one of the deacons."

"No. Not a confession," I say. "I come to you as family and because I trust you."

"Ack, my Katie is better at personal advice than me. Do you want me to get her?"

I shake my head.

He pulls over a crate and sits down, spreading his hands and waiting for me to begin.

"At the quilting bee yesterday, Ruthie Mae said something to me, and I want to ask you about it."

"What'd she say?"

"She said...well, she implied that Korwin won't be baptized in August with the rest of the candidates because Deacon Lapp thinks he isn't ready. But when I confronted her about this, she let on that there was more to the deacon's decision than Korwin's readiness. She said 'too many people changing minds these days.' I think she might be angry that Jeremiah and I didn't end up together. Maybe Deacon Lapp believes Korwin could change his mind about Hemlock Hollow or I will change my mind about Korwin. Regardless, it weighs heavy on my soul that judgments about me might keep Korwin from God or his proper place in our *Ordnung*."

He rubs his calloused palms on his thighs. "I was afraid this might happen."

"You were?"

"Folks liked the idea of you and Jeremiah."

"But... we weren't courting or published."

He nods. "I reckon there are two types of folks in Hemlock Hollow—those that embrace the new ways and those who cling to the old."

"New ways?"

"You're too young to think of them as new. Let's just say, as much as things have stayed the same around here, we've also changed. There are folks... more than a few... who think we are much too dependent on the Englishers and all too accepting of their ways."

I furrow my brow. "I don't understand. We live behind a wall. We rarely see the outside world."

"A few think we should lock the gate and never go out again."

"What if someone got sick?"

He ran a hand through his beard. "God's will."

It's hard to believe anyone would be ignorant enough to think we'd never have a justifiable reason for visiting the Green Republic. Clearly, those folks who do have a different understanding of right and wrong than me. It dawns on me that the bishop is sharing this information for a more personal reason than bettering my understanding of *Ordnung* politics.

"Korwin is from the outside. He's an Englisher. What must they think of him?"

Bishop Kauffman nods. "Folks had it in their heads about you and Jeremiah. His family feels cheated. He shows no interest in anyone now, and they think the scar on his face will keep others from being interested in him."

"There are people who want Korwin to leave," I say as understanding seeps in. "They think I ruined Jeremiah. It's not true. Many girls find Jeremiah an attractive man, with or without the scar."

He snorts. "No. You didn't ruin him. He'll get to know an available girl. Korwin, though, seems he's sufferin' the consequence of a sin he didn't commit."

My mind flashes to the paintings, to the sin Korwin *did* commit, but I do not mention them. Instead, I keep the conversation focused squarely on what I feel is the problem at hand. "For certain. Ruthie Mae says she thinks Korwin and I should have to wait until next year to be married, but such a long courting is too much temptation. I'm eighteen now, as of April, and my father has given his blessing. You know Ruthie Mae has the deacon's ear."

"And Abram is probably dragging his feet on the baptism to appease her."

I nod once.

He sighs. "What do you say 'bout I talk with Korwin and if he expresses a desire and readiness to commit to the *Ordnung*, I will discuss this with Abram and see what can be done?"

"Yes, please. Thank you. Thank you," I say, feeling like my heart will explode with gratitude. I stand, moving toward the door. "I won't take up any more of your time. Excuse my interruption."

"Lydia?"

"Yes."

"Do you truly believe Korwin is ready?"

"Of course! I wouldn't ask you about it if I didn't."

"Good. Because in our world, behind the wall, all we have is each other. Now that you've been to the English world, I'm sure you realize how detrimental it would be for us to allow an outsider in who wasn't fully committed. Our lives depend on our law."

"Our lives depend on our law," I repeat, nodding my agreement. "He's ready. He's committed. Korwin will never go back to his old life."

Bishop Kauffman smiles and slaps me on the shoulder. "Now, we both have work to do." He picks up his sandpaper.

I slip from the barn, anxious to get home and start dinner for my father.

FIVE

"Lydia! Frank! Come quickly!"

The harried cry comes from the road outside our farmhouse, and I wipe my hands on my apron before scrambling for the door. My father is quick on my heels, not even bothering to put on his hat. At the end of our drive, Jacob Bender turns a dark horse in tight circles, kicking up pebbles. His face is as pale as the sky behind him.

"What is it, Jacob?" I yell.

"Bishop Kauffman. He's d-dead!" Jacob sobs.

"No," Dad says. "How?"

"Come to the farm. The family is there praying with Katie."

Dad and I nod, and Jacob takes off toward the next farm.

"I'll hitch up the horses," my father says.

I jog into the house, remove the beans I have warming on the stove for dinner, and grab my father's hat. By the time I'm out the door, Dad has the buggy ready to go.

We ride to the Kauffmans' place in silence, night creeping in like a toxic fog. I replay my last conversation with John Kauffman in my head. He did not look thin or pale. In fact, his skin had a healthy, ruddy glow from his work. Sure, he was older than my father—gray bearded—but always healthy and active. How could he have died? Was he killed in a farming accident?

The yard in front of the Kauffmans' house is filled with visitors, so I tie our horse on the side of the lane. Solemnly, my father walks with me to the house where we join our cousins in the crowded space. That's when I see John Kauffman's body. He's been laid out on a narrow bed at the back of the room, a quilt covering him to the shoulders. I hug my way into the room, comforting each person I greet as best I can.

The whisper among the crowd is "heart attack" and I gather this was Doc Nelson's assessment. Most of the talk, though, isn't about how he died but how he lived and the sure and certain hope of his salvation. People cry and hug and make arrangements to keep Katie and her three children in meals. John's boy is too young to work the farm and Isaac Bender and his son, Jacob, volunteer to help.

And then I see Korwin.

"I'm so glad you came," I say. "It's horrible. Have you heard what happened?"

Korwin frowns and steps in close to me, lowering his voice. "I was the one who found him."

I widen my eyes, desperately wanting more details, but it isn't appropriate here. Already we are the target of pointed stares, standing too close and whispering too quietly for a public gathering. I lower my eyes and angle my body away from him. Mary is there and gathers me into her arms.

Korwin whispers, "Tonight."

* * *

Wide awake, I lie in bed, waiting for Korwin. I stare out my window, wondering what the future holds for Hemlock Hollow. John Kauffman was a true man of God, gentle and kind. He handled all things with judicial integrity and courage. It wasn't just that he upheld the *Ordnung* but that he seemed to understand when to break the rules and when to stick to them. He was my father's cousin, but I loved him like an uncle. His loss is an iron cage of grief I fear I will never escape.

In our *Ordnung*, the bishop, deacons, and preachers aren't elected like leaders in the English world. Any baptized male can be nominated by anyone in the congregation. Those with three or more votes become candidates. Someone will hide a Bible verse in one of the hymnals and then each of the candidates randomly selects one of the bound books. The one who draws the hymnal with the verse in it is named to the role. It's completely up to God, and God's will can have big consequences.

Clink. A pebble hits my window and I pop up. A Korwin-shaped shadow waves at me through the foggy glass. Still in my dress, I don't bother with shoes, but creep from the dark house and join him under the mulberry tree in my front yard. I wipe under my eyes, but there are no tears left to cry.

"Thanks for meeting me," he says.

"What happened today? You said you were there when John Kauffman died?"

"He came to see me at the Lapps'."

A chill courses through me, although the night is warm and there is nary a breeze over the cornfield behind us. "What did he say?"

"He came to talk to me about my baptism. He asked me if I felt ready. Carried on the entire conversation in Pennsylvania German. I think he was testing me."

I squeeze my eyebrows together over my nose. "How did it go?"

"He asked if we could walk in the field behind the Lapps'. Said the fresh air would do us good. You know how he could never hold still."

"Sure."

"Well, I answered his questions best I could, and he said he thought I was ready to be baptized."

"He did?" I give a small smile despite the knowledge that the story does not have a happy ending. "But then when did he become ill?"

Korwin takes a deep breath. "We came across another flasher in the field."

I inhale sharply. Korwin and I have kept an eye out during our regular chores and have not seen another one. We thought we were safe. "Did it go off?"

"It did. While the bishop was leaning over it. I told him not to. I told him it looked dangerous, but he didn't listen to me." Korwin removes his hat and holds it in front of his waist. His lip trembles slightly. "I had to fry it," he murmurs. "You know I did. I couldn't let it transmit his picture."

An image of John electrocuted passes through my mind, and I take a step back. All the blood rushes from my head. I wobble and brace myself on the tree trunk.

Korwin holds up his hands. "I didn't hit him." He sounds offended. "But between the flasher and the lightning, it must have been too much for him. He grabbed his left arm, said it hurt. He wasn't feeling well. I helped him back to the house, all the way trying to explain the possibility of heat lightning. I needn't have. He died in the Lapps' main room."

I brace myself against the tree bark and fresh tears come to my eyes. "The Green Republic claims another one of my loved ones." I take a deep, shaky breath and blow it out my nose.

"Do you think it was me?" Korwin said. "I tried to be discreet about it. I had my back to him when I sparked."

"I don't believe it was you. When it happened to us, I could not discern the light from the flasher and that from your hand. I'm sure John couldn't either. Poor John. Oh, Lord Jesus, save us from the darkness we've brought upon our world." I cover my eyes with my palms as a fresh wave of guilt plows into me.

"I'm sorry, Lydia. This is my fault. You had a good life here, a better life than I could have ever imagined before coming to Hemlock Hollow." He snorts and looks away, toward the reactor. His eyes mist and he shakes his head.

I place my hands on his cheeks. "No. Stop. It wasn't your fault. I chose to go on *rumspringa*. No one could've known what awaited me on the other side of the wall. You brought me back here. You saved me, Korwin."

His gaze rises to meet mine in jerky increments and a tear hits my fingers. He is not the type to cry. Our connection comes alive and I can feel the guilt he caries, the thought that he had something to do with John Kauffman's death.

"Everything's going to be okay," I say. "We just need to put our faith in God that he'll take care of the flashers. One hard rain and any that are left will probably short out or get buried in the mud. Bishop Kauffman wasn't your fault. His death was God's will, as all of our lives and deaths are. Everything to His purpose, yeah?"

Korwin nods. "So they keep telling me in baptism school."

"Don't you believe it?"

"It's a new concept for me. I guess I think human choices play a larger part in this world than you guys are giving credit for."

I lower my hands. A question comes to mind, one I don't want to know the answer to but feel compelled to ask. "Can I ask you something? But I want you to answer honestly."

He gives one quick nod.

"Are you happy here?"

"I'm happy with you."

"That's not what I asked."

He sighs, leans his back against the tree trunk, and turns his face toward the moon. "This community doesn't take kindly to strangers."

"The longer you stay, the less of a stranger you'll be."

"But I'll always be the asshole who stole you from Jeremiah."

I glance away. "They'll get over it. You'll see. Once we're married, they'll slowly forget and in a few years, they won't remember anything but Korwin and Lydia Stuart."

"Can I ask you something?" Korwin asks. "But I want an honest answer."

With a small laugh, I say, "Seems only fair."

"Do you miss Jeremiah?"

When I open my mouth to deny it, I stop myself. I'm about to tell a lie. I expected the truth from Korwin and if we are to be married, he deserves the truth from me.

"Yes. I do miss him. We were best friends once. I know you see me with Mary now, but before it was Jeremiah and me."

"So I did come between you."

"Life came between us. Boys and girls play together here, but not men and women. We'd outgrown our friendship. If we didn't court and marry, we would have had to end our relationship anyway. It would have been inappropriate."

"Hmm." Korwin sighs. "So you never loved him?"

I thread my fingers over my stomach. "In truth, I did love him, but only as a friend or family."

Korwin doesn't move. It's as if his muscles have frozen into place. But his eyes burn. I watch him swallow—slowly, deliberately.

I try to explain. "Before I met you, I thought there was only one kind of love—the comfortable, family kind. I thought marriage would be an arrangement." I rub my hands together and take a deep breath. "I might have been happy with an arrangement before I met you. The making of a life around managed expectations and prayer is a common occurrence here. But I'm afraid you've spoiled me."

"Oh?" he says, voice trembling.

"When I'm with you, Korwin, I'm not thinking about who will make the bread tomorrow or who will till the field next year. I'm thinking about kissing you, and my skin on your skin, years of whispered dreams and made memories. I see us old and gray, stuck to each other in the morning and inseparable at night. Speaking our own language through this thing that connects us." I step toward him and reach for his hands. "With you I have passion. I love you, Korwin. You've spoiled me because now I know what real love is and I could never settle for anything less."

For a few heartbeats, I simply stare into his eyes, the tingle of our connection starting at my scalp and working its way down. And then, Korwin's face changes. He rushes me, sweeping me into his arms and landing his mouth on mine. The kiss is hot, wanting. His lips search mine as if they can't settle on the best source of connection. My fingers are in his hair and he's spinning me around while we both hold back the electric beast inside.

By the time he stops kissing me, I've broken a sweat and the smell of singed cotton hangs in the air around us.

"I'll work harder to prove to Deacon Lapp and Preacher Yoder that I'm committed. I'll prove to them I'm ready for the August baptism and to be married this fall. I can't wait another year."

Smiling, I slowly drop my hand.

A knock on the front window of the house startles me, and I jump back from Korwin. My father beckons from behind the glass.

"I guess I'd better go in," I say.

He agrees and climbs into his buggy as I jog inside the house, anxious to explain everything to my father.

SIX

On Tuesday, less than two days after John Kauffman's passing, I climb into our buggy dressed in my best black dress. Preacher Bender, who led the two-hour funeral service, helps load the coffin into a long wagon along with my father and the Lapps. Korwin is driving a separate buggy with two of the Lapps' younger children and is parked just ahead of us. Once the casket is buckled into place, Dad walks back to me, looking old and tired, and takes up the reins.

I place a hand on his. "*Gut Arwet.*" It means *good work* in Pennsylvania German.

He smiles weakly.

We follow a long parade of buggies to the cemetery. The wall around Hemlock Hollow is an imperfect circle and is about thirty miles from one side to the other. Our cemetery is in the area closest to the reactor, northwest of the gate. No one ever goes there. Unless someone dies.

An Amish burial is a solemn affair. The men dig the hole and lower the body in perfect silence, as if every word was said and note sung at the service before. It takes a long time to mound the grave or maybe it just seems long, burying our dead in the shadow of a twelve-foot concrete wall. As if God is as upset about the loss as we are, it starts to rain. And then it is done. A plain wooden cross marks the grave, without a name or a date. It has always been so for us. He's not there, in that grave. Just his body. John Kauffman is somewhere else. Somewhere better.

All of us, soaking wet and weeping softly, climb into our buggies for the long ride home.

* * *

"The Bible tells us that for everything there is a season, a time to sow and a time to reap. A time for every purpose under heaven." Isaac Bender preaches at the front of the rows of wooden benches, his voice soft as the spirit moves him. "Here, in Hemlock Hollow, we live by the word. Our very lives depend on trusting the will of God. We've been farming this land for close to four hundred years, in the same ways as our ancestors and under the same laws. My grandfather and his grandfather passed down the old ways, ways that come from this book." He thumps his Bible with his hand. "We've always been separate. Always done things our own way. God's way. The Englishers on the other side of that wall—" he points at the side of the Stoltz-fuses's house, toward the wall that lies beyond, "—they think they've put us in a cage, in a preservation to keep them safe from what we are. They think they've set them-selves apart from us. But in truth, we are set apart. It is they who are in the cage of the devil's making. Their God is sin and selfishness. Be ye warned, my brothers and sisters. I

Peter 5:8—*Be of sober spirit, be on the alert. Your adversary, the devil, prowls around like a roaring lion, seeking someone to devour.* Some of you have been on the other side. Some of you are fixin' to go. It's scary how close we must come to the enemy. Stay vigilant..."

I tune out Isaac's words as I look to my right and three rows up where Korwin sits straight backed on the hard wooden bench. He is as attentive as any of us. The last few weeks, I can tell he's been trying hard, always working and as helpful as a saint. Coming home from the last Sunday Singing, he said he'd been helping with Katie Kauffman's land too. Still, there is an extra inch of space between Korwin's shoulder and Abram Lapp's. Perhaps I'm imagining the distance, but I stare at that gap of air and wonder what the space would say if it could talk.

Isaac Bender finishes his preaching and Abram Lapp stands up and takes his place. "I will now announce those men nominated for the position of bishop." He unfolds a square of worn yellowed paper. "Frank Troyer." Startled, Dad rises slowly, eyes darting around as if there must be some mistake. When no one tells him to sit back down, he takes his place at the front of the room.

"Jeremiah Yoder."

There is a murmur in the crowd and everyone turns toward the Yoders, who have three generations of Jeremiahs in the same pew. Certainly it wouldn't be my friend. He's much too young for such responsibility.

"Ruthie Mae's Jeremiah," Abram clarifies.

I chew my lip as Jeremiah's grandfather rises and ambles forth. He's in his eighties and has a reputation for strict enforcement of the old ways. Rumor has it, the reason Ruthie Mae still cooks over a wood stove is because the technology that converts pig chips to methane has a few parts that can only be made in the English world. Unlike the rest of us, Ruthie Mae spins her own yarn and makes her own cloth. Although all of us dress plain and sew our own clothes, most homes don't even own a spinning wheel. We obtain modest cloth from the English world when needed, trading with English neighbors for meat or wood-work. A bishop like Ruthie Mae's Jeremiah would be a harsh dictator, nothing like John Kauffman.

"Benjamin Samuels," Isaac reads.

Mary's older brother stands and prayerfully joins the small group of men.

"These are our three candidates," Isaac says. "Please, each of you select a hymnal from the stack behind you."

The three men turn toward the stack on the Benders' kitchen table, which has been pushed up against the wall to make room for the benches. My father goes first, sliding the middle hymnal out of the stack. Ruthie's Jeremiah selects the top hymnal, and Benjamin takes the last one. The men open the covers and start flipping through the pages. My father breathes a sigh of relief when his does not contain the scripture. His body language is subtle, but I can tell he did not want the responsibility of being bishop. I have to think it is for the best with him not being married and managing the farm with no one but Korwin and me to help.

Ruthie's Jeremiah clears his throat and all eyes fixate on the elderly man. He grips a rectangle of paper in his gnarled hands. "Psalms 74:6-7—*For not from the east or from the west and not from the wilderness comes lifting up, but it is God who executes judgment, putting down one and lifting up another.*"

We have a new bishop.

And just like that, the air in the Benders' house shifts.

Mary sits up straighter and even her mother smoothes her dress. A general unrest falls over the rows of benches as the men return to their seats. The truth roars in the silence and darting glances. Everything will change now. Everything has changed.

SEVEN

"IT'S FOR THE BEST, LYDIA," MY FATHER SAYS AS HE sweeps the chimney of the wood-burning stove. We're lucky our house had one, previously used only for heat. Other families have to install the stoves.

"For the best? Less than a month has passed since Bishop Yoder's assignment and already the ripples of change have reached every corner of Hemlock Hollow," I say. "It's like he enjoys making our lives difficult."

By Bishop Yoder's decree, we can no longer use our gas stove or refrigerators. I don't mind about the stove. I can make do with the wood version, although the house will be unbearable in the summer. The fridge is another story entirely. We won't have ice to put up until winter. Not only will we have to build an ice shed to keep it in, but until then, the task of preserving food falls on me. We'll be eating more canned meat than I'd prefer, and it's a lot more work.

"It's been this way from the beginning," Dad says. "We follow God's will. God sent us the new bishop."

"God giveth and God taketh away." I cross my arms. "I wish God would taketh sooner."

"Ack. It's not all on you, you know. We can't use anything from the English world in the field anymore. Don't get me started on the buggies. No new rubber for the tires. Let's hope ours remains intact until the next bishop." He whispers the last with a smile on his face, although there is nothing funny about it.

A knock on the door catches our attention. "Do you think he heard us?" I whisper, as if Bishop Yoder had ears everywhere. Dad gives a low chuckle and moves to answer the door.

"Mary Samuels, what brings you by at this late hour?" my father says.

She glances toward me and back at my father. "I'm sorry to be the bearer of bad news, but I thought you'd want to know."

"Well?" My father motions with his hand for her to continue, a gesture left over from his days as an Englisher.

"There's been a fire... in the Lapps' barn. They think it started in the haymow."

"Good Lord above us, is everyone well?" my father asks. "Have they put it out?"

"Do they need our help?" I ask.

"No. It's out. Luckily, Abram had just filled the water trough for the animals. He caught it early and they were able to extinguish it."

I press a hand into the space at the base of my neck and hold my breath, terrified about what she might say next. I can see it coming like a runaway horse, but I can't move out of the way. Not from this.

"They're blaming Korwin, Lydia," she says. "Nathaniel told about the canvases and the paint."

"He didn't."

"He did. And he's suggesting it was the cause of the fire.

That the chemicals got too hot up there and started the hay. Abram found some pieces in the ashes."

"Where's Korwin now?"

"They've gathered at the Lapps' farmhouse. I think you should come." Her lips purse and she wrings her hands. This is nervous Mary. She knows more than she's letting on. I look to my father for approval.

"We'll both go," he says.

Mary nods and says her goodbyes.

A few minutes later and we are in the buggy on our way to the Lapps'. "What will they do to him?" I ask my father.

"I don't know, exactly. They can't shun him since he isn't baptized."

"Good."

"But they can delay his baptism."

I sigh deeply and bury my face in my hands.

"What was he painting up there? I don't suppose it was the landscape," he says.

I shake my head. "He was painting me."

"No! You didn't—"

"Not with my permission! Just from memory. When Mary and I found them we painted over each one. I thought Korwin was going to get rid of them." My thumbnail catches on my apron and rips at the edge. I pick at the torn nail, trying to decide to rip it off and risk exposing my nail bed, or let it to catch on something else. It's low and deep. I decide to let it be.

"Did anyone know the paintings were of you?" My father's tone is low, a warning.

"Nathaniel and Mary."

He rolls his lips and taps the side of his nose nervously. "You can be shunned, Lydia."

"I didn't do anything wrong!"

"I believe you. But be very careful today. If Bishop Yoder thinks you were part of this, there could be hell to pay, quite literally."

Suddenly, I feel sick. I've only been part of one shunning, a boy named Jonah who wouldn't stop stealing. After six months of folks finding their missing tools and animals at Jonah's residence, his parents admitted to their son's sticky fingers. He was shunned. No one would talk or eat with Jonah. The boy was isolated, even when he was among us. His own parents barely acknowledged him. Eventually, he left and never came home. That was four years ago. We all assume he's living in the English world, but we will never know for sure. Not unless he comes back and repents, and odds are, that's not going to happen.

We pull into the Lapps' drive and I wipe my sweaty hands on my blue skirt. What I thought was about Korwin has become about me, too. In my head, I ask God for help navigating these strange waters.

"Hoi, Frank. You must have heard about the fire," Abram says solemnly.

"Do you need our help? Was there much damage?"

"No. No. Nathaniel and I got it under control, but I'm glad you are here. Bishop Yoder has come. Decisions need to be made." His eyes bore into me. My limbs are heavy and sluggish as if they're filled with wet sand.

We follow him into the house where Bishop Yoder is waiting, back as straight as the chair he's sitting in. Korwin sits rigidly on the sofa, his hat in his hands.

"Hello," Korwin murmurs. As I return his greeting, I notice I am the only woman in the room. Nathaniel, Abram, my father, and Preacher Isaac all find seats. No one looks happy.

"Let's get down to it," the bishop says, scowling.

"There's been a fire. A fire caused by the sinfulness of a member of our community. Vanity and pride." He fixes his eyes on Korwin. "Nathaniel has confessed his sin of silence in the matter of your... artwork."

Korwin frowns. "I am so sorry if my paintings had anything to do with the fire."

The bishop's face twists as if he's smelled something bad. "The fire? Don't be sorry about the fire, boy. Be sorry about the sin!"

Korwin's throat cracks. "Where I come from, painting isn't considered sinful."

"I told him," Nathaniel pipes up, waving a finger in Korwin's direction. "I explained weeks ago why he needed to stop."

The way he says it almost seems like he wants to condemn Korwin. The corners of Abram's mouth turn up slightly, almost imperceptibly. He is proud of his son. Korwin's surrogate family isn't being a family at all.

"It must be confusing," I say, "having been raised one way and now to live another. Korwin isn't even finished with baptism classes. I'm sure this was something he did a long time ago, before he fully understood our *Ordnung*. Perhaps he just hadn't found a way to dispose of the paintings after Nathaniel brought it to his attention."

My father nods and squeezes my hand.

The bishop sighs. "Unfortunately, that isn't the case."

I glare at Korwin. What has he done? His jaw tightens, and he keeps his eyes focused on the floor. "How do you know for sure?"

"One of the paintings didn't burn. It was of you, Lydia."

My jaw comes unhinged, and I take a loud breath. Mary and I painted over every canvas. True, Nathaniel had seen the paintings before, but the bishop is referring to a new painting. That means Korwin didn't stop when I asked him to. My chest constricts and when I close my mouth again, all the muscles in my face and neck tighten. I feel betrayed. I can't even look at Korwin.

"How do you know when it was painted?" my father asks.

"It was of John Kauffman's funeral—Lydia and the other girls watching the coffin being lowered into the ground."

I bury my face in my hands and shake my head.

"I take by your actions that you were unaware Korwin was painting you," the bishop says.

"Of course she was unaware," my father says.

I wipe under my eyes and warm wet tears coat my fingers. Korwin doesn't even look at me.

"I'd like to hear it from her," the bishop says.

Korwin straightens. "She didn't know. Never did Lydia pose for me or give me permission to paint her. I did it without her knowledge."

I notice the nuance to his words. I did not pose. I did not give permission. But I did know. Still, everything he has said is true.

"Lydia?" the bishop prompts. My father squeezes my hand.

"What Korwin says is true. I did not pose, and I never gave him permission. I am disappointed in him for painting me."

Korwin's head snaps up, and this time his eyes do meet mine. I'm surprised at what I see in his gaze. He isn't sorry and if anything, he looks disappointed in *me*. As if I am the problem here.

"We all are," Abram says.

"Korwin," the bishop starts, "if you had been baptized,

I'd ask you to repent, confess publicly, and ask for forgiveness. Instead, since you are still *rumschpringe*, I will ask you to repent and confirm to me your intent to be baptized."

Korwin lowers his head. "I am deeply sorry for what I have done and promise to follow the rules from now on. I ask your forgiveness and wish to be baptized." The repentance is genuine and heartfelt. I pray it will be enough.

Abram scowls but says nothing.

"Very well. You are welcome to stay, but I feel I have no choice but to delay your baptism another year. Full commitment to the *Ordnung* is essential to our community."

A sob breaks my lips, but Korwin seems unaffected by this news. His elbows rest on his knees and his face is hard, as if carved from stone. He shakes his head. "I think my apology and repentance is evidence enough of my commitment, not to mention the months I've spent working side by side with you in your fields and attending your services." Korwin's voice rises. "I even learned your secret language!"

"Now, there's no need to raise your voice," Abram says, shaking his head. "Don't disrespect, boy, or you'll find yourself back where you came from."

Korwin's neck blushes red. "Disrespect? I have done everything you've asked me to without question. I'm not disrespecting you. I'm asking you to reconsider and treat me like you would Nathaniel."

"Nathaniel is a member of this *Ordnung*. You are not. Not yet." Abram crosses his arms over his chest.

Bishop Yoder makes a low throaty sound and exchanges a glance with Abram. My father squeezes my hand and begs me with his eyes not to speak.

"If you stay, you wait another year," Bishop Yoder says.

"*If*...If I stay," Korwin's eyes dart around the room, "and do this for another year, then you'll let me be baptized and marry Lydia?"

"If you prove you are ready," Bishop Yoder says, exasperated.

"Let me get this straight." Korwin crumples his hat in his tightening grip. "Two years of servitude, of eating, sleeping, and praying side by side with your community is not guaranteed to be enough to prove I'm committed?"

"There are no guarantees. This life isn't for everyone."

"You mean, it isn't for me. Because I'm an Englisher. That's what you mean, isn't it?"

The room plunges into silence. No one moves. No one breathes.

"He doesn't mean that," I finally say. I turn to Bishop Yoder expectantly, but he doesn't deny Korwin's accusation.

Korwin meets my gaze again. "I'm not sure I can live in a place where I'm not wanted, where creating art in the privacy of your own home is a capital offense. I'm not sure I can live in a community that claims to be so forgiving, but judges you at the first opportunity." He turns his head and faces Abram and Nathaniel. "I'm not sure I can live in a house for another year with people who have it in for me because they can't find it within themselves to trust an Englisher."

Abram's face turns the color of a freshly roasted beet.

"What are you saying, Korwin?" My father's voice carries a hint of warning.

Korwin stands. "I'm saying, I think I should go."

My next breath hitches in my throat. What should I say? What can I do? The situation has gone from bad to worse.

Abram stands from his chair. "Get your things. You are

not welcome here anymore." The words slice through the room.

"No. No," I say. "Korwin, apologize. Make this right!"

Korwin sneers at me as if the thought of apologizing makes him ill.

The bishop stands, turns his back on Korwin, and walks from the room. It is done.

Weeping softly, I watch Korwin practically jog into his room and come out with a small bag, already packed. He walks right past me and out the door. None of the men follow him, but I do. I break from my father's arms and push through the door, feet pounding over the porch and down the stairs.

"Korwin!" I yell.

He stops and turns around, pointing a finger in my direction. "Stay, Lydia. Find someone who can make you happy. This life is more important to you than me. You belong here. Obviously, I don't, and they," he motions with his head toward the house, "will make damn sure I never will."

What? Does he mean the Lapps? I shake my head. "Don't do this. Stay. We can work something out."

"Tell Abram I'll leave his horse at the gate."

Abram's mare is saddled and tied to a post. Strange considering Amish don't ride horseback often, preferring to go by buggy. It's almost like the Lapps had it ready for him. Korwin mounts and takes one last look at me. "Be happy, Lydia. Goodbye." He prods the horse around.

"Korwin," I yell. "Korwin!" I run after him but he's gone, his horse heading for the wall at a full gallop. Strong hands grip my shoulders and stop me in the middle of the road. Nathaniel.

"Let him go," he says. "He doesn't belong here."

I tug my shoulder out of his hands. "Don't touch me. He does belong here. He's always belonged here. If you had any compassion, you'd go after him right now." I can't contain my hands, and my animated gestures catch my hangnail on my skirt. It tears and bleeds. I suck the drop of blood from my thumb and stomp back toward the house where my father waits next to Bishop Yoder and Abram. Abram's wife, Ebbie, has joined him in the drive and stares at me, shaking her head.

"I'm going after him," I shout. "He'll repent. We can wait another year." The people in the drive say nothing, but there is no name for the expressions on their faces. Even from a distance, I can see a mixture of embarrassment, sympathy, and condescension. I ignore them. I have to convince Korwin to stay. There has to be a way to make this right.

Flustered, I stumble on loose stones on the shoulder of the road. In my haste, I've neglected to watch where I'm going. Arms out, I stagger off the road, trying to regain my footing. I succeed in keeping my face from planting in the dirt, but as I stray toward the rows of corn in Abram's field, a bright blue flash blinds me.

It's a reflex. My lower arm snaps from the elbow and I fry the flasher, leaving behind six inches of scorched earth and a hunk of twisted metal. Only after I've done it do I think about the men and women watching me. Nathaniel's jaw drops and his mother and father begin to pray. Bishop Yoder glances between my father and me and then rubs his eyes as if he can't believe what he's seen.

Only my father seems to know what to do. He walks toward me in a panic. "Did it get ya?" he calls. "I never seen heat lightning do that before." He looks up at the clear blue sky. "Are you all right?'

"Yeah, fine," I say. "Shaken though. Did you see how near it came to me?" I close the space between us, and my father pulls me into a hug.

"Looked like it... connected with your hand," Nathaniel says.

"Looked like it came from your hand," Bishop Yoder says.

"Ridiculous," I say. "Lightning is so fast. I bet it was a trick of the light."

Abram and his wife frown and whisper to each other as my father leads me toward the buggy. I could be mistaken, but I swear Ebbie Lapp mouths *witch* to her husband.

"I'll take her home." My father says to the stunned faces. "She's had quite a scare." He pushes me into the buggy and closes the door. Before I can string two thoughts together, he snaps the reins and our horse heads for home. I stare at my hands. It's been so long since I used my power, it feels foreign to me.

"We have to go after him," I mumble. "We have to catch up to Korwin."

"We will not," he says.

"Dad—"

"He made his choice, Lydia. He could've stayed and waited. He could have begged for mercy and sworn to turn from vanity. Instead, he made a scene and stormed off. It looked to me like he wanted to go."

"No." Tears slip down my cheeks.

"This life isn't for everyone."

I rest my head against the window, feeling tired and confused, like my whole life has been tossed to the wind. Like everything I've ever loved is as scorched and ruined as the earth around the flasher.

EIGHT

Korwin is gone. This is the first thing I think of when I wake and my last thought before falling asleep. In between these two thoughts, I go over what I've come to refer to as "The List," which is an argument I have with myself that goes like this:

You should have followed him.

He didn't want to be followed.

But you loved him and people who love each other should stay together.

If he loved you, he wouldn't have made you sacrifice your family and religion to be with him.

You might have convinced him to stay.

He would have resented you if you succeeded.

You should have followed him.

He left you.

You'll never see him again.

If you'd followed and he'd rejected you, there would be no coming back. You'd be shunned.

He didn't love you the way you loved him. If he had, he wouldn't have chosen painting over you.

Korwin is gone. It's been three weeks, and I have thought of little else but him.

"Are you going to the Sunday Singing tomorrow night?" Mary asks. She's across the kitchen table from me, cutting corn off the cob for canning. The golden nuggets land in a mountain of kernels between us.

"I don't think so. I'll probably go to bed early," I say.

"I think you should go. You should go."

"Why?"

"Because you're not dead."

"I feel dead." The corn in my hands grows blurry as tears fill my eyes.

She grimaces. "Well, it's time to come alive again. Hiding in your house doesn't give the Maker glory."

"Everyone knows what happened. It's embarrassing."

"No one cares. They loved you before Korwin and they'll love you after."

I discard my naked cob into the pile for the pigs. "Maybe next time."

"It's not just about you, you know."

I pause, a new golden ear of corn in my hand. "It's not? I think putting myself forth as ready to court again should be about me in some way."

"Your father isn't getting any younger. If he passes, are you going to run this farm on your own? Courting isn't just about finding a husband, it's about finding a man."

The kernels fall off the cob into the pile at the coaxing of my knife. Mary is right. In Hemlock Hollow, I have never once known of a woman to run a farm on her own. A widow with sons maybe, like Katie Kauffman, but even in those instances it usually isn't long before she remarries or moves into a *dowdy* house with one of her married children. In

Katie's case, the community is helping her work her land until one of those things happens.

I groan. This is not the English world where women are doctors and engineers. This is Hemlock Hollow, and here I'm expected to find a husband.

"Okay," I murmur. "I'll go."

"Good," she says. "Because Nathaniel and I are still courting and I need you there to keep me from thinking immoral thoughts."

The mention of Nathaniel's name makes me grind my teeth. "Mary, has Nathaniel ever said anything about what happened with Korwin?"

Her face falls, and she pauses her work. "The story he told about his leaving was... strange."

I raise an eyebrow. How much does she know? And what spin has Nathaniel's loose lips put on the happenings of that dreadful day?

"He said Korwin made a scene and left."

I frown but say nothing.

"He said... there was lightning." She squints at me.

"Yes. Came close enough to raise the hair on my arms."

"He said it looked like... almost as if it came from your hand."

"Hogwash. You've seen lightning, Mary. It all happens at once and branches every which way. Obviously, it was the angle and a trick of the light." I hold out my hand. "If I'd been struck in the hand, I'd have been burned."

For a moment, she works silently, shucking ear after ear of corn. Then she pauses again and wipes the cornsilk from her hands.

"What are you doing?" I ask. "Do you have to go?"

Without comment, she retrieves something from her

pocket and sets it on the corner of the table. It's a charred flasher, legs bent in on itself like a dead spider.

"Where did you find that?" My voice is breathy and I freeze at the revelation.

"On the burnt ground where the lightning struck. Nathaniel took me back there and it was lying in the burnt bits of grass."

"What do you think it is?" It's not a lie for me to ask her what she thinks it is, but certainly my inflection is carefully crafted to make her believe I am not familiar with it.

"I don't know," she says. "I was wondering if you might."

I scowl. "Looks like something from the outside. Who was the last to come back through the wall?"

"I don't remember. I'll have to ask Nathaniel," she says flatly.

Yes, ask Nathaniel, I think, *because the boy has his nose in everyone else's business.* I pause my work to set the big pot on the wood stove to boil. I move the mason jars to the table, gesturing at Mary to make room.

She picks up the flasher and puts it back in her pocket.

"What are you going to do with that?"

She shrugs. "Maybe show it to my grandchildren." A smile turns her cheeks, and she winks at me.

"Be careful Bishop Yoder doesn't see it. He'll say it's a source of vanity," I say bitterly.

The smile fades and Mary grabs an unshucked ear of corn and gets to work again, peeling back the leaves almost violently. "Nathaniel hated what he had to do, Lydia, but he felt like he was saving you."

"Saving me?"

"You were in the picture they found. You might have been shunned if he hadn't told about Korwin's history.

Nathaniel warned Korwin to stop again and again. He knew you and I had seen the paintings, and he didn't tell that part. He protected us. He just couldn't protect Korwin any longer."

"Oh?" My face feels hot.

"He's a good man."

I nod once and bite my tongue. Nathaniel could have done more. He could have told me Korwin was still painting. But all of it is water under the bridge now. No changing it.

Slowly, I force a smile. "You and Nathaniel are still serious?"

"Very," she says, raising her eyebrows.

"I know someone with extra celery in her garden if you plan to be published quickly."

We giggle weakly, but in the end the sadness of my offer hangs over the room like a cloud.

* * *

I'M GLAD MARY CONVINCED ME TO COME TO THE Sunday Singing. She blows the pitchpipe and kicks off one of my favorite tunes: "My Roots and Wings." My heart is light for the first time in almost a month. Even though the barn is sweltering in the August heat, even with it being dark outside and all the doors and windows open, my soul is buoyant with singing.

The spot across the table from me is empty, as if no boy was presumptuous enough to take Korwin's place. I appreciate the gesture. I haven't even worn my *for-gut* dress today, as I am completely uninterested in attracting any sort of attention. But in the far corner, I notice Jeremiah looking at me and occasionally whispering to Jacob Bender when there is a break in singing. Are they talking about me? Is he saying I got what I deserved?

I've never known Jeremiah to be cruel and his face is consistent with that assessment. He looks sorry for me and a little sad. And so, I become more and more curious about his eyes on me, and I meet his gaze more than once during the evening.

When we finish the last song, unsurprisingly Mary pairs off with Nathaniel. The rest of the young men and women either climb into their own buggies, bikes, scooters, or accept prearranged rides from their suitors. I begin the walk home as today's singing is in the Benders' barn, just a little more than a mile from my place. I pause when Jeremiah's horse, Abe, trots up beside me.

"Ride home?" he asks.

I scratch the side of my neck. "I can walk. Don't put yourself out."

"Not a courting ride home, just a Good Samaritan ride home," he says.

I look behind me. Everyone is gone, swept up into their own lives, their own worlds. "Okay." I walk behind the buggy and climb in next to him. Déjà vu strikes. This is how it all began. I rode with Jeremiah in this buggy, pulled by this horse, to go on *rumspringa*. That ride changed my life forever. Or had it? I was back where I began, wasn't I?

Jeremiah urges Abe into motion, and I'm lulled by the rhythmic *clip-clop* of our journey. "Would you talk to me about something?" he asks.

"What?"

"Have you missed me these last months?" The grin he gives me is part jest, part arrogance.

"I could ask you the same," I quip.

"Yes," he says. "I missed our friendship." He pauses for

a moment and takes a drink from a jar he has on the dash-board. He offers me some but I shake my head. "I stayed away out of respect for Korwin. It's not appropriate for men and women to be friends here after a certain age."

"I know."

"Dumb rule, I think," he says. "There's been a lot of dumb rules lately."

I huff. "I agree. More than I care to speak about."

He smiles, the corner of his eye wrinkling as he glances in my direction.

"Do you think, if there had never been a Korwin, that we would have ended up together?"

With a deep sigh, I fold my hands in my lap and look away from him, toward the reactor in the distance. "Proba-bly. That seemed to be the way things were going."

"Do you think, now that there's been a Korwin, that we might ever end up together?"

I swallow hard and choose my words carefully. "Before or after Korwin, I think the outcome might be the same. Successful marriages have been based on a lot less than a friendship like ours. I suspect we'd laugh a lot and things would be... comfortable."

He gives me a wide grin, eyes twinkling.

"But... you must know... I could never love anyone the way I loved Korwin. I'm not sure I can explain to you the connection we have. It was like, being with him, I came alive. Every part of me."

"Are we talking about marital relations?" he asks, the corner of his mouth rising.

I smack his shoulder. "No! We didn't do anything like that. I just meant being in his presence. Being near him. It made my heart swell every time."

"And now it doesn't swell."

I try to stop but tears well over my lower lids. "No," I whimper. "I wanted him to be happy here. I wanted him to fit in, but he never seemed to. Do you think it was me? Maybe I could have helped him fit in a bit more. Maybe he didn't love me the way I loved him."

Jeremiah pulls the reins and stops the buggy. I turn my tear-stained face in his direction, wondering what he's doing. His eyes are wet as well, and he looks as sad as I've ever seen him.

"There is no possible way that Korwin loved you less."

A slight sob is all the response I can give.

"There is a reason I never courted you before we went on *rumspringa*. A reason I never kissed you. Something it has taken me this long to admit to myself."

"What?"

"I think of you as a friend, Lydia. I always have. Since we could walk, people here have treated us like a matched set. They've whispered and assumed we would court and be married. I always thought it would happen and that God would magically turn the protective and companionable feeling I had for you into something more. I tried to foster it. Held your hand. Stared into your eyes. Tried to say and do the right things. I even convinced myself I was waiting for you to become more wifely. But I never felt the attraction that I saw between you and Korwin. The night I saw you kiss...I didn't wish to be kissing *you*, I wished to be kissed like that."

"Oh Jeremiah."

"I didn't put it all together until now. Even at the end, I thought he had taken something from me. I realize now, we never had that. No matter how much we wanted it. No matter how easy it would have made things."

"I know. I understand." A whisper of relief fills the cab,

and I filter through my thoughts for some other way to explain it but come up short.

"So, now that you know my feelings, Lydia, I want to give you a choice."

"What kind of choice?"

"If you want to live out your days with me, in a marriage based on friendship, I would like to court you. There is no one else in Hemlock Hollow I am interested in, and we will be, as you say, comfortable."

Frozen with shock, I remain silent, his offer twisting through my brain, both a source of despair and relief. Despair that I will never love again the way I loved Korwin, a loss that I will grieve until the day I die. Relief that if I say yes I would not have to pretend with anyone else. Jeremiah has put it all on the table, in full and honest truth. I chew my lip, wondering what to say and how to say it.

"Before you answer, there is something I have to tell you," Jeremiah says. "Something that could change your mind about wanting to be here at all."

I turn toward him, wondering if I heard him right. "Be here at all?"

"Jacob Bender overheard Abram confessing to his father. He wasn't trying to eavesdrop. Just in the wrong place at the wrong time."

My back stiffens. What does this have to do with me?

"He said that Abram confessed to starting the fire in his barn."

"What? No. Jeremiah, what is this evil you speak of?"

"Abram never liked Korwin because he thought you belonged to me. He only volunteered to take him in, not out of a desire to help Korwin, but to make it hard on him. He wanted him to quit Hemlock Hollow from the beginning.

Jacob says he worked him harder than all the other boys combined, and Korwin never complained."

I shake my head, but all at once I know it's true. This is what Korwin was trying tell me the day he left. *You belong here. Obviously, I don't, and they will make damn sure I never will.* "The horse was ready for him," I mumble.

"What?"

"The day Korwin left, the Lapps' horse was saddled and ready to go. They expected him to leave, or else they expected to kick him out." I frown. "Why didn't I see it before?" But then maybe I had seen it. The space between them at service. The delayed baptism.

Jeremiah grabs my hand. "None of us saw it for what it was, Lydia. Jacob says that Abram started to get worried that Korwin would actually succeed here. After my grandfather was elected, Abram found the paintings. He had to act, but he had the option of handling it in his own home."

I nod. "He could have punished Korwin privately; he wasn't baptized yet, after all. Even if he had been, a real father would try to handle it himself first, before getting the *Ordnung* involved." My stomach twists at the epiphany.

"Exactly. Instead, he calls the bishop. Poor Nathaniel thought it was such a strange thing to do that he told about seeing the paintings. He thought it was about him, that he would be shunned or you would be. But the entire focus was on Korwin. It was always about Korwin."

"I thought it was just the new bishop's way," I mumble. "I was so afraid that I'd be shunned, I didn't see the situation for what it was!"

Jeremiah shakes his head. "Abram orchestrated the entire thing to pressure Korwin to leave, and if my grandfather knew anything about it, he looked the other way."

"It's too awful. Oh, Jeremiah, why would they do this? How could they do this?"

"Hemlock Hollow doesn't like outsiders, Lydia. When was the last time someone moved here from the English world?"

"My father was an Englisher."

"Your father was an Amish teen who never came back from *rumspringa*. He has blood here. John was his cousin. Not only did Korwin not have family, the circumstances of his arrival made him stand out like a sore thumb. He healed too fast. He was too strong. Everyone was constantly reminded he was different."

"Lord help me. Jeremiah, what should I do? I let him leave. I barely tried to help him. I blamed him for what happened."

"Like I said, you have two choices." He stares straight ahead over the reins. "You can forget and forgive and marry me. I'd be a good husband. We could be comfortable."

"Or?"

"Or you can leave Hemlock Hollow and find Korwin."

"And then what? Bring him back here?"

Jeremiah blinks slowly. "You know as well as I do there's no coming back. The bishop will never give you permission to go. If you leave he'll charge you and shun you. You will be excommunicated. You can't come back."

I cup my hands over my face and sob.

"I'm sorry I had to tell you this, Lydia. I never wished to hurt you. This is the only way I can see things working out, having it all in the open like this."

"I don't blame you. Thank you for telling me. It explains some things that have bothered me since he left."

"What will you do?"

I look him in the eyes, those cornflower blues that

always seem to hold sunshine for me. From this angle, I can clearly see the scar that runs from his eye to his chin. The one he got on *rumspringa* with me. This is part of it, the part he's not saying. Just like Ruthie Mae, Abram, and his grandfather believe that his disfigurement was my fault and will leave him without a wife. Perhaps they assume I changed my mind because of the scar.

"I don't know," I say. "Do you need my answer today about the courting?"

He snorts. "No." A moment passes in silence. "But, if you choose to leave, I want a chance to say goodbye."

"There's something I need to know to make my decision."

"What?"

I lean across the seat and place my lips on his. His kiss is warm and soft, slightly moist, and his breath holds the hint of alcohol, which I assume comes from whatever he's drinking from the jar. I reposition my mouth and so does he, even placing a hand on the side of my face. I cup the back of his neck. We kiss for a good minute or two, but my pulse does not race, and there is no tingle. No current of heat runs through me. When I return to my seat, it is easy to break the contact.

"Nothing," Jeremiah says, shrugging.

"Me neither," I say. "But at least I know my electrokinesis won't hurt you."

"Not even a shock."

"I love you, Jeremiah."

"I love you too."

"I really wish that was enough."

"Me too."

NINE

"Do you see that?" I ask Jeremiah.

An orange glow flickers in the distance—my front yard. "Fire." Jeremiah snaps the reins.

"What? No!" I jump from the buggy while it's still moving. Orange flames lick from a life-sized doll ablaze in the front yard of my farmhouse. It's tied to a stake, its consumption sending sparks toward the night sky. My father stands on the porch with a rock in one hand and a scrap of paper in the other. The stupor he is in scares me and I wonder if he's having another stroke.

"Dad!" I rush to his side and take his hand.

"Lydia," he rasps, "for a moment... I thought it was you." He means the stake. He thought it was me burning. A chill passes through me even though the night is hot and we can feel the fire on our cheeks.

I search his eyes. "You thought it could be me?"

"These are strange times," he says. "Strange times."

We look back at the fire at the same time. Jeremiah races forth with a bucket of water from the hand pump. He douses the doll and the fire ebbs with a protesting hiss.

"Who did this?" I ask. "Did you see them?"

"No. I heard this hit the door." He holds up the rock and the note.

"Give it to me. I know the handwriting of everyone in Hemlock Hollow. We'll be taking this to the bishop."

My father shakes his head as Jeremiah joins us on the porch, the bucket still in his hand. "What does it say?" Jeremiah asks.

"Not handwritten," I say with disappointment. "Typed. Cut from a Bible." A wave of dizziness passes through me and I have to grab the porch rail.

Jeremiah takes the page from my hand. *"Thou shalt not suffer a witch to live*. Is this some kind of a joke?" he says.

"I find nothing about this remotely funny."

"Nor do I," my father says.

"This is about me, about what happened at the Lapps'. It must have been Abram and Ebbie. Nathaniel was with us, and the bishop wouldn't do this."

Jeremiah scratches behind his ear. "There've been rumors. It could've been anyone who wasn't at the barn tonight."

"I know Nathaniel told about the lightning." I place my hands on my hips, thinking of Mary.

"I'm not sure it was just Nathaniel who told. Seems Abram has had loose lips lately," Jeremiah says.

Mind reeling, I stare at the burnt doll and the scorched stake it's tied to and feel so tired I can hardly move. "You should go home, Jeremiah. Your parents will wonder why you're late. Please don't tell them. Don't tell anyone."

He nods. "I won't say a word." He won't. I'm sure of it.

As tired as I am, I trudge to the shed on the side of the house and retrieve a shovel.

"What are you doing?" Dad asks.

"Go inside. I'll take care of this."

At first, he hesitates, like he's thinking he should help me. I pause in the yard next to the scorched witch, the smell of singed hay and cloth stinging my nose. An execution in effigy. "I need to do this, Dad. Alone."

Dad rests his closed fist on the banister for a moment, gives a shake of his head, and disappears inside.

The celery I'd planted taunts me. By moonlight, I pull it out, bunch by bunch, and make a stack in the corner of the garden. Then I dig. The hole might as well be a grave, though not as deep. By the time I am done I am covered with loose dirt. I toss the shovel aside and return to the site of the burning. With both hands, I pull the stake from the ground and fill in the resulting divot with my toe.

"Rest in peace," I say as I toss it into the hole and bury it. On a whim, I replant the celery atop the heap. It's not ready for harvest. The roots will take again, I am sure. When I'm done, an outsider would never know about the burning. No humiliating evidence remains. Exactly how I want it.

I dust off my hands and leave my muddy boots next to the mat. Inside at the table, Dad looks up from his Bible, eyes rimmed red, the silver trails of drying tears on his cheeks. I sink into the chair across from him. We don't speak. The gas lamp hisses above our heads. He's using gas, not candles, an act in direct opposition to the recent changes in Hemlock Hollow. I scratch my cheek and my hand comes away dirty.

"Jeremiah gave you a ride home from the singing." Dad plays with the corner of the page, his callused fingers two shades darker than the yellowed parchment.

"Yeah."

"Does that mean you two are courting?"

I squirm in my chair. "Is that what you want for me?" It seems an odd question after the night's drama.

He leans back from his Bible and rubs his palms on his thighs. "I'm not good at talk like this—almost like you want me to make a decision only you can make. Marriage is a holy union, not be entered into lightly. Only you can decide who you might want to court."

"But you like Jeremiah."

"Of course I do. I liked Korwin too. It has only been a few weeks since he left."

The lamp flickers above us and, for a moment, I'm lost in its light. "Jeremiah says that Abram Lapp started the fire in the haymow to frame Korwin."

My father inhales sharply. "That is some accusation. Is he sure it's true?"

"It's not like Jeremiah to spread gossip. He said Jacob overheard Abram confessing to Isaac. He admitted he never felt Korwin belonged here." I shift in my seat. "I saw it, Dad. The way Abram always kept a space between himself and Korwin. How they had the horse ready the day he left. Why did the Lapps need to involve the bishop anyway?"

"Abram was often cold to the boy, but I'd hoped it was his way of challenging him. Makes sense though. If Abram had simply found the paintings, that would not be reason enough to call the bishop. The fire, maybe."

"A fire that was already out? A fire that was so under control that it failed to burn the painting of me?"

Dad sighs. "And now another fire. Accusations of witchcraft." He holds up the Bible passage left wrapped around the stone on our porch, crumples it in his hand, and tosses it into the wood stove. "Abram's actions were sinful. He must have known they were sinful or he wouldn't have confessed to Isaac. And to think the bishop was accusing *you*. Now this."

"Korwin did paint the paintings, Dad, and they were of me. But I didn't support him at all. I wouldn't be surprised if Korwin hates me for not defending him. I protected myself. If I'd admitted that I knew about the paintings, Abram and the bishop wouldn't have had such an easy time kicking him out."

He scoffs. "They might have shunned you *and* kicked him out!"

"And Nathaniel? I doubt it. Even so, if we were both kicked out, we'd still be together. We might have been allowed to confess and repent together. Instead, my lie of omission isolated Korwin. What choice did he have but to leave?"

"You love him."

"Yes."

"Are you going after him?"

I stare at him for a beat, feeling empty. "Even if I succeeded in finding Korwin and convinced him to come home, what if the *Ordnung* doesn't let us back in? Someone in this community thinks I'm a witch. What would it mean for him here, when he can't even be baptized for another year? And then, after the year's up, will they make good or will we both be old and gray before we're allowed to marry?"

"Only God knows for sure." He scrubs his face with his hands. With a scrape and rumble, he pushes his chair back and paces the floor. He's had a limp since his stroke but usually it's imperceptible. Tonight, his fatigue is evident by his uneven gait. "I'm concerned for your safety," he says.

"Do you think I should marry Jeremiah to smooth things over with the *Ordnung*?"

"Marrying a boy you don't love isn't going to solve the problem. Bishop Yoder wants to take everything to the extreme. The day Korwin left, well, I've never known a man to enjoy others suffering the way he did."

I'm shocked my father is saying anything against church leadership. Yet every word is true. I'm not naïve enough to think that the burning on our lawn is the last. The seed of untruth planted, rumors about the lightning would fester, entertainment for the small minded and unoccupied. Marrying Jeremiah might help my position in the community. It might keep me safe. But it wouldn't solve the problem. Not really.

I shake my head. "I'm baptized. My loyalty is to God first." This is perhaps the most important reason I should marry Jeremiah, to uphold the vows of my baptism.

"God travels with you, on the inside. He's not here or there. He's everywhere. It's just a matter of remembering you are His. That's why we do this, the clothes, the way of life. We are constantly reminded that we are His."

"You think I should find Korwin."

"I think you should listen to what God is telling you to do and do it."

I rub my eyes. "I wouldn't even know where to start looking."

"Of course you do." Dad tilts his head toward the side of the house, in the direction of the wall.

"The reactor? You think he's joined David and the opposition?"

"Where else would he go?"

"But Korwin hates David. David is the reason his father is dead. He'd never work with the man or go back to that life. We spoke at length about it."

"Again I ask you, where else would he go? He's a wanted man."

A wave of panic constricts my chest, making it hard to breathe. I should have stuck up for Korwin or at a minimum told the whole truth about what I knew. Then we'd be in this together. Instead, I saved myself but made him compromise his principles. The Liberty Party will use Korwin. Maybe not how the Green Republic would, but joining the rebellion comes with a price. Then again, not joining means almost certain death at the hands of the Greens.

Dad scratches the stubble on his face, and then rubs the back of his neck. "Seems like there's only one thing to do."

"What?"

"I think, perhaps, you've become ill, and I insisted you go seek treatment."

"But Dad. I can't let you lie for me."

"Not a lie if you count heartsick as being ill." He threads his fingers over his stomach. "It is your choice. Always your choice. Maybe I've spent too much time among the Englishers. I'm supposed to be the head of the household." He shakes his head. "I couldn't live with myself if I made the wrong choice for you. You have to decide this one for yourself."

It's still dark when I wake, heart pounding in my ears. I have no desire to close my eyes again. The sliver of sleep I endured was wrought with nightmares. Green uniforms chasing me through dark passages, my body burning with the power within. I've worked so long and hard to put that part of my life behind me, but as I rise from my bed, I start packing without even thinking. The journey is too long to carry my suitcase, but I find an old fabric bag among my things, something I sewed to help with gathering onions. It has handles I can slip my arms through and wear like a backpack.

I change into my emergency Englisher clothes, the ones we all have now that Hannah and Caleb are on the lam. When they were running the safe house, we could rely on them to provide appropriate dress and identification on the outside. Now, no one leaves Hemlock Hollow for any reason without an Englisher disguise. My costume is a pair of jeans and a stretchy T-shirt with a jacket. In the August heat, the modern material is cooler than my cotton dress.

When I emerge from my room, my father is sitting at the table, his Bible open in front of him, as if he never went to sleep. With weary eyes, he scans me from head to toe. "I'll take you to the wall."

Life can be measured in heartbeats. Two to the buggy. One hundred to the fields. A thousand or more to the woods. Each beat is a threat, like a clock ticking down. I am leaving Hemlock Hollow. In what must be hours but feels like minutes, we reach the gate and Dad gets out to unlatch the crossbeam and push it open. I rush to him.

He catches me in his arms as if I am still a little girl, and I sob onto his shoulder. "Oh Dad, I can't, I can't do this."

With a hand on each of my shoulders he thrusts me away and gives me a little shake. "Of course you can. You are the strongest young lady I've had the privilege of knowing, my pride and joy. Make it to the reactor. Use the spark if you have to. Don't look back."

"I'm not sure I can. Besides the flasher, I haven't practiced in ages," I say. "I'm not sure I have the control I used to."

"You can do this. You will do this."

I hug him, hard. "I'll miss you so."

"If you choose to come back with Korwin, I'll help you. There'll be consequences but nothing we can't work through."

I nod. "Tell Jeremiah where I've gone. I told him I'd say goodbye. You'll have to apologize for me."

He nods. "I'll explain everything."

One more tight hug and I back across the threshold. It's still dark and this will be my first time going into the Outlands alone and on foot. I slip my thumbs under the straps at my shoulders. My fingers tremble. My father closes the gate as I stand paralyzed with apprehension. Through the narrowing gap, I see him shake his head. "The choice is made. Don't waste the darkness."

The thunk of wood against wood seals my exodus.

TEN

THE FOREST IS DARK, ALL TWISTED TREE TRUNKS AND slippery shadows. I shuffle across a soft mat of pine needles in the direction of the reactor, unwilling to pick my feet up too high or walk too fast for fear of tripping. Even with a full moon, full sight would be impossible under the thick mesh of branches. Tonight, I have but a sliver of light in the heavens to guide my journey and still several hours until sunrise.

The grinding shrill of cicadas accompanies my slow, deliberate steps. I fall into a rhythm and soon forget myself. Perhaps it is a type of self-defense, this blank meditative state that comes over me, or else a product of extreme fatigue. Either way, I approach the base of the reactor before first light.

Dawn comes like a slow leak, the darkness draining, mixing with the paint of tomorrow to create a dim silver glow among the trees. A snap to my right, a branch breaking, pulls me up short. I hold my breath and listen. There's rustling about one hundred yards away. An animal? I squint against the dim, wishing the sun would rise faster. A shadow stretches from tree to tree behind me and I strain to make it out. Even adapted to the dark, my eyes can't distinguish anything in the trees. I pull my hood tighter around my face in fear of being recognized, only to witness a rabbit hopping from my suspected source of sound. With a breath of relief, I place a hand over my heart and pivot to get back on track.

A flash of silver passes by me and impales the forest floor near my feet. Squinting in the dim light, I approach the long rod that protrudes from the ground at a forty-five-degree angle. On the very end are feathers that look like they are made from strips of glass.

"An arrow?" The hair on my neck stands on end. I see myself in the training room at CGEF with a crossbow in my hands. David is explaining the virtues of a Solarbow, a weapon with technology to change the trajectory of an arrow in flight using solar energy. When the sun rises, this arrow will be a heat-seeking missile. The memory grows stronger as I pull the arrow from the ground. Images flash through my brain. A city at night. A soldier chasing me. An arrow circling a building and landing squarely in my stomach.

Sweat breaks out across my forehead and I grip my uninjured stomach. This is not my memory; it's David's. But the experience feels real. Another flash of silver passes over my shoulder and impales a tree beside me. My borrowed memory urges me into motion.

I take flight, weaving between the trees in a zigzag pattern. A crossbow requires a straight shot. My attacker will have four arrows before having to reload. Most soldiers can't fire while running, so my best bet is to pour on the speed and make aim difficult.

Another arrow follows, but I dodge it with skill I never

knew I had. It skims the bark of a tree next to my shoulder, grazing the fabric of my bag. That's three. One more and he'll have to reload. I run fast, stealing glances over my shoulder at my attacker. I see nothing but dark clothing and the glint of the cross-shaped weapon.

UGG! Half my body slams into a tree and the intense pain makes me double over. My stomach clenches as if I'll vomit. There's a pause and a click, the swish of feet in pine needles. Another arrow is loosed.

This one veers around the trees and nicks my shoulder before landing in the bark next to me, covered in my blood. Without a doubt, I'm in grave danger. I've never seen an arrow travel like that. My borrowed memory is true. The sun is rising. I have mere moments before my attacker has full capabilities.

A series of scrapes and clicks in the distance signals that my attacker is reloading. I force myself forward, my injured shoulder soaking the arm of my hoodie in warm blood. The tickle at the back of my brain urges me to spark. I could protect myself with my power. I could fry my enemy with the flick of one hand. But I hold back. If the person hunting me is from the Green Republic, the worst thing I can do is reveal who I am. Even being shot is better than being detected as a living, breathing Lydia Lane. They'd take me to CGEF immediately, and I'd end up Dr. Konrad's plaything.

The first rays of sunlight beam between the trunks of the trees. The low twang of another arrow being released cuts through the woods around me. I'm out of time. I cut sideways, behind a tree, and the arrow takes out a chunk of bark near my ear. With a yelp, I bolt forward, sprinting for the next tree. Cold steel barely misses my cheekbone and this time the next twang comes faster. I dive for the shelter of a thicket.

I'm not fast enough.

The arrow bites into my calf and drives deep, burrowing to the bone. I trip, crumpling, instinctively guarding my internal organs. My cheek plows into the forest floor and I squeeze my eyes shut against the onslaught of pine needles and grit. My exposed skin shreds. I groan in pain. Mercifully, I come to a stop in a mass of ferns, soft enough and with some coverage of my injured body. From this angle, I can see the arrow protruding from my calf. I reach for it and it buzzes in response, vibrating in the wound it's caused. It burrows deeper. I can't help it. Despite my desire to hide, I scream.

Black boots step toward me, the business end of a crossbow just within my field of vision. "Don't move or it'll break your bone," a man's voice orders.

The voice sounds familiar and I turn my bloodied face to see my attacker. "David?" I rasp.

"Oh crap. Lydia?" David reaches for me and I make the mistake of reaching back. The sound of my leg bone cracking seems to echo. He curses under his breath and grabs the end of the arrow, pushing a button near the feathers. "This is going to hurt," he says, and then he rips it from my flesh.

* * *

My eyes flutter open inside a bright white room. I'm lying on my back on a narrow bed with my injured leg elevated on a large pillow. I try to lift it and notice it's wrapped in a soft, rubbery material filled with liquid. There's a cord running from my ankle to a place I can't see.

My lower leg throbs in protest with my movement, and I drop it back onto the white padding.

"Don't move it. The bone is shattered." David approaches the bed. He's replaced his black outfit with light-wash jeans and a loose-fitting white shirt. His hair is longer than I remember, almost to his shoulders. "Dr. Stone did surgery to set your tibia, but it's going to take a few days to heal, even with your superhuman qualities and the healing boot. If we had a full-body tub like the Stuarts, it might go faster, but that was one of a kind."

"Where are we?" I ask, glancing at the white cabinetry and the rows of bottles and boxes around the room.

"Infirmary. Inside the reactor. I'm sorry I shot you, but I thought you were the enemy. It's been months since I visited the preservation. I wasn't expecting you to change your mind."

"You must've known I'd eventually come for Korwin," I say. "Where is he? I need to speak with him." My eyes flick toward the door. All I want to do is tell him how sorry I am for what happened. I've let him down in the worst possible way. I should have stood up for him. And he should have fought harder for me.

David's brows dip over his nose. "Korwin isn't here."

I stiffen, searching his face for some sign he might be joking. All the blood drains from my head and the icy chill from its loss seeps lower. "He left Hemlock Hollow three weeks ago." I push up on my elbows. My temples pound and the room spins. One side of my face feels like it's on fire. My shoulder gives out under the effort of sitting up and I flop back down, moaning.

"Whoa," David says, gently pressing my shoulders into the narrow bed. "The anesthesia we have here isn't like what you get in the hospital. Your nervous system is going to need some time to recover. Not to mention, you've suffered some serious injuries."

"I hurt everywhere." I close my eyes against the pain.

"The Solarbow arrows are heat seeking. When there's enough sun to power them, they lock onto the target and are programmed not to stop. Without intervention, the arrow would have either passed right through your leg or burrowed deeper into your body. Makes hunting out here a hell of a lot easier but can do some real damage to a human being."

"I know," I murmur, swallowing hard. "I remember. Not just my leg but you being hit in the stomach. Thank you, Nanomem." I roll my eyes. I mean it sarcastically but David doesn't seem to take it that way.

He smiles and pulls up the corner of his shirt. Just above his waistband is a jagged scar, raised in sections like the stitches were hastily made or maybe the wound became infected before it healed. "I thought your defensive maneuvers were exceptional." He smoothes his shirt back down. "Good to know the Nanomem is still working. But why didn't you spark?"

"I thought you were a Green. I'm not going back to CGEF. Not ever."

"Understood." He nods his head. "Smart girl."

I roll my head back on the pillow and stare at a white wall, trying to block out the pain. "I need your help to find Korwin. What if he's been captured by the Greens?"

"We would have heard the drumbeats. Even if it wasn't made public, we've got eyes and ears all over Crater City."

"But then where could he be?" My voice is high and tight.

"I don't know."

Images of the day I found Korwin, wired to the drainer,

white faced and spotted with sores, make my stomach turn and my heart flutter. Pressure builds within my skull, and I push myself up again, ignoring the pain. I can't rest. I can't be here if Korwin is captured again. "You have to do something! You have to find him."

He shoves me back against the mattress, harder than before. "Easy," he commands. "I'll send the word out. The Liberty Party is broken but it's not dead. We'll find him."

Our eyes meet, and his cold blue stare softens slightly. David is a harsh trainer, a selfish teammate, and an accomplished triple agent. He knows how to fight and he knows how to lie. Still, I believe him. He'll look for Korwin if for no other reason than to try to convince us to join up with his cause.

"Why would Korwin leave Hemlock Hollow if he wasn't coming here?" David's eyes narrow and I can see him processing the risk. To the Liberty Party, Korwin is like a missing atomic missile, too dangerous to be unaccounted for.

"He was kicked out."

"For using his power? Did he kill someone?"

"No," I say emphatically. "He was caught painting a picture of me."

"Painting?"

"Art is considered vain and without purpose to plain folk."

"Plain folk." David laughs. "Does anyone there know just how un-plain you are?"

Ashamed, I turn my attention to a row of drawers across from my bed. Each one is labeled with a name scrawled in black marker. One says David, another Charlie. I stop reading when David shifts into my line of sight.

"When they kicked Korwin out, why didn't you go with him?"

"I'm baptized. I committed to the *Ordnung*. I couldn't leave without risking excommunication. I hoped Korwin would return and repent, be accepted back into the fold."

"What changed?"

"I might have been shunned if I stayed."

"Why?"

I hesitate at first, not wanting to admit what I've done, even to David. He's a killer and the last with any right to judge, but my instinct is to hide my sin. I chew my lip but eventually crumble under his expectant stare.

"There was a flasher."

David's expression is carefully blank. "A drone flasher?"

"The only kind I know of. Korwin and I found one and destroyed it. I found another. I fried it before it could transmit. That's why I had to leave."

"Because plain folk don't shoot lightning from their hands."

I nod. My eyes swim in unshed tears.

He turns away. "I'm going to get the doctor. He'll want to check on your recovery from the anesthesia. Once we get you up, we'll introduce you to the rest of the team. Hemlock Hollow might not need you, Lydia, but we do."

"No need," a man's voice says. "I'm here." The doctor extends his hand toward me as he strides confidently to my bedside. Under the white lab coat, I can tell he is a soldier, straight backed like David but broader through the chest. His hair is dark but graying and he has a wide scar on one side of his forehead above compassionate brown eyes. He looks familiar, although I can't place him right away. "I'm Dr. Charles Stone, Charlie. Welcome to the new headquarters of the rebellion. We're glad to have you here."

Dr. Stone. Charlie Stone. A memory flashes through my brain and the white walls melt away. A younger Charlie holds the end of the arrow protruding from my—I mean, David's—abdomen. He presses a handful of snow against the wound. "This is going to hurt," he says. Snow blows across my cheek. I squeeze his hand and take a deep breath.

The echo of my scream as he pulls the arrow from my side bounces off the white walls. My body is shaking hard enough for David and Charlie to have to hold me down.

"What's happening?" Charlie asks David.

"The arrow," I rasp to Charlie. "You pulled it from my stomach."

Charlie looks at David in horror. They help me turn on my side as my body seizes and vomit rises in my throat.

ELEVEN

When I can think again, David is gone and only Charlie remains in the room. He's working at the counter, peering through a microscope with his back to me.

"You're one of the Alpha Eight," I whisper. My throat burns. How long did I throw up?

Charlie glances over his shoulder at me. "You're awake. Are you in much pain?"

I think about the question for a second. I'm stiff and foggy but as long as I don't move, there is no pain, only numbness. "Just a little stiff," I say. "And it's hard to think."

"Good. I gave you some morphine. It's got some side effects compared to the newer drugs, but it works in a pinch. Unfortunately, it's all we've got out here."

"How are we able to be here at all? I thought the reactor melted down?"

"Rebels have used the reactor since the meltdown," Charlie says. "One of the original Liberty Party founders, an activist named Louis Kowalski, developed the technology to absorb the radiation from the environment. Even the Green Republic can't do what he did all those years ago.

And thankfully, they don't know it's possible. Those of us who survived did so by coming here. Unfortunately, Louis died from radiation poisoning implementing his life's work. Little did he know, he saved the rest of us and your entire community."

"Wait, so there *was* a meltdown?" I ask from my bed. "I thought it was faked."

"Oh, the meltdown was very real. Louis was working here as a pre-revolution scientist when it happened. When everyone else evacuated, he saw the writing on the wall and stayed, sacrificing himself to lay the groundwork for the rebellion. He'd used his background in proteomics and biogenetics to engineer bacteria that could feed on radiation. The project was something he hoped he'd never have to use but his foresight mitigated the effects of the meltdown. We use a synthetic radiation alternative to keep the Green Republic scientists believing this area is uninhabitable."

Most of what he's saying doesn't make sense to me. Proteomics? I grab my throbbing head.

"Are you all right?"

"Headache," I say.

"You seem to be having a reaction to the anesthesia. Nanomem causes rogue memories but usually not seizures. I think your unique physiology wreaked havoc on my dosing calculations."

"Yeah?" I rub my temples. "Will it go away?"

"With time." Charlie stares at me for a moment, a pensive look in his eyes. "As soon as you're feeling better, there's much more you need to know. Now that you are part of the team, we need to bring you up to speed."

I shake my head. "David should have told you, I'm not

part of the team. I came to find Korwin. That's all. I don't want to be part of your war."

"Our war. *Our* war!" He plunges his hands into the pockets of his lab coat and glares at me, obviously angry or offended, although I'm not sure what I've said to cause such a reaction. "Are you ignorant enough to think this isn't about you?"

"I'm sure it affects me, I just want no part of it."

"And you think you get to choose?"

"Of course I get to choose. You can't make a person fight if they don't want to. I'm a pacifist."

He tilts his head and gives me a long, hard look. "Even pacifists learn to fight when something's worth fighting for. The Green Republic won't wait for you to grow up and figure out you don't have a choice. If you aren't fighting for us, you're fighting for them."

I open my mouth to say that I'm not fighting for anyone, but I don't get a chance. An alarm sounds from a watch on his wrist, and he taps a button on the dial.

"While I sincerely hope you change your mind about helping us, I'm afraid this conversation needs to wait until another time."

He turns to the drawers on the wall and opens the one labeled *Charlie*. Inside is a gadget that looks like a gun with a vial behind the trigger. With practiced agility, he removes a replacement vial of blue liquid from the drawer, flips off the cap, and with a twist of his pinky finger drops the old vial into a red bin. The new vial snaps into place.

"Seven o'clock," David says to no one in particular as he enters the room and pulls open the drawer with his name on it. He loads his own gun as Charlie shrugs out of his lab coat and lifts the corner of his shirt slightly. He presses the barrel of the gun to his abdomen and pulls the trigger. The blue fluid drains into his body.

David presses the gun into the side of his neck. I flinch when he pulls the trigger, thinking the injection site looks particularly painful. The entire process flows like a dance, choreographed and efficient.

"How often do you have to do that?" I ask.

"We've got the formula down to twice a day," Charlie says. "Every time the clock hits seven."

"And you make it yourself now?"

"At first, no. We stole some, and I was able to make a weak alternative. But thanks to David and what he stole from Konrad when he escaped, we were able to analyze the formula and reproduce it, even make it better."

"No one told me," a woman's voice says from the open door.

My eyes shift from Charlie to the newcomer who is ghost white and frozen in the doorframe. I cannot process her appearance. The woman in the doorway could be my twin if not for her age. Honey brown hair, green eyes, my height.

"Why was I not informed she was here?" she demands of David. She stares at me, dumbfounded, then approaches my bed. "What's happened to you?"

"I...I..." I can't make my brain produce words. She's so familiar. Tears gather and spill from her green eyes. "Do I know you?"

She shakes her head. "No. But I know you. I've prayed for years that I would get the opportunity to meet you." Her fingers burrow into my hand at my side. "My name is Laura Fawn."

The name evokes a memory, and this time it is not David's but my own. I see the picture of the Alpha Eight and David's finger tapping near the woman who looks like me.

"You're my mother," I mumble, because my voice isn't working right. My head is spinning and dark spots dance at the corners of my vision.

She nods and smiles. "I am."

The whole room starts to shake as flashes of a younger Laura and Michael Fawn come back to me. David's memory of her belly round with child inside a glass prison. Laura holding me in her arms. Laura using her power to blast her way through a crowd of green uniforms. The memories come fast and hard and shake me to the quick.

"She's seizing!" Charlie yells, and then they turn me on my side again.

TWELVE

"You need a break from the healer," Charlie says when I'm myself again. "It loses its effectiveness if you wear it for too long." He removes the electric boot from my leg.

"Where's Laura?" I look around the room.

"I asked her to leave so you could rest. The anesthesia has left you... fragile."

"I want to see her. Why didn't anyone tell me my mother was still alive?" My voice cracks.

"I met you on the operating table. As for David, he'll have to answer that himself."

"But, you... all of you knew where I was. David, Hannah, and Caleb, they all knew about Hemlock Hollow. Why hasn't she looked for me?"

"Again, not a question I feel I should answer," Charlie says. "However, as for my part, by the time we knew who you were and where you came from, you were back home on the preservation and Jonas and David made it clear you wanted to stay there."

"They never told me. I want to see her."

"You should rest."

"I feel better."

"Don't be fooled. The bone is in the early stages of healing. It'll snap like a brittle twig if you're not careful."

I give him a stern look.

He sighs. "No question you're her daughter. You are as hardheaded as she is." From the cabinet, he retrieves a black boot. "This is called a walking cast. It will protect your bone while it's healing." The boot opens at the touch of a button and he fastens it around my injured calf.

"How long until it's back to normal?" I ask.

"A few days."

I swing my legs over the side and wiggle my hips to the edge of the bed until the foot of my good leg slaps the floor. At least the hospital pants and tunic I wear allow me room to maneuver. The walking cast forces me to angle my injured leg to the side where I can put very little weight on it.

"Try this." Charlie hands me a cane. A few practice steps and I have the rhythm down.

"It feels pretty good," I say.

"Excellent. Come on. We'll find Laura."

With his hand behind my back to steady me, I hobble through the door. The hallway is freshly painted and lined with colorful art. There's a black door every fifteen feet or so labeled with a room number. "This isn't what I expected," I say.

Charlie smiles a mouthful of teeth I think must be artificial because they are too straight and white. They don't match the scar on his head or the gray in his hair.

"Because the reactor melted down you assumed this place would be in ruins? They use the term *meltdown* any time radiation breaches the outer wall. In this case, the structure was preserved and the Liberty Party rebuilt from there."

"How? I can't imagine any of you can walk into a Green Republic store and pay with units."

With a snort, he looks at me from the corner of his eye. "Don't you come from the preservation?"

I nod.

"And your people have been obtaining things for decades, if I understand correctly."

"Yes, but we use false identifications obtained with help from Englishers."

He spreads his hands. Of course, Hannah and Caleb, the same people who obtained false identifications for Hemlock Hollow, used to work for Maxwell Stuart. Although their cover was blown, it makes sense that there are others doing the same thing. "I guess I underestimated how organized the Liberty Party was. I thought after the rebellion failed..."

"You thought we lost our best and brightest and retreated with our tails between our legs."

I raise an eyebrow in affirmation.

"You don't organize a revolution in a matter of hours, Lydia. Jonas understood the odds were against us. Still, he did his best to send a contingent in. It was rushed and sloppy. We almost won CGEF thanks to you and Korwin, but in the end, it became clear someone on the inside had leaked information about the rebellion to the Greens—a mole at the fire station. The Greens were expecting us and we couldn't pull the numbers to overcome their militia. With more time, maybe." He shakes his head.

"Are you saying the loss was somehow our fault?" I ask

incredulously. "Because we *rushed* you?" Korwin and I almost died taking the transformer down. My blood boils at the thought the effort wasn't appreciated or fully utilized. "If the Liberty Party wasn't ready, they should have helped us get home without risking our lives."

He raises a hand defensively. "All I meant was the losses we suffered were great but not terminal to our cause. Jonas acted conservatively. We lost the battle but not the war."

A woman in a blue uniform approaches us, carrying an unmarked brown box. "Good morning, Dr. Stone," she says with a nod.

"Morning. Are those...?"

She nods. "I'll put them with the others."

"What was that all about?"

"Medical supplies. Every day we get closer to state of the art."

We've reached the end of the hall and the room opens, *really* opens. I am at the base of an anthill with hundreds of blue uniforms scurrying where the ants should be. The funnel shape of the room is my clue that we are inside the concrete tower of the reactor, but that is where the similarities end. As opposed to the cold outer appearance of the concrete, inside is a bustling metropolis. I count twenty-three railed floors, each well lit and populated with smiling faces going about their day.

"There are so many!" I say.

Charlie grins. "Did you think Stuart Manor was the entire resistance? The Liberty Party has doubled down. We will not go quietly."

"Where do you get the power?" I stare up at the bright internal lighting. "Is this scamped?"

"No need. The reactor is working again."

My head snaps around. "Now? It's working now?"

"Yes. Safely." He pats my shoulder. "We have the best and brightest scientists and engineers on board—thorium experts. The rebellion used to scamp from the Greens in the beginning. That was before my time, of course. But over the years they leveraged what was already here on a smaller and safer scale. This reactor uses liquid fluoride instead of steam. We have an endless supply of energy."

I know less than nothing about nuclear science and shake my head at the magnitude of what he's saying. The reactor is working. The Liberty Party has its own energy. "How in the world do you keep this a secret?"

Charlie is cut off when a boy in a blue uniform calls my name. "Lydia? Lydia Troyer, is that you?"

I perk at my given name. He removes his cap when he reaches me and his spiky brown hair is as untamed as ever. "Caleb! What a relief to see you." I accept a brief hug. "So this is where you escaped to after the raid?"

With a wink, he slaps me on the shoulder. "You didn't think Hannah and I would go down so easily, did you? Once we handed Jeremiah off to Maxwell, we escaped in the tunnels under Lakehurst and made our way through the forest. Took a couple of scary nights in the woods to make it here on foot, but we did."

"Thank the Lord."

"Are Korwin and Jeremiah with you?" Caleb looks between Charlie and me.

"No. I came here looking for Korwin. He left Hemlock Hollow without me. I assumed he'd be here. Jeremiah stayed behind."

Caleb frowns. "Korwin's not here *or* in Hemlock Hollow?"

I shake my head. Out of the corner of my eye, I see Charlie lock eyes with Caleb. Both men look equally concerned.

"Don't worry, Lydia. Now that you're here and safe, we can put out the word. We still have contacts in Crater City. We will find him. The Liberty Party needs both of you."

"I want to help find him," I say quickly. "As soon as my leg's healed, I want to help look for him."

Caleb laughs as if the thought is inconceivable. "Don't you worry, they'll send a team. It's too dangerous and you're too important. We need you here. Hasn't anyone told you how bad the Greens have become? They are out of control. The entire continent is a slave to Chancellor Pierce."

"Chancellor? You mean Senator."

Caleb shakes his head. "You've been gone a long time."

"Maybe this is a conversation for her to have with the council. We're on our way there now."

Charlie grips me under the elbow and guides me away.

"Nice to see you again, Lydia. I'll tell Hannah you're here." Caleb gives me a little wave as I hobble away.

I am led to a bright white conference room where five people wait at a long silver table: Jonas, David, Laura, and an elderly man and woman who I've never met. My eyes lock on Laura. I can't look away. I have so many questions, but for her part, she keeps her head down, her gaze glued to the pad of paper in front of her.

"Welcome, Lydia," Jonas says, standing and pulling out a chair for me. "Please, have a seat."

I lower myself into it, thankful for the rest. My leg is already sore and the injuries on my face and shoulder are throbbing slightly.

"As I understand it, you've already met Laura and David."

I glance between the two, suddenly anxious to speak given the formality of the meeting. "Yes," I say softly.

Jonas aims one hand toward the elderly couple across the table from me. "This is Mirabella and Warden Grant."

"Pleasure to meet you," I say politely as they reach across to shake my hand. Mirabella has a diamond ring on her finger almost as big as my thumb, and her gold bracelets clatter when she pumps my hand. Warden's watch and sweater remind me of something Maxwell Stuart would wear, expensive and tailored.

Charlie takes an empty chair next to Warden and folds his hands on the table. "This is the Liberty Council," Charlie says. "We are the ruling body for the resistance."

Confused, I chew my bottom lip. Last year, Maxwell held a party at Stuart Manor for the Liberty Council, to show them what I could do. The only person I remember meeting was Jonas and of course, David, who was posing as Maxwell's butler.

I glare at David. "Why didn't you tell me my mother was alive?"

David sighs heavily and leans back in his chair. "You didn't want to know. You just wanted to go home, remember?"

My eyes dart to Laura. "Did you know? Have you known this entire time?"

She raises her green eyes to mine. "You were safer with Frank."

Frank. She knows my father's name. I recoil in my chair. "How long have you known?"

"Since just after you surfaced at Maxwell's. I kept you a secret for so long. I didn't think it was possible you could still be alive after all these years. He eventually proved you were my daughter from your blood."

"Maxwell knew about you?" I stare at her incredulously.

David scoffs. "Turns out Maxwell had more than a few tightly held secrets. Some he managed to keep even from me."

I ignore David and stare at Laura. "And you never sought me out? Never thought to introduce yourself in over a year?"

Laura's eyes brim with tears. "It would have been too risky, for both of us. But you're here now. I'm looking forward to getting to know you."

Jonas, who has been standing during our exchange, lowers himself slowly into the chair at the head of the table. "Now that that's settled, we have business to discuss."

"Nothing is settled," I snap. Anger boils within me. I don't trust any of them. Not Jonas, not David, not the wealthy strangers across the table from me, and certainly not the woman who is my mother by biology only. I don't understand any of this. "Why is David on this council when he was the one responsible for having Maxwell killed?"

Jonas shakes his head. "David did what he had to do to protect you. Maxwell made too many mistakes. He became disconnected from the Party's goals in pursuit of his own. Killing those people in the West Hub bombing was just the beginning."

David spreads his hands. "Konrad had Natasha. He was pulling my strings. Still, I tried to keep you out of it. I sent you and Jeremiah to your father, hoping you'd find each other and make it home with Frank. I didn't think you'd be stupid enough to walk through the front door."

"What did you expect me to do?"

"I expected you'd use your head and steal the identity of a night nurse or something, not make up a name and walk past the facial recognition cameras. My plan was to have Korwin go after you. I liked the kid; I didn't want anything to happen to him. But he insisted on getting his father involved."

"It's water under the bridge," Mirabella says in a soft, sophisticated tone. "We've got to move on. My understanding is the other asset is missing."

I glare at her. "The other asset?"

"Korwin," Warden says with a tight-lipped smile. "We must bring him to safety and prepare for war."

"You want to find him, don't you?" Mirabella adds.

"Yes." I grit my teeth at her description of Korwin as an asset. "When will you go looking? I want to help."

She shakes her head. "Out of the question. You're too important to us. We will put the word out to our people in the trenches. Once we have a lead, we'll send a contingent."

"How long will that take? He's been gone for weeks. Konrad could be draining him as we speak. We can't wait for someone to stumble upon his whereabouts."

Jonas holds up a hand. "Lydia, in the time since you've been gone, things in the Green Republic have changed. In fact, they've grown far worse. After our failed revolution, Senator Pierce declared martial law and named himself Chancellor Pierce. Along with the Bureau of Republic Affairs, he has turned the nation into a military dictatorship. There is no longer any semblance of free trade. The Greens control everything. Every unit of electricity, every bite of food, every job, and every drop of information communicated to the populace. They say they do it for our safety." He snorts derisively. "They do it for power. They do it for control."

I interlock my fingers on the table and look Jonas in the eye. "What does this have to do with finding Korwin?"

"We can't risk exposing ourselves. We are going to find Korwin, but we can't be reckless. We have to keep the end goal of revolution in mind."

"The war has nothing to do with me. Thank you for fixing my leg and for your help finding Korwin but once we do, the two of us won't be staying. I'm going to take him home."

Mirabella brushes her long gray hair behind her ear, her green eyes dart to her husband's. "You're a very young girl. Perhaps that is why you think this does not pertain to you. Allow me to put it a different way: The Green Republic has been looking for you, diligently enough that men in hazmat suits roam the forests of the Outlands on occasion. As I'm told David has shared with you, the compound at Stuart Manor is controlled by the Greens. We have yet to determine if the classified data there has been compromised, but we've seen flashers fall from drones on a regular basis. We've taken measures to minimize the risk to us and to you, but the risk is there and so is a very real possibility they'll find something that leads them to us. If that happens, it's only a short distance to Hemlock Hollow."

"Are you threatening me? Are you saying you'd tell them where to look for me?"

"Oh, we wouldn't do it on purpose. I simply want you to understand that the Liberty Party is the only thing keeping the Greens from the Outlands, and the Outlands are the only thing keeping them from Hemlock Hollow. Now do you see? If we fail in our attempts at revolution, you're next."

For a moment, I stare at my hands and let what she's said sink in. My head is pounding and I'm more worried than ever about Korwin. I can't even process what she's saying.

"I think I need to lay down," I say to Charlie. He nods and helps me out of my chair.

"Another time then," Jonas says, more an order than a question.

I limp through the door, aware that each of them is staring at me and none of them look happy.

THIRTEEN

CHARLIE TAKES ME BACK TO THE INFIRMARY TO REST and hooks me back up to the healing boot. I fall asleep almost instantly, although my rest is riddled with nightmares. I picture tanks and huge bulldozers plowing through the wall to Hemlock Hollow, crushing me, my father, and everyone else in their wake. My *Ordnung* is obliterated into a dust of crushed bones. Our homes are flattened under metal treads, and even our animals are killed in cold blood.

I wake with a sharp intake of breath, my eyes moist with tears. Thankfully, the nightmare is not reality. The infirmary is quiet, the lights dimmed, and I find David asleep in a chair by my side. I can't find a clock.

Lights on the rubbery contraption around my lower leg blink green. I sit up in bed, fighting the ache of my shoulder and face. Incredibly, the pain in my leg from my earlier walk is completely gone. I run my fingers along the edge of the healer, feeling the hum of electricity beneath my fingertips. Charlie said this worked similarly to the bathtub Maxwell Stuart made for Korwin, but it was localized. Can I help things along?

Closing my eyes, I find the glowing blue tickle at the back of my brain. It seems like forever since I communed with it or practiced controlling it. Sure, in Hemlock Hollow I suppressed it, a type of control, but that particular skill was far different than safely wielding it. It was a stupid thing to do. A potentially fatal mistake. My power is a stranger to me again in many ways and in this world of the Englishers could be an important defense.

With a deep breath, I carefully peel back the bandage on my shoulder and inspect the crusty gouge of bloody flesh. I place my hand over the wound and then carefully allow the tickle in my brain to travel both to my hand and down my neck to the spot under it. My shoulder glows blue through my fingers and I watch as tiny segments of skin knit together beneath my touch, a spider's web that thickens to cover the deep wound. The place of injury fills in, turning bright red, then purple like a bruise. My body lurches, and the boot on my leg blinks red again. The tickle within shifts, power flowing from the boot, up to my heart and back to my shoulder. It takes me a minute to figure out what's happened. The source of my healing power has shifted from my inner reserve to the charge of the boot. The deep bruise beneath my fingers heals to normal flesh, my skin taking on the distinctive blue glow of a Spark.

I remove my palm from my shoulder and work at the tape holding the bandage to my face. Even before I have it off, I can feel the healing energy working, warming the skin of my cheek. By the time I toss the bloodied bandage to the floor, my skin is smooth and pain free beneath my touch. Why didn't I think to do this before?

Again I close my eyes, and this time, I turn my intention within. My injuries are more than skin deep, and I mean to heal them all. I concentrate on the tips of my toes, then scan up my legs, inch by inch, relieving any tightness or pain, setting things right and trusting my instincts. I scan my knees, my thighs, my hips, my abdomen. Once the warmth and light is in my head, it joins the source of the tickle in the back of my skull.

An alarm rouses me from my meditation. The device on my leg is blinking green and ringing like an egg timer. I fold in half and slap the buttons on the side, trying to turn it off.

"Allow me," David says. He stands and brushes my hands aside. A series of beeps later, the device splits in two and my calf is freed. "How does it feel?"

I bend and straighten my leg, then roll my ankle. "Good. Fine." In one motion, I swing both legs over the side and kick my feet. "Stronger than before."

"Easy," he says. "How's your head? We don't want another seizure. Charlie told me to make sure you don't get up too fast until we know the anesthesia is out of your system." He holds a hand near my shoulder as if he'll catch me if I fall.

I cast him a sideways glance. "I'm not sure I'll ever be safe from seizures with the Nanomem in my system. Is that another side effect?"

He shakes his head. "You saw Laura at the council meeting and didn't seize again. I don't think it was the Nanomem. It's more likely from the anesthesia."

"Both things injected into my body without my permission."

"Come on, Lydia, you know I had no choice about either of those."

"You had no choice but to inject me with a toxic substance untested on my biological makeup?"

"Konrad was watching," he says through his teeth. "What was I suppose to do? I couldn't teach you what you needed to know any other way. You should be thanking me. If it wasn't for me, you'd still be Konrad's pawn."

I jump down from the table and take a few experimental steps without the walking cast. I have no pain and everything seems to be working fine. "Why didn't you tell me about my mother?"

"I didn't know. I thought she was dead."

I scoff.

"After your parents escaped with you, Natasha and I were recaptured. Your father's body was found, as were the Villeneuves. The Stones and your mother were presumed dead. As it turned out, they made it here. Charlie had managed to steal enough serum to keep them alive for a time. His wife, Rebekah, succumbed to electroscurvy before they could synergize an alternative in the lab here. Even then, what they came up with wasn't enough for them to thrive on until I brought them vials of the newest formula when I escaped."

"If that's true, how did you know to come here?"

"I followed Jonas here after Natasha passed. Once it was clear the rebellion had been compromised, Jonas ordered a retreat and saved as many soldiers as he could by bringing them here while the Greens were distracted with you. He was quick to get the word out about Stuart Manor and the fire station. He re-established Liberty Party headquarters here."

"Charlie mentioned someone on the inside knew about Maxwell's plan and leaked it to the Greens. Did Jonas ever find out who it was?"

"No."

"Was it you?"

"No! How could it be me? I was huddled on the landing

with my wife dying in my arms, Lydia. Not exactly prime time to get chummy with Konrad and Pierce."

"But you knew about Maxwell's plan. The rebels had tried it before. And you were all too willing to share enough with Konrad and Pierce to get Maxwell shot."

David holds up both hands. "It wasn't me."

I hang my head and stare at the tile floor. "Where are my clothes?"

"They were cut off when Charlie did surgery on you, but there are new ones in room 212 upstairs. Your new room."

"Can I get there on my own, or do I need a key or something?"

His eyes bore into me. "All Biolocks."

I head for the door to the hall.

"Charlie says you're supposed to wear the walking boot. Your leg isn't completely healed."

"It's fine," I call behind me. In truth, I have no idea if it's fine. It doesn't hurt at the moment and that's all that matters to me.

I find the room easily enough and pop the Biolock. David wasn't lying. They've prepared the room for me with a closet of size-adjustable clothing and formal blue uniforms. I take a long, hot shower before dressing in dark pants and a shirt, with a stretchy, metallic-looking hoodie sporting the weatherproof properties I've come to expect from English clothes. Socks on, I look for shoes. All that's available is a heavy pair of steel-toed military boots. I pull them on. If my bone isn't completely healed, these will do to keep it relatively safe. I poke my feet in and lace them up, then braid my hair, missing my *kapp* out of habit. When I emerge again, David is waiting outside my door.

"It's the middle of the night. Why don't you get a good

night's rest, and we can talk in the morning about finding Korwin?"

I shake my head. "If you think I'm helping you or the Liberty Party while there could be any chance of Korwin being used as a human battery by the Greens, you don't know me very well. In fact, if you ever want my help, you'd better show me the door and point me in the direction of Crater City."

"Crater City? Do you plan to walk through the front door of CGEF and ask at the front desk for him?" He laughs incredulously.

I huff. "I don't know. Sometimes I can... feel him. We have a connection. If I drive around the city, I might be able to sense him."

"Ever widening circles until you reach the ocean? Somehow eating and sleeping without being discovered?"

I shrug. "Do you have a better idea?"

For a long time, David just stares at me, hands on his hips, a calculating look in his eyes. He licks his lips. "Lydia, I understand what you're feeling. The pull you feel to find Korwin is only natural given your connection and your relationship." He pats his chest over his heart. "I've been there. I loved Natasha more than life. But this is reckless. You're barely healed. Chances are as good you'll get caught as rescue Korwin."

"You say you loved Natasha. Would you have waited for the council to put together a team to look for her... *if* they heard a tip about her whereabouts?" I ask cynically. "Can you honestly tell me you would wait?"

His head rolls forward on his shoulders but he doesn't answer me.

"You owe me this, David. After all the things you put

Korwin and me through, after what happened with Maxwell. You owe me. Help me. Help me find him."

His eyes snap to mine and he grimaces in silence. After a few tense moments, he shakes his head. "There's only one other place Korwin would likely try to go."

"Where?"

"If I help you and you find Korwin, do you promise to return here?"

"Like you said, where else am I going to go?"

"Promise me."

I grind my teeth together for a moment. A promise to David is a promise to the devil. "If you know something about where he could be, you'd better tell me or I will never trust you again."

"Promise me."

"I promise," I hiss. "Now, where do you think he is?"

"Come on."

David leads me through a maze of corridors to a garage half full of vehicles. There's a large white van and a Humvee with the logo of the Green Republic on the side. I look at David, puzzled.

"How'd you get one of theirs?"

He raises an eyebrow. "We're resourceful," he says darkly.

"You killed the driver," I accuse.

"No. But I think you did during your tantrum down Fifth Street."

I recoil, shaking my head, and he bursts into laughter. "I'm joking. You most certainly did not kill the driver of this vehicle. I did. And he had it coming."

"That wasn't funny," I say.

"Get over it. You're in the English world now, and it's a world at war. Either you kill or you die. The faster you accept that, the more likely you'll survive the next twenty-four hours."

"You are a ruined man, David. You have no soul," I say through my teeth.

His wayward grin melts as if my words sting a little. He shivers slightly, casting my insult off and covering the motion by striding away from me, toward a cabinet on the wall. He unlocks it and rummages through its shelves.

"Which way is the door?" I ask.

"You can't leave on foot. We're too far from the city. If anyone sees you, they'll know there's something wrong. No one walks out here."

"I don't know how to drive."

"Ever ride a bike?"

"Sure. Every day."

"Perfect." He turns from the cabinet and throws something round and hard in my direction. I catch it in my stomach. "What's this?"

"Helmet. Put it on." He leads me to a type of bicycle I've never seen in person. I only know what it is from the book about the Englishers we keep in Hemlock Hollow. A motorcycle. It's got two fat tires, a seat as wide as a horse saddle, and a dashboard between the handlebars with a full keyboard and an array of blinking lights. "This is a Toma-hawk Infinity. They are rare and very fast."

"I can't drive this."

"It will snap to the grid just like any other vehicle and expect you to supply the coordinates of where you're going."

"I don't know where I'm going, and I can't drive this."

"If you want to go manual, you simply hit this blue switch." He points to one of the flashing lights. "Otherwise, all you have to do is turn the key and steer. This bad boy does the rest. Even has anti-crash technology, but hold on if it engages because you are in for one hell of a ride."

"David!"

"What?"

"I don't know how to drive a motorcycle."

He grins at me and taps the side of his head. "But I do. So why don't you climb on and see if you can figure it out by the magic of Nanomem."

I stare at him for a moment, scared to the point of trembling. What if I do remember? Will the memory cause another seizure? Or worse, will the reaction be delayed and occur while riding the strange machine. I rotate the helmet in my hands.

"You haven't even told me where you think I should look for Korwin. You said there was only one other place he could have gone." I shift my weight from foot to foot, staring into the helmet as if something within its confines will give me an idea of Korwin's whereabouts. No answers appear within the headgear.

David hooks his fingers beneath a cord around his neck and pulls a small vial out from under his shirt. Delicately, he unhooks it from the cord and holds it out to me between his thumb and forefinger. "Take this and pay Stuart Manor a visit?"

"Stuart Manor is occupied by the Greens. What is this?"

"A vial of Maxwell Stuart's blood. He provided it to the council in the event of his death. They won't be happy that I took it."

"Eww. Why would I want this?"

"As you will recall, the secret entrance into the basement compound of Stuart Manor is locked using a biological key. This is it."

I accept the vial, turning the small steel cylinder between my fingers. "Korwin would never go there. The place is crawling with Greens."

"Not the compound. You heard Korwin, even if they tortured it out of the man they caught, they'll never get in without the biological key. I have reason to believe that Maxwell provided Korwin with the location of a similar vial before they were arrested. He knows the security codes and enough about the compound to find a way in unnoticed. Once inside, there's enough resources for you both to live safely for months."

"This is your theory? That with a price on his head Korwin would rush to a place he knows will be occupied by government officers under the odd chance he can recover a vial of blood from some hiding place and break into the compound."

"Think about it. Where else would he go? True, he knows the Greens are there, but it's been almost a year since they took the manor. Now that they have the place secured, there will be a skeletal staff keeping it that way. They are not going to waste staff policing an empty house. Korwin is smart enough to get inside without being seen. He's probably living inside the compound as we speak."

"Living in a house secured by the Greens?" I hold up the vial.

"The manor has hundreds of hidden rooms and passageways. Korwin knows them all. The Greens don't."

I cross my arms.

David spreads his hands. "Where else would he go?"

With a sigh, I nod and place the helmet on my head. "It's as good a place to start as any."

"One more thing." He reaches around the back of my head and I feel him push against the helmet. A bright green grid forms in my field of vision, light splitting down the center and then widening to the full visor. A bunch of numbers appear in my right peripheral vision, next to David's face. His hands are on his hips again and his intense stare makes me squirm.

"What?" I say. My voice sounds different, robotic, nothing like my own.

"Inside the compound, behind Korwin's palomino painting, Maxwell Stuart's most important experiment is stored in a safe. The safe will only open with a drop of this blood. It is imperative that you retrieve the specimens inside while you're there. Just a few vials. Easy to carry. By loaning you his blood, I'm giving you my only way in and out of that place. It's a huge sacrifice for our cause. The least you can do is obtain what we need and keep Maxwell's work safe from the Greens."

"I'll do my best," I say. I've already promised to come back. How hard will it be to bring a few vials with me?

"Good." He rummages through the cabinet again and pulls out a black backpack with a hard outer shell. "There's a false bottom in this that will keep the vials frozen for several days. The main compartment holds a change of clothes, a dopp kit—do you know what a dopp kit is? It's a military-issue bag with a toothbrush and hairbrush and things."

"Okay." I shrug.

"There's emergency provisions under the clothes. Put it on." He hands me the heavy pack.

I do as he says, suddenly impatient to leave now that I know where I will start my search.

"Lydia, block," he commands. His heel flies toward my stomach and I rotate my forearm down to block the kick. He smacks my shoulder and I connect with his jaw. He scrambles behind the bike and the adrenaline, coupled with the weight of the backpack and the image of the Tomahawk, bring back a flood of memories.

"I have it," I say. "The desert. You fought off three masked men."

He nods. "I thought that might do it."

About the time I swing one leg over the seat, I am deep within the memory—a good memory. Through David's eyes I am speeding into the sunset, nothing but wide open desert ahead and Natasha waiting at the end of the road. I give my head a little shake.

"See? No seizures. It's getting easier." He grins.

"I know how to drive this."

"Of course you do."

I turn the key and the engine roars to life and rumbles under me, a horse chomping at the bit. I'm in the Outlands, so I switch to manual and engage stability control, anticipating rough terrain. David lifts the garage door. It rattles to a stop over my head and warm moist air fills the space between us.

David approaches my side. "The green projection on your right relays the temperature, speed, and fuel level. The helmet is state of the art. It will disguise your voice and has other helpful capabilities. Don't stare at the interface. Keep your eyes on the road—or the trail as the case may be. And Lydia..."

"Yeah."

"If you get into trouble, do not pull over. You have no identification."

"Then what should I do?"

He guides my hand to the side of the backpack. There's a zipper on the side. My fingers caress the ridged grip of a semiautomatic pistol.

"I won't use it," I say defiantly.

"Fine. Fistfight the bastards then. But for God's sake do not remove your helmet or use the spark. If the Greens find you, they will stop at nothing to bring you in. Stay safe and find your way home. We need you."

Find my way home? My home is a place in Hemlock Hollow. What he means is find my way back. He thinks, when I return, it will be to stay. But he's wrong. Once I find Korwin, I'll do as I promised but then I plan to take him home, to face whatever the *Ordnung* has in store for us.

"Well? Day's a-wastin'. Go," David says, pointing both hands toward the door and the silver light that heralds the coming dawn.

"Goodbye, David," I say. Then I pump the accelerator.

FOURTEEN

Once, when I was seven, I was in a runaway buggy. Later, my father would tell me a snake scared our newly broke horse. The Morgan gelding reared and leapt, sending the buggy and me flying. What I remember most is the weightless lurch, the way my stomach dropped as the seat pulled out from under me. For a moment, direction had no meaning and my breath caught in anticipation of the inevitable collision to come.

Riding David's motorcycle is a similar yet infinitely more terrifying experience. The slightest rotation of my wrist rockets me past him and out of the garage. I grip the seat with my thighs and lay my body flat against the fuel cells, clinging to the handlebars for dear life. Pebbles fly all around me as I race down the gravel road and take my journey into the forest.

I veer around one tree and then the next, allowing my instincts to take over. As long as I don't think too hard, don't allow myself to contemplate the untenable speed in the corner of my vision or the branches that occasionally brush the top of my helmet. My instincts tell me when it's time to slow down, when the trees have become much too close for comfort.

Only then am I able to appreciate the beauty around me. I'm riding on a carpet of pine needles, surrounded by deciduous forest in full summer splendor. Sunrise filters through the branches. The shades of green alone are breathtaking, from deep pine to the pale birch with its paperwhite bark. "Thank you, Lord, for this. What a beautiful day you've given me." My prayer is muffled within my helmet.

Flash! The blast of whitish-blue light blinds me and makes me jerk the handlebars. My vision recovers in time to brace myself for collision with a massive oak tree. Instead, the accident avoidance technology kicks in, and I veer around the trunk, wheels skidding in loose leaves and pine needles as the bike veers right then left to avoid tree after tree. I tap the brake until I regain control, then drive back to the source of the flash. Before I've even reached the mechanical spider, I fry the thing with a surge from my hand.

I stop the bike to make sure I haven't started a fire in my overzealous destruction of the flasher. *Tick-tick-tick.* The sound of a beetle scampering across a wood floor brings my gaze up to the trees. Flashers. Everywhere. They creep up trunks and branches, climb from tree to tree with their spider legs, en masse. The swarm is close, too close. With a sharp turn, I retreat.

The mechanical sound of hundreds of flashers turning is louder than the Tomahawk. Flashes explode around me. Blinded and terrified, I lay my chest against the fuel cells and hang on for dear life. The bike takes over, ricocheting through the woods as its sensors work to avoid the trees. Instead of tapping the brakes, I crank the accelerator. My only hope is to go far and fast enough that the only thing the Greens see is a black blur.

"Please Lord, make me brave. Give me strength." Tears flow over my cheeks. "I can't do this without you."

A massive figure darts in front of me, and I slam on the brakes to keep from colliding with it. My back tire skids through the pine needles. I am thrown from the bike, my back and head slapping a nearby tree. I crumple to the dirt. Only the backpack and helmet save me from being seriously injured. Even with the helmet, my head hurts from the impact, and a small crack appears in the corner of the visor. The bike halts perpendicular to the trail, its stabilizing technology righting itself.

The source of movement stares at me from between the trees. A wolf. At least I think it's a wolf. The animal is unnaturally large, as big as a bear and silver-white with frosty blue eyes and tufted, attentive ears. I freeze. A wolf this size could tear through any one of my limbs without much trouble. The pack wouldn't be far behind to finish the job. I brush the pistol in my backpack with the tips of my fingers and chide myself for even considering it. The animal is too beautiful. Too proud. It takes a step closer to me and I snap my hand out from the elbow, feeling the elastic tickle stretch from the back of my brain. I'll protect myself if I have to, but I won't kill it intentionally. A few thousand volts will knock it out.

But this is a dangerous plan. If there are more flashers in these woods, the last thing I want is for the Greens to have a picture of me using my power. I hold back, heart pounding, and swear to only act if the creature attacks.

The wolf sniffs the air, then lowers its head. I hold my breath, afraid even the rise and fall of my chest will cause the beast to attack. It stares at me in the oddest way, as if she can see inside my soul. *She*. I sense she's a girl. A remarkable calm comes over me in the grip of her stare. For a moment, I take it all in, this wild animal accepting me while I accept her, without reservation. We are two creatures, surviving and curious.

Without warning or pageantry, the wolf attacks. I call out and cross my arms in front of my helmet, closing my eyes and expecting hundreds of pounds of wolf to barrel into me. But it never does. Well, not physically. A firm pressure passes through my skin and settles over my heart. I open my eyes and scan my surroundings, my breath heavy inside my helmet. The wolf is gone. Only, she's not. I feel her… inside of me. Am I losing my mind?

On shaky legs, I stand and remove my helmet. I turn a circle, looking for the beast. I'm alone. My eyes linger on the carpet of pine needles. No footprints. I rub my throbbing temple. She wasn't real. What does it mean? Did God answer my prayer with the vision of the wolf? Or was it simply a coincidence that I imagined her at the moment I opened myself to divine guidance. If there is meaning in the encounter, I can't put words to it.

I return to the bike—trembling, overwhelmed. With one last look toward the forest, I don the helmet again, turn the accelerator, and continue down the path.

The forest opens up. I'm on the road that passes the Adamses' residence and 54 Lakehurst Drive, the house where I found out I was a Spark. A Green Republic squad car is in the driveway, the government seal on the door. Just the sight of the emblem fills me with dread. David taught me what it represents: the laurel wreath is the symbol of Next Generation Ag and represents synthetically developed food; the lightning bolt, Nucore, naturally acquired energy; and the hammer, the Evergreen Party, military strength. It is a symbol of the three organizations who formed the Green Republic and now own the country.

Anxious to put miles between the emblem and me, I pump the accelerator. Not the smartest idea I've ever had. The rev of the engine draws the attention of the Green officer in the front seat. I check my speed and slow to the posted limit, seventy-five in Willow's Province. I'm relieved when time and distance separate me from the symbol of the Green Republic.

Miles later, a beep on my dashboard lets me know I'm approaching the grid. The road ahead of me looks exactly the same as the road behind me. I have a fading memory of riding in the back of Officer Reynolds's squad car my first day in the English world. Invisible or not, if I lock to the grid, the road will take me to my destination using its own energy. It will save fuel and get me where I'm going faster. Tentatively, I flip the glowing blue switch from manual to automatic on the dash.

Looking for network... Red letters flash in my peripheral vision. *Enter coordinates or touch map to search.* I tap the map of North America. It lights up, showing the entire empire of the Green Republic. Beyond is nothing but blue representing the ocean. I tap the northeast sector and it expands to take up the entire viewing area, then Crater City, and then the dark outskirts that I know as the dead-zone. There's an access point that will take me to the manor. The coordinates load.

Warning: Destination requires manual override. Fuel: 40%. Select LOCK to join grid.

I'm not sure how far I'll have to drive off-grid. Is forty percent enough? Movement in my side mirror garners my attention. The Green Republic squad car creeps into view on the horizon. He's followed me, although he is keeping his distance. "Forty percent will have to do," I say to myself. I tap the LOCK button.

The motorcycle's engine roars beneath me and I cling to the handlebars as it lurches forward. In my helmet, I watch my speed increase from seventy-five to one hundred, one fifty, two hundred. I can no longer make out individual trees. They've become a blur of color and light. By the time my speed reaches three hundred, my belly is flat against the fuel cells and I can hear my panting breaths behind my visor. The engine isn't rumbling anymore. It's as quiet as if I'm parked, but my speed is a steady three hundred miles per hour, powered by the road beneath me.

I squeak when my front wheel lifts from the ground and my body pitches sideways. Am I flying? No, a ramp, but I can't make out the road I'm riding on any more than the cars that pass around me like shooting stars. I've heard the upper grid is nothing but a sheet of mesh wire, enough to hold up your vehicle if the power goes out but almost invisible from the ground. There's no shoulder or guard rails. The empty air below me is both exhilarating and terrifying.

A familiar pang of guilt courses through me. Good Amish women do not ride motorcycles in stretchy black pants. They do not hurl through the sky as if they are challenging the angels themselves. Surely this is a sin, this feeling of being on top of the world, in control, strong, fast, and powerful. "Forgive me, Lord."

The image of the wolf appears to me, staring at me in my mind's eye as if she is my own private message from the beyond. For a second time, I am overwhelmed with the sense the animal is a sign from God. Twice, the wolf has come to me when I've prayed. But what does she mean?

The motorcycle slows, jarring me from my reverie. My stomach drops as I descend and I sit up straighter. In my peripheral vision, the green numbers roll down from three hundred and level out at seventy-five. My dash blinks at me. *Manual override engaging.*

The engine purrs to life and the map on the dash indicates I should turn left at the bottom of the ramp. I stop at the intersection and signal. I'm definitely entering the deadzone. The buildings here are rundown, with boarded shut windows, broken glass, and hanging wires. After looking both ways, I squeeze the accelerator but pause when red lights flash in my mirror. The officer from Willow's Province is behind me. He's followed me.

"This is a routine inspection," booms a robotic male voice from the vehicle. "Please remain in park with engine running."

I curse under my breath. The recording is for me. There is no one else in the vicinity. What if the flashers transmitted my picture? Why else would he follow me this far? The rhythm of my heart kicks off a drum line in my chest. *Boom, deboom-boom.* The officer steps from the vehicle and approaches me. Should I stay or run? *Boom-boom-boom.* Too late, he's by my side. *Boom-boom.* He has a tablet in his hands that he presses against the side of my dash.

"Candace Beckwith, thank you for stopping," the officer says. "What were you doing in Willow's Province and now in the deadzone?"

I swallow, my mouth so dry I can hardly speak. A half-truth comes to me and I say, "Out for a ride. I like to open this baby up every now and then. The freedom is exhilarating."

The officer laughs. "You must be well off to afford a Tomahawk Infinity. Your dad work for the Republic?"

He's staring at the device in his hand and it occurs to me that if he knows the owner of the bike is named Candace

Beckwith then he probably has information about who her family is. David's words echo through my head. *Do not pull over. You have no identification.*

"Something like that," I say.

"Hmm." Without taking his eyes off the screen, he takes a step back and lifts the device so that it's blocking his face. I calm my breathing in an attempt to act natural. Maybe he'll buy my story and let me go if I cooperate. "One more thing, Candace. Please remove your helmet."

He's taking your picture, I conclude, whether from intuition or David's memories. *I can't remove my helmet.*

I do nothing. I stare at the back of the officer's device thinking, absurdly, that I've never had my picture taken and the only time I've ever appeared on film was for the Green Republic's purposes. Korwin's painting of me was the first time I saw an image of myself in a favorable light. I don't know, maybe Bishop Yoder is right and it is vanity, but all at once it bothers me beyond the immediate threat to be photographed by the Greens.

"Ms. Beckwith? Your helmet."

My eyes flick down to the scrambler on his belt. What's wrong with me? I'm playing with fire. If I run, he'll probably catch me. Who knows what technology he has to disable my vehicle at close range? If I remove my helmet, I'm done for. If I fry him, I send up a flag that Lydia Lane is in the dead-zone. None of those options is acceptable. *Fistfight the bastards then,* I hear David say.

I place my hands on the sides of my helmet. "The clasp is stuck. Can you help me?"

The officer approaches, a look of annoyance on his face. As soon as he's within striking distance, I jab his throat, leaving him gasping. I punch the device from his hand, sending it skidding across the pavement. He reaches for his scrambler, but he's too slow. I elbow a tendon in his shoulder to debilitate his arm and head-butt him as hard as I can. It works. For a moment, he's stunned. I'm off the bike in one lithe move. Thumb to wrist, I bend his arm into submission behind his back, spinning him to face away from me.

"Down on the ground!" I yell. I kick the back of his knees and he collapses.

"Consider the consequences, Candace," the man shouts from his prone position, cheek pressed into the asphalt. My foot lands in the center of his back. His eyes flick to the squad car behind us and I follow his line of sight. How could I be so stupid? Of course there's a camera in the vehicle recording all of this. It's only a matter of time until more arrive.

Efficiently, I deliver a blow to the back of his head and render him unconscious. I'm back on the bike in a flash and accelerate into the deadzone. I can already hear sirens. Pouring on the speed, I drive deeper into the abandoned part of the city, cruising past the occasional man or woman curled up on the sidewalk. This is the deadzone, where defectors of Green Republic society come to escape. I'm not sure how they survive here without home, community, or farmland, and no power to live the modern way, and I don't have time to think about it.

The sirens grow louder and I pull through a wide door into a space that used to be a garage for fixing vehicles. An automobile the color of a robin's egg sits rusting in the darkness. I park behind it, in the pitch dark. It's tempting to remove my helmet; the heat and humidity are suffocating.

Flashing red lights slink by the open door of the garage, sirens off, and I flatten myself against a section of wall. They're close, too close. Fumbling behind me in the darkness, I feel for somewhere to hide. A car door slams on the street outside. They're looking for me on foot. My fingers close around a knob—a door! I pivot and take a closer look, flipping my visor up and using my power to create a faint glow so I can see. I'm in luck. The lock has a keypad—not a Biolock but electronic. I place my fingers over the pad and the tickle moves down my arm to pulse the lock. It pops open at my prodding.

A teeth-clenching metal-on-metal clang gongs above my head when I open the door—two hubcaps on a chain, rigged to clash when the door is opened. Great. A figure appears in the entrance to the garage, the light breaking around the officer's silhouette. I slip behind the door and close it noisily behind me, but I can't relock it now that the wiring is fried.

I'm in an office. No way out. Footsteps approach outside the door. This is it. I'll have to fight again. Another set of footsteps joins the first. Can I take on both of them?

"Identify yourself," a man's voice says.

I open my mouth to answer *Candace Beckwith* but pause when the officer grunts in pain. There's a scuffle. The clang of metal on metal. The sizzle of a scrambler hitting flesh. The thud of a body against concrete. The doorknob turns. I flip my visor down and step into a fighting stance, ready to face off against the officer.

The door swings open. "If you know what's good for you, you'll come with me."

FIFTEEN

THE MAN IN FRONT OF ME IS VAGUELY FAMILIAR. I search my brain for where I've seen him before but come up empty. He looks to be in his thirties with cropped brown hair and a scruffy face. His tunic has been mended in multiple places—places consistent with stab wounds. There's a strip of red cloth tied around his upper arm. This I recognize, and it makes me shuffle deeper into the room. He's a Red Dog—one of the gang of deadzone miscreants that tried to rape me last year.

He pushes his sunglasses to the top of his head. "Listen, girlie, I got no beef with you." He points at his chest. "But this is Red Dog territory. Either you come with me to visit the alpha or I toss your ass out to the Greens."

Red Dogs or Greens? I've survived the Red Dogs before. Definitely an easier opponent than the Greens, not to mention their headquarters is near my point of entry to Stuart Manor. I might get a free tour guide and protection all in one swoop. Unlike my first encounter with his kind, he doesn't have a knife to my throat. I appreciate that.

I nod. "Okay."

He pulls a red bandana from the pocket of his drawstring pants and approaches me cautiously before tying it around my upper arm. "I'll need you to remove the helmet."

I hesitate.

"Don't worry about it. All the Red Dogs have familiar faces. You get me?" His voice is kind but demanding. Maybe I'm tired or scared but my intuition tells me to do what he says. I need his help, and I highly doubt he's going to take me where I need to go with it on my head.

I reach up and pull the helmet off.

He winces like he smells something bad. "Maybe you'd better put it back on." I don't understand until he starts laughing.

"Are you suggesting I'm ugly?" I run a hand over my tightly braided hair.

He wipes his smile away with the back of his hand and stares at me through narrowed eyes. "I remember you," he says. "You gave me water when I was living on the street."

Recognition dawns. He wasn't a Red Dog then. His hair was longer and he was thinner, almost skeletal. But the smile is the same. "I helped you then. Now, I need your help."

He grunts. "Leave the helmet with the bike. Sometimes they can trace the technology to link one to the other."

Since he's standing between the Tomahawk and me, I hold out the helmet. He doesn't take it. Instead, he wraps his hand around a rope dangling near the door hinge. He takes up the slack as he slowly opens the door. There is no gong of metal on metal. "The tension keeps the hubcaps apart." He motions with his head for me to pass through the door. I do. He follows, closing the string within the door to keep it taut.

I place the helmet on the bike seat and balk at the body

of the Green Officer near my feet. He's bound but breathing. Carefully, my Red Dog guide steps over him. The officer groans and twitches.

"We'd better move," he says, motioning for me to follow. "Be careful where you step." He picks his way over a slew of strewn tools and parts to another door near the front of the garage. This one, he opens with a key, and we venture into a long corridor. He locks the door behind us.

"What do I call you?" he asks.

"Candace," I say too quickly.

He raises his chin and one eyebrow, clearly skeptical of the name.

"What do I call you?" I ask, trying to turn the interview around on him.

"Pit Bull."

"Like the dog?"

He rolls his eyes at me. "Yes, Candace," he drawls. "You can call me Pit. So why are the Greens after you?"

I roll the question around in my mind. Lying doesn't come easily to me, especially not when I'm face to face with someone who has been kind. "Misunderstanding," I say, settling for a half-truth.

Pit chuckles. "There's always a misunderstanding when it comes to the Greens."

We've come to the end of the passageway. He pokes his head out into the alley and then pulls it back in like a scared turtle. "Place is crawling with Greens. Your misunderstanding must have been more complicated than most."

"Why are you helping me?" I blurt. "This could end badly for both of us."

He looks at me and narrows his eyes. "We've got to make it across the alley to the slaughterhouse. You can't miss it. The door has a big X painted on it. You go first. I'll be right behind you. If you get caught, you're on your own."

Maybe his intentions aren't so altruistic after all. I poke my head out. The emblem of the Green Republic passes by at the end of the alley and I tuck myself inside once more.

"Now," Pit says. "Before the Green gets too curious."

I dart across and deeper into the alley, looking for the door with the X. When I find it, I hesitate. The X is drawn in blood and the smell coming from behind the door makes me gag. I stretch the sleeve of my hoodie over my thumb and cover my nose and mouth with it. Uncertain, I glance back in the direction of Pit. He waves me on. The swirl of red lights on the pavement at the end of the alley spurs me on, and I push the door open.

Death. Everywhere. At first the muscle and sinew dangling from hooks in the ceiling look almost human, and I spark in response, filling the space with a bright blue glow. But in the increased light I can see the pointed snout and elongated jaw of a sewer rat. The stench is suffocating. The cleanliness, deplorable. Dried blood lines the drain in the floor.

The door behind me opens. I tuck my power back inside, hopefully fast enough to hide it from Pit, who presses his red bandana to his nose and mouth.

"You might have warned me what I was walking into," I say from behind my sleeve.

"Needed to know you could follow directions. You do as I say, you'll be fine."

"And if I don't?"

The leathery brown skin of his cheek tightens with his scowl. "The deadzone is a dangerous world. Bad things happen to little girls without protection. You might wish the Greens had found you."

His words are chilling. Even though I trust God to protect me, and Pit is my best chance of escaping the Greens, the feel of Red Dog hands on my body is something I won't soon forget. These men have no rules and I shouldn't confuse his help for kindness.

I nod. Pit leads the way along the wall, our shoes sticking to the blood and grit. When we reach a stairwell, we descend into pitch-black. I'm tempted to spark so I can see but don't. I can't give myself away.

Pit's hand grabs my shoulder to stop me. "Wait a minute." I hear a metal-on-metal sound like beads in a tin can.

"What are you doing?" I ask.

"Would you rather walk in the dark?"

I'm confused until a minute later the front of a metal cylinder glows to life in his hand. "Runs on kinetic energy. Takes a minute to charge it."

"Handy," I say.

He points the light ahead of us. If possible, the corridor is filthier than the slaughterhouse, lined with garbage and peppered with what looks like animal feces. He leads the way, picking through the waste. I'm careful to stay close behind and within the ring of light.

"Don't touch anything," he says with a wry grin. "The meat upstairs starts out down here."

"Is it safe?"

"Safer than facing the Greens."

Our footsteps echo and the silence reminds me how hungry and tired I am. It must be after noon, and I have had nothing to eat or drink today. I remember the provisions in my backpack, but now is not the time to partake in them. My stomach growls conspicuously.

"Can you cook?" Pit asks.

"Of course," I say, and then remember that not all English women can.

"Not just NGA kibble, but meat, fresh meat?"

NGA? New Generation Ag. He's asking if I know how to prepare non-synthetic food. This must be an even rarer skill, one I'm hesitant to admit to. "Yes," I murmur. "Why do you want to know?"

"It's a requirement for being a Red Dog woman."

I bite my lip to keep from declaring that I will not be a Red Dog woman. I plan to escape as soon as I am sure the Greens can't track me. Hopefully, Pit is bringing me closer to the sewer access point to Stuart Manor. All I need to do is bide my time and stay quiet. For now, I need Pit to get me out of here.

He leads me up a steep staircase and opens a door for me. "Welcome to the kennel."

I remember this place. We are in an enormous warehouse, bigger than a barn, all concrete and steel. We're on the main floor in an atrium-style room, the ceiling three floors above us. Pit makes a whooping sound and one by one dark silhouettes come to the railings of the floors above and stare down at us. All the men are dressed like Pit, in worn but mended clothing in various shades of gray, the same red band around their left biceps. The women are something else entirely. They are dressed the modern way, some with new dresses, high heels, designer shirts. They wear heavy makeup and have brushed hair and fair skin. But every one of them wears a shiny red collar around her neck, two inches thick with a big silver buckle.

A man walks toward us, stopping inside the line of shadows from the floor above. "What do you have there,

Pit?" he asks in a raspy, low voice. He steps into the light. He's big. Huge. On appearance alone, he is formidable. At least six feet tall with bulky muscles I've never seen the likes of. I suspect some sort of chemical augmentation. No one gets that big naturally. A ponytail of long black hair falls down his back and piercings in his lip and eyebrow glint in the light. At first I think he's wearing a long-sleeved shirt, but as he comes closer, I stand corrected. His arms are covered in tattoos. I tremble under his intense scrutiny.

"A woman, Alpha. I found her near the slaughterhouse, running from the Greens," Pit says.

"Do you give this woman a name?" Alpha asks Pit.

"My name is Candace," I say.

Both men ignore me. Others form a circle around us. I grow increasingly uncomfortable. What if one of them remembers me? I'd zapped a man named Hambone and another called Patchwork last year. If one of them recognizes me, they'll know my secret. Eyes rake me from head to toe. One man comes close enough to touch my hair and I have flashbacks to my first time here, when my body reacted and fried everyone who touched me. This time, I hope to make it out without hurting anyone. But just the brush of the man's fingers makes a cold sweat break out over my upper lip.

Pit clears his throat. "Stella," he says. "I claim her."

What? My eyes dart from Pit to Alpha and I stare in horror as a woman runs forward with a bright red collar. "What are you doing?" I whisper to Pit.

"Keeping you safe. Women don't survive in the kennel without a keeper." Pit takes the red collar and moves to place it around my neck. I back away. The men behind me grab my arms and pull my hair to restrain me. Panic lights the spark within and a plan of escape plays out in my brain. I ready myself to do what I have to.

"I challenge."

Everyone's head snaps around, and I cannot believe my eyes. Korwin hovers, arms folded, next to Alpha. His eyes bore into me.

"This woman's name is Lydia, and she's *mine*."

SIXTEEN

My lips part to say his name, but with a curt shake of his head, Korwin shuts me down. He disguises the movement by cracking his neck and backs into the open space at the center of the concrete. "She's mine," he says again, beckoning Pit forward.

"So be it." Alpha gives a genuine laugh. "She is a pretty one, isn't she?" Pit looks distraught as the big man removes the collar from his grip and steps toward Korwin.

A dozen hands reach for me, and I am swept away, up a set of stairs to the second floor. The Red Dog women force me to the front of the railing. From here I have a clear view of the kennel below. But everyone in the kennel also has a clear view of me. Long, manicured nails are in my hair, removing my braids and fluffing the wavy tresses.

"Let's see what's under the jacket," a woman with black bobbed hair says. She forcibly removes my backpack.

"Hey," I protest, reaching for the leather strap as she shifts it to a platinum blonde behind her.

"Relax," she says. "You'll get it back in a minute. We're just going to show the boys what they're fighting for. She unzips my hoodie and strips it from my shoulders. I am thrust against the railing again in nothing but a snug black T-shirt, the waves of my hair thrown over one shoulder. I feel naked like this, and totally vulnerable.

"Quite a prize, boys!" Black Bob calls, pushing my upper body over the railing. I consider fighting her but Korwin's eyes fix me to the spot. His expression couldn't be clearer if he followed it up with *stay put*.

The men have formed a circle around Korwin and Pit, Alpha between them with the collar. Korwin is taller, but Pit is older, more experienced. He carries himself like a battle-worn veteran of the ring.

"Does anyone else challenge for this woman?" Alpha booms.

Korwin clenches his fists and turns a circle. The other men seem intimidated by his presence, even Pit who stands with his hands on his hips. No one says a word.

"You'd better pray Pit wins," the redheaded woman behind me says. "Ace is cruel. I'd never want him as a keeper."

"Sophie!" snaps the platinum blonde holding my backpack.

The kennel grows quiet.

"Very well," Alpha says. "Win the collar, win the bitch. Go!"

He drops the red leather ring between the two men and shuffles out of the way. At first the men circle, sizing each other up. Korwin hangs back, fists raised and eyes narrowed. Pit lunges first, striking at Korwin's jaw. Korwin slaps the fist away and lands a sidekick into Pit's ribs. Pit curls but doesn't quit. He ducks under Korwin's next punch and rams his shoulder into Korwin's gut. The blow rocks him off balance and Korwin stumbles back a few steps. But before

Pit can regain his footing, Korwin grips his hips and lifts the older man's feet off the floor, sending Pit tumbling. The stocky man tucks into a ball, somersaulting into Korwin's knees. Korwin leaps out of the way, straight up, pivots in the air, and delivers a front kick to Pit's left kidney before the man can scramble out of the way.

An audible groan rises from the crowd. Pit crumples but Korwin doesn't quit. He kicks Pit repeatedly in the ribs, head and back. I've never seen Korwin like this. Pit is effectively helpless but Korwin continues, feet and fists flying. Blood spills on the concrete next to Pit's head. Even from the second floor, I can tell his nose is smashed and the skin of his shoulder is split.

"Match!" Alpha says, grabbing Korwin by the waist and pulling him from the fight. "Korwin take your prize."

To my horror, as soon as Alpha releases him, Korwin attacks Pit's prone body again. Lips peeled back from his teeth, he pounds Pit in the head and lands a boot in his ribs. It takes three men to drag him off and by that time Pit is a bloody, bruised mess. Only when Alpha forces the red collar into Korwin's hands does he seem to remember himself. He scans the rail until he finds me, then takes the stairs two at a time, shouldering through the crowd to me. I turn around, gripping the rail as he approaches. I do not know this Korwin. His expression is feral, and he has blood sprayed across his face. Sweat stains his gray muscle shirt and the red band around his arm.

He unbuckles the red collar and steps in close to place it around my neck. "I am Ace," he says, locking eyes with me. "I'm your keeper." He hooks a finger into the silver loop at my throat and yanks me forward. I gag a little and grab his wrist with both my hands, but he doesn't let up.

"Where are her things?"

The platinum blonde tosses my backpack and hoodie at him like they're hot and backs away. Korwin snatches them from the floor before half-dragging me up another flight of stairs to a room on the third floor. He pushes me in by the neck and slides the door closed behind us.

I stumble into the space, gasping for breath and rubbing my neck. "Korwin, I—"

He body slams me against the wall, the length of him pressing me into the concrete. "My name is Ace," he says into my ear. "Things are different here. Women don't speak unless spoken to." One arm slips around my back, making me arch off the wall. His hand lands under my breast while his other one grips my jaw. There is no space between our bodies and his hot breath hits my face. Despite his nearness, something is missing. The usual connection I feel to him, the warmth behind my breastbone, is gone. I have the fleeting thought that this is not Korwin at all.

"You should be used to taking orders from a man, given where you come from," he hisses, remedying that suspicion. He threads his fingers into my hair and tips my face so we are eye to eye. I part my lips to speak but the look he gives me makes the words halt in my throat. His eyes are hard and violent. In his tight grip, I am suddenly afraid.

His hand grips my neck harder through my hair, and his lips crash against mine. The kiss is brutal, invasive. I struggle against him. Not my best effort. I want the kiss, and before long both of us have softened into each other and the spark within me comes alive again.

I'm glowing blue by the time he pulls away, panting.

He gives his head a hard shake, then grabs the hem of his shirt and lifts it over his head. My eyes widen at the sight of his bare chest, and I shake my head, not willing or ready for more than the kiss we just shared.

"Don't flatter yourself," he says. He throws the blood-and-sweat-stained T-shirt into a basket in the corner. "I'll send Sophie to show you where to do laundry." He digs another shirt from the dresser against the wall and pulls it over his head.

"Where are you going?"

"To find you something acceptable to wear." The door to his room is wide and slides like a barn door. He opens it and moves into the hall. With a sideways glance he says, "Stay away from the men. I don't want to have to hurt anyone when I return. And don't try to leave. We have unfinished business."

I stare at him blankly as he walks out. The big door rumbles shut behind him. My knees give out and I crumple, tripping backward. My bottom lands on a hard mattress. With face in hands, I lower my head between my knees and weep.

* * *

"Hey," the redheaded girl called Sophie says, pressing a tissue into my hands. I didn't even hear her come in over my own weeping.

"Hello," I mumble.

"Ace gave you a rough initiation, huh?"

"Yeah." I wipe my swollen eyes. I hate that she calls Korwin *Ace* and that she *expects* my welcome to this world to be violent.

"What did he name you? Lydia, right?"

I nod.

"Do you need a painkiller? My keeper got me some."

"No. Thank you." Medication won't help the type of pain I'm feeling.

"It's hard in the beginning, but you'll get used to this life after a while. Ace is the beta, so you're like a princess here. Plus, the Red Dogs keep their women safe and well fed."

"The beta?"

"Second-in-command." She smiles. "I'm sorry about that crack I made about not wanting him as your keeper. He's a catch. Honestly." Her face gives her away. She's lying.

"Violent though," I say, cupping my cheek.

She sighs. "Yeah."

"So, I'm a prisoner here?" I ask.

"Some girls have left," Sophie says. She tangles her fingers over her stomach. "I'm not sure why. There's nowhere worth going anymore."

Korwin must know I could leave whenever I want, but he trusted me to stay. What Sophie says is true. I have no place else to go. I came here to find *him*. If I leave, what then? Return to the reactor? Join the Liberty Party? Not the worst idea, considering the circumstances. What has happened to him? Deep down, the real Korwin must be in there, buried under this violent-and-aggressive version of himself.

My eyes dart around the room, looking for any clue that the man I once loved lives here. The place is a pigsty— clothes everywhere, dirty dishes on the floor, a pile of books scattered next to the bed, garbage strewn on the dresser. Behind a folding screen in the corner, there's a sink and a toilet that look as if they've never been cleaned.

"He wanted me to do his laundry," I murmur.

"Okay," she says, following my gaze around the room. "I'll get you started on that and then, maybe, you can help Ace clean this place up. I can see why he wanted you. This place needs a woman's touch."

"I've never seen a room like this," I say, staring at the sliding door.

She laughs. "That's a good thing. This used to be a prison. The old-fashioned kind where the bars are on the outside of your body." She walks to the wide door and bangs her fist on the bars on the back of the wood paneling. "These were cages for criminals."

The thought makes me feel claustrophobic. "Would you mind opening the door?"

She does. I take a deep breath of stale air, missing Hemlock Hollow so badly I think I might cry again. But I'm here for a reason, to bring Korwin home. I need to stay long enough to save him, to retrieve him from this life of violence.

"An idle hand does the devil's work," I say. I pick up the basket and begin to gather the dirty clothing strewn around the room.

"You talk funny," she says. When I move to strip the linens from the bed, she helps with the wool blanket and pillowcases. "Who's the devil?"

"You know, from the Bible," I say.

She shakes her head. "I don't really read. I was born in the deadzone, so..." She brushes her red bangs from her eyes and I'm struck by how young she is. Young and impossibly thin.

"You were born here?"

She shakes her head and changes the subject. "The laundry is next to the kitchen on the main floor. We don't have units to waste on the washers, but we do have water and detergent. Come on. I'll show you."

She leads me downstairs, her four-inch heels clicking on the tile floor. Sophie is the opposite of plain in a blue wrap dress that ties above the hip. I wonder how she gets anything done at all in the outfit. She stops in a large white room where a dozen washtubs with ancient-looking wringers are lined up on three long tables. I grimace. Bishop Yoder would approve. Even my wringer washer in Hemlock Hollow is more advanced. There's a box of detergent at the end of each row and clotheslines stretched from one side of the room to the other in the empty space over the unused washers.

"Normally, there are more girls down here, but they're all preparing dinner at this hour. I'd introduce you, but if Ace says you need to do laundry, you need to do laundry."

"Do I cook for... Ace?" I fight my temptation to call him Korwin.

She scratches behind her ear and smoothes a hand over her bright auburn hair. It doesn't need smoothing. "The pack women cook for all the men, not just their own. The ratio here of men to women is twenty to one, so it's a lot of work, but the mutts take care of it most of the time."

"The mutts?"

"The lower class. There are four pack leaders. Ace is one of them. That means you are not a mutt. A pack leader's woman has her own expectations, but we don't have to cook."

Expectations? I frown. After all these weeks, I still think of Korwin as my fiancé. But the way he kissed me was brutal. If Korwin still has feelings for me, they are something altogether different than what they were before. I bristle thinking of what his expectations might be.

Sophie fidgets with the tie of the blue dress she's wearing. "Sink's over there to fill up. Do you need help getting started?"

"No. I've done this before."

Sophie scoffs. "Where are you from that you've had to wash clothes by hand?" She squints at me.

Internally, I chide myself for my big mouth. Of course most people would never use a tub like this in the English world. To buy some time, I lift the washtub and bring it to the sink, then turn on the tap. The water is ice cold. "I'm from Willow's Province and my parents liked to conserve units." Without making eye contact, I shovel a scoop of soap flakes into the running water.

"Oh." Sophie seems unconvinced. "Because if you're from a rival pack, you'd better divulge that information pronto. That's the type of thing Alpha takes seriously. The type of omission that could get you in trouble, even killed."

"I'm not from a rival pack. I'm from Willow's Province." This time I meet her eyes. I grab a shirt from the basket, plunge it into the soapy water, and start scrubbing.

Sophie drops the subject of my origins and marches to a basket under the sink. "Here," she says, handing me a pair of rubber gloves. "It's good you have some experience because you have your work cut out for you with this mess."

I see what she means as I dig through the basket. "Why are all his shirts covered in blood?" I accept the rubber gloves she offers and wipe my hands on my pants before putting them on.

"The blood is because Ace is the pack's prizefighter."

"Like a protector? A soldier?"

"No. That would be Pit and most of the others. Ace fights men from other packs for units. Every Friday is fight night. It's a huge event. The packs take turns hosting, and people bet black market units on the fight. That's why your keeper is beta now. He hasn't lost a match since he arrived. It's a bloody job." She raises her eyebrows and tips her head, as if there is something glamorous and enviable about being a fighter.

I scrub and plunge, scrub and plunge. Everything about what Sophie says bothers me. Korwin hurts others for profit, and worse, people find it entertaining. I place the washed shirt in a second tub, ready for rinsing, and start in on the next.

Sophie sighs. "I'm going to go check on dinner. I know you're new and all, and your keeper scared you tonight, but don't try to leave. Bad things happen to girls who leave, one way or another."

I pause my scrubbing to meet her eyes and lower my chin in assent.

"I'm glad we understand each other." She motions for me to get to work and *click-clacks* her way out the door.

SEVENTEEN

I finish the laundry and hang each of Korwin's garments on the drying line. Several of them look almost new. Compared to the mended rags I remember Pit wearing, they might as well be luxury goods. In some ways, I'm glad Korwin ended up here. He's surviving, safe from the Greens, and hasn't compromised his integrity by rejoining the Liberty Party. Still, I stare at the shirts, seeing the faint remnants of sprayed blood I wasn't able to work from the fabric, and fresh tears anoint my cheeks.

Our lives have spun out of control, as distant from the life we'd planned as night from day. The future I imagined, white house, farm, a baby on my hip, church on Sunday, it all dissolves in a flash of blue light. Still, he has claimed me. Despite the *Ordnung's* rejection of him, and my delay in coming to find him, he still chose me. He still fought for me. That, at least, tells me that things between us aren't completely broken.

I run a finger under the red collar around my neck. My father would explode if he saw it. A child of God treated like a common pet. I should be livid. I should stand up for myself. Who would stop me if I tried to leave? No one I couldn't burn like forgotten toast. So why do I stay, hanging laundry with a collar around my neck?

It comes down to hope. Maybe, if I do this for him, stay and be his woman here, we can regain what we lost. If I can reach the Korwin I remember, the kind and decent man who lives under the harsh, violent exterior, I can bring him back from this godless life. I resolve to win his love again. And when I do, we can return home and leave all this behind us.

"Good, you're done," Sophie says as I hang the sheets. "Let's go get you dressed for dinner." She *clip-clops* to a mirror on the wall and fluffs her hair.

"I only have what I'm wearing," I say. "And another outfit like it."

With a disapproving scan of my outfit, she shakes her head. "Oh, honey, you can't wear that." She takes me by the elbow and leads me from the room. "It's your keeper's duty to provide you with something more... eye catching. You're his woman now. He'll want you to dress the part." She pats my arm. "I'll get you started in the bath and find you something."

She ushers me down the hall to an unassuming gray door. Inside is a small room that doesn't belong in the concrete bunker. There's a fireplace with a lively fire burning and a painted cast-iron kettle resting near the flames. At the center of the room is an antique porcelain bathtub on an exquisite woven rug. There's a small sitting area.

"This is... unexpected." I trip on the word, as if it isn't quite adequate. The room is surprisingly posh, with velvet curtains and textured walls.

"Add the entire kettle," she says. "Without the boiling

water, it makes for a cold bath." She hands me a hot pad and motions toward the fireplace. "Towels are over there in the cabinet with anything else you might need. Do you need a clip for your hair?"

"No. I'll manage."

"Good." She turns to leave.

A question comes to me and I can't help myself from asking. "Sophie? Do all the Red Dog women get to use this room?"

She laughs. "No. Just pack leaders and their women."

I clear my throat. "I never asked, but who is your keeper?"

She smiles. "I thought you knew. I'm Alpha's girl."

"Oh."

"Now, be quick. You do not want to be late for dinner your first night here." She tips her chin up for a moment. "That could be a mistake you regret later."

"Why? What would happen to me?"

"Let's just say that Red Dog men do not withhold physical punishment." She slips out the door, leaving me alone in the flickering firelight.

As Sophie suggested, I pour the entire contents of the kettle into the bath. It's enough to make the water blissfully warm, and I intend to take advantage of it while it lasts. Quickly, I strip down and lower myself into the water. The heat radiates through me. I groan and rest my head, allowing my still-dry hair to fan out over the edge of the tub.

How long have I been awake? When was the last time I ate? With no clock in the room, I can't divine the answer, only that the excitement and adrenaline that have fueled me to this point are gone. I slip into a dreamy state of almost-sleep, where images of Korwin mingle with home.

The rattle of the door opening brings me to my senses.

"Have I taken too long?" I ask, eyes still closed. I presume it's Sophie bringing me my dress.

"Well, this is an amusing turnabout." Korwin's voice. Not Sophie.

I sink deeper into the water. My face warms as I turn and catch a glimpse of him behind me. "Kor—"

His hand clamps over my mouth. "Ace."

"Ace," I say when he pulls his hand away. I lower my voice. "You have to leave. I'm... naked."

"First, I seem to recall a day at my father's house when you not only walked in on my bath but reached in and pulled me to the surface." My ears grow hot remembering. "And second? I don't have to do anything." He turns his back to me and digs through my pile of dirty clothes. He holds up the red leather collar. "Cast it aside already, did you?"

"Surely you didn't expect me to wear it in the tub?"

"No."

"I don't like wearing it at all. I'm not property."

"This isn't Hemlock Hollow, Lydia," he says through his teeth. He turns toward me, collar in hand, the fire illuminating his face in a warm glow. "If you aren't my property, you'll be someone else's before sundown, and I guarantee they won't honor your virtue like I will."

I cross my arms under the water and look toward the fire. "Do you call pressing me against the wall of your room preserving my virtue?"

"Take accountability. How we left things, I was more than a little shocked at your arrival today. Would you rather be sharing a marriage bed with Pit?"

I turn to face him and there isn't an ounce of humor in his expression. I reach for the collar.

"Allow me," he says, placing it around my neck.

"You know I'd never let Pit touch me. I'd fry him to ash before he came close."

Korwin finishes buckling and reaches for something beside him. A hairbrush. He pulls up a chair behind me and grabs a handful of my hair, methodically brushing out the knots. I try not to think about the fact that the water is a poor concealer of my naked flesh.

"Now, tell me what your plan is to return to Hemlock Hollow," he says.

I furrow my brow, not expecting him to be open to the idea so soon. "We can leave tonight. We'll have to be careful because the Greens are looking for me, but if we travel by sewer—"

He stops brushing. "We?"

"Yes. I came to get you, to bring you back home, so we could face our discipline together."

The brush strokes down my hair again—slowly, absently.

"Our discipline? I don't recall you being punished for anything."

"The day you left... there was a flasher. I took care of it, but Ebbie Lapp saw. Some people are saying I'm a witch."

He grips my hair in his hand, forcing my head back painfully, although I don't think he does it intentionally. "They punished you for being a witch?"

"Not exactly. I wasn't outwardly disciplined. Someone made a doll to look like me and set it on fire in our front yard." Korwin's sharp inhale coincides with a sharper tug on my hair. I place my hand on his, and he loosens his grip. "Whoever did it left a note. *Thou shalt not suffer a witch to live.* So, um, I was not asked to leave as you were, but my father thought that it was safer for me."

"Lydia... I don't know what to say. They burned you at the stake in effigy?"

"Jeremiah thought if I agreed to marry him people would forget and accept me again."

"Go back. Do it," he says without hesitation. "This place isn't good for you."

I strain my neck to look at him, placing both hands on the side of the tub. "I don't want to marry Jeremiah."

He releases my hair and rises from his position. "You could go to David. The Liberty Party could keep you safe."

"I went there first, looking for you."

He snorts derisively. "Of all of the places, you must have known I wouldn't go there."

"Where else would I think you might go?" I say, gripping the sides of the tub. "How did you end up here anyway?"

Korwin picks up a towel and holds it open in front of him. "Come on. We're going to be late. You need to get dressed."

"I know you don't believe me, but I regret not following you the day you left. I should have stood up for you and—"

"Stop." His voice is stern, threatening. "First, I wouldn't have let you go with me. Second, there was nothing you could have said or done to change what happened. Now, stand up. Get dressed. We're going to be late."

I stand and wrap the towel around my body. There's a plastic dress bag resting on a bench near the tub next to a paper sack.

He faces the wall while I towel off and unveil the dress he's brought for me. Conscious of my nudity, I slip it on as quickly as possible.

"Korwin, I can't wear this." I stare at myself in the mirror on the wall. The dress is purple and stretchy. The material crosses low between my breasts, cinches at the waist, and extends barely to the middle of my thigh. In the paper bag, I find a pair of knee-high boots in beige suede. I put them on experimentally, teetering on the high heels.

"Are you covered?" he asks.

"If you can call it that."

He pivots. When he sees me, his eyes widen for a moment and then his mouth stretches into a wry smile. "What's wrong with it?"

"This is not modest."

"No. No, it is not."

I spread my hands and stare at him disbelievingly.

His lips purse and he places his hands on his hips. "You say you came here for me, Lydia. This is the life I lead now. This is how the women here dress."

"But now that I've found you, can't we just go home? I mean, a bite to eat would be nice, but do I have to do this?" I circle my hand in front of the dress, ending by pointing at the collar.

"I'm not going back," he says, shaking his head.

"What?" I whisper.

His jaw hardens. "Let me put it plainly, Lydia. Either you wear the dress and act the part or you go back to Hemlock Hollow with your tail between your legs and beg Jeremiah to marry you. He can beg the bishop to take you back. I won't do it."

I tug at the dress, but there is no way to make it cover more of me. My cheeks warm with shame looking down at myself.

Korwin holds up his hands. "I can walk out now, accidentally leave the door unlocked, and you can hijack a car and be home by morning, but if you think I'm returning to that hateful bunch of self-righteous men and women you call a community, you are mistaken." He turns to leave.

I have only moments to decide what to do. He crosses the room. His hand is on the door. "I'm not going anywhere," I blurt.

He stops and looks over his shoulder at me. Our eyes lock. For a moment, it's back—that feeling, deep in my chest, like I'm connected to Korwin by a stretched rubber band. I take one step, then another as it tugs me in his direction. When I reach him, he gathers me into his arms as if he can't help himself, his breath coming quick and ragged in my ear.

"I've missed you," I whisper. I think he might kiss me again but instead he pushes me away. The brief connection fades as he turns his head away.

"We have to go." He threads my hand through his elbow and helps me walk to the door.

"Wait, should I clean up here?" I ask.

He shakes his head. "There are people to do that."

"Oh."

As he opens the door for me and leads me down the long hall, I whisper, "Why did you name me Lydia?" He knows what I mean. Everyone else has a fake name, a new persona.

Korwin frowns toward the wall and murmurs, "Because I couldn't bear for them to call you anything else."

EIGHTEEN

WITHOUT KORWIN HOLDING ME UP, I WOULD HAVE never made it to dinner. As it is, I struggle to lower myself into the chair he offers me without falling off my sky-high heels. The other pack leaders are already seated when we arrive. My chair is across from Sophie, on the other side of Alpha who sits at the head of the table. Korwin takes the chair on my right.

The table itself is something out of a dream. On a raised platform at the front of the dining hall, it's drenched in candlelight and dressed with crystal goblets and gold-edged plates. The majority of Red Dogs eat from orange acrylic trays, sitting on the wood slats of folding tables in the main section of the cafeteria. Some eat with their hands. They wait in line to serve themselves, cafeteria style.

"Don't stare at the mutts, Princess." Alpha grabs my chin between his thumb and forefinger and turns my head back toward the table. "It enrages them."

Mutts. That's what they call everyone else here. Everyone who is not a pack leader.

I look away obediently. One of the female mutts fills my

glass with a deep red liquid. I want to ask for water but none of the other women are saying anything. I don't know if I'm allowed. I lift the goblet to my nose and give it a good sniff, then put the glass back down without taking a sip.

"It's wine," Korwin says. "Real stuff. Old; from before the West Coast was covered in ocean. I think you'll like it."

Four men have earned the ranks of Red Dog leadership: Alpha, Korwin (known as Ace), Sting, and Jake. Aside from Korwin, the men look like mutants, excessively tall and muscled with abnormally broad foreheads and a smattering of gruesome scars. No one in Hemlock Hollow looks like this, and I can't help but suspect again that chemistry has played a part in their warped appearance.

In contrast, the women at the table are beautiful beyond words. Sophie, Alpha's mate, wears a deep blue strapless gown. A plush swag of auburn hair covers one eye before curling over her shoulder. Her face looks carved in the candlelight. Sting's wife, Bella, I remember from the challenge. Her black bob is sleek and sophisticated. She's dressed in a black leather bustier and has a silver heart charm dangling from her red collar. Jake's wife, Bailey, is platinum blonde with blunt cut bangs over enormous blue eyes. She's wearing a red dress with a corset that looks like it's made of rubber. The outfit is so suggestive I can't look directly at her without feeling dirty.

I try not to think about my own dress, or the fact that my hair is down and uncovered. It's shameful, but Korwin is right. Anything else would stick out here, and it is clear the status of these men is based in some part on the appearance of their women. For now, until I can convince Korwin to return to Hemlock Hollow with me, I need to be a good Red Dog woman. I take a drink of wine, my face twisting at the taste of alcohol when I swallow.

"You've never had liquor?" Sting asks, staring at me.

I shake my head.

"Where on Earth are you from?" He breaks apart a roll and slathers it in butter while everyone at the table stares at me, waiting for a response.

"Willow's Province," I say. "My parents rarely let me out of the house. I was sort of a prisoner."

"Hmm." Jake leans back in his chair. "How'd you get away?"

"Father died," I say. Korwin's eyes dart in my direction. He's probably surprised at how easy it's become for me to lie, but by now I'm well practiced.

"You look young to be in the deadzone all by yourself. Especially young to have the Greens chase you here," Jake says. He pauses, roll in hand, and points his butter knife at me. "Why do the Greens want you so badly?"

It suddenly strikes me as strange that none of the Red Dogs recognize Korwin or me, but then there is no television here, and all of these men must be outlaws or outcasts in some way or they'd be living on the grid. "Misunderstanding. Nothing worth worrying about." I make my voice sound sweet and young. Innocent.

There's a moment of silence while they stare at me, as if waiting for me to spill my secrets. When I say nothing, tension builds until Alpha breaks into laughter. "Well, drink up, young'un. You're not in Willow's Province anymore." He chuckles and clinks Korwin's glass, almost as if he's congratulating him on capturing naïve me.

Korwin smiles, raises his glass, and says, "I plan to teach her lots of things."

The comment makes my face heat and the table bursts into laughter as I stare into the empty copper charger in front of me. Thankfully, at that moment, dinner is served.

A plate of dark meat, whipped potatoes, and carrots lands in front of Alpha. The server is there and gone in an instant, as if she is afraid to interrupt him. The same food is placed in front of me, but Korwin grips my wrist beneath the table, warning me not to eat. All the men, including Korwin, cut into their meat and take a bite. Only after they've chewed and swallowed does Sophie pick up her fork. I glance toward Korwin. Am I supposed to start?

He nudges me with his knee. I pick up my fork and knife, shoveling in a bite of potatoes. They taste real, like the kind we have back home, and I dig in, hungry from the day's drama.

"Word on the street is that the Knights have five thousand units on a contender for Friday," Alpha says through a mouth of half-masticated food.

"I've heard," Korwin says. "I'm confident I can take him."

"Good, because I'm considering upping the stakes," Alpha continues.

"To what?"

"Ten thousand." Alpha lifts his goblet of wine and takes a large gulp.

A collective murmur is audible over the scratching forks and clinking glasses.

"That's a heavy investment," Korwin says, raising his eyebrows.

Sophie gestures for me to keep eating. The other women are hyper-attentive to their plates. Perhaps I appear too interested in a conversation that is not supposed to concern me. I cut into the meat and try a bite. Venison, I'm almost positive. I wash it down with another swig of wine. This time I'm accustomed to the taste.

"The Red Dogs have grown with the expansion of the

deadzone. Your woman here is a prime example." Alpha points the finger of his goblet-holding hand at me. "We need more units to support the troops. Can't do without refrigeration here, and come winter, we'll need the heat and the light."

"I don't know the fighter. I've heard he's new to the deadzone," Korwin says.

"You've never lost," Jake says through a mouthful of meat. I notice for the first time that one of his eyes doesn't move like the other one, even though it seems like he can see out of it. Sophie taps my shin with her foot and I focus on my plate again.

"Believe me, I appreciate your confidence. I'm just saying there's a risk. There are no rules in the cage. And the Knights are especially sick of losing."

That makes the men laugh and drain their glasses. I take another sip and notice I've reached the bottom of my goblet as well. I must have drunk it all listening to the conversation. I set the glass down and it is filled again before I can pull my hand away.

"I have every confidence in you, Ace," Alpha says. "You know, that cell you're living in is hardly big enough for two. Win this one and we'll spend the manpower to build you something more appropriate."

I've cleaned my plate and finished my second glass of wine. My head swims and my body feels floaty. In my altered state, I try to digest the implications of what Alpha is saying. It sounds like a reward, but there's a threat latent in the words.

Korwin must have caught the threat part too because his expression is wrought with anxiety. "And if I lose?"

Alpha groans and spreads his hands as if it's anyone's guess what might happen.

"You won't lose," Sting says in a voice strangely high and feminine for his bulky body.

A lengthy pause has everyone concentrating on the wine. Finally, Alpha sighs as if a suitable punishment has just come to him. "If you lose, you go back to the mutts."

Korwin pales, although he keeps his expression carefully impassive.

"You won't lose," Alpha says with a chuckle. "But if you do, I promise you I'll keep Lydia in the lifestyle she's grown accustomed to." His hand brushes my knee under the table.

Noisily, I jerk my chair away so that my knee is out of his reach. This puts me almost on top of Korwin and gains the attention of everyone at the table. "Grown accustomed?" I repeat inquisitively, the wine making my lips feel slightly numb. "I've been here less than a day, and you said yourself that Ace's room is hardly accommodating. I won't require any special treatment if Ace loses."

Alpha's face turns a bright shade of beet and his lips purse.

Korwin forces a laugh and pulls me into his side. "What's all this talk about losing? I haven't lost a fight yet."

Sting picks his teeth with his fork. "Some people think there isn't a challenge you could lose."

Alpha straightens and gives Korwin a narrow look. I have no idea what's going on, but the tension at the table is enough for me to take another sip of wine. The smooth liquid is barely down my throat when I hiccup. A loud, open-mouthed sound that brings everyone's attention back to me. I try to stop, to hold it back, but another one comes. At least this time I keep my lips closed.

"Sorry," I say, hand over mouth. I hiccup again. This one sounds like a muffled squeak.

Korwin pushes his chair back from the table and rises.

"Please excuse me. It appears *my* woman needs to be put to bed."

The entire table erupts into laughter and before I know it, I am tugged into Korwin's side and led from the dining hall.

"I feel funny," I say, hiccupping between *feel* and *funny*.

"That's because you're drunk. Why didn't you hold off on the wine?"

"You didn't tell me it would make me drunk."

"People in Hemlock Hollow drink alcohol. It's not some new Englisher invention."

"Yes, but I've never had it before. I thought it would take more to feel the effects."

By the time we make it to his room, I don't feel like myself. The world comes to me in flashes of light and color. Korwin props my back against the wall and lights a few candles before closing and locking the door.

"I'm going to fall off these boots," I say, trying to lift one foot to take them off and tumbling, ungracefully, into the wardrobe. The heavy piece of furniture rattles ominously.

"Wait. Let me help you." He kneels in front of me, unzips one boot and slides it from my foot. I brace myself on his shoulders to keep my balance. My fingers automatically knead the muscles there. It's a pleasurable experience, touching Korwin, and I run my thumbs along the side of his neck as he removes my other boot. The footwear hits the floor with a thud when he casts it aside, and for some reason this strikes me as supremely hilarious. I laugh from my belly and can't stop.

"There. I won't have you breaking your neck your first night here." His hands are still on my leg, one under the outside of my knee and the other skimming my inner thigh. He raises his face to look at me, and I stop laughing. Full lips parted, a spark of blue lights up the irises of his hooded eyes.

"You're so beautiful," I mumble. I mean it to be an internal thought but it pops out from between my lips of its own accord.

A crooked smile graces his lips. "You're drunk." His wrist reaches the hem of my dress, mid-thigh, and I lean harder into the cool wall in an effort to balance the heat he's putting off.

"Maybe," I agree. He strokes higher, until a shiver travels the length of me, from the place where he gently rubs to the roots of my hair.

There is something I'm supposed to say now, something I'm supposed to do. I can't remember. I could no sooner hold a thought within the wavy confines of my brain than capture the flicker of the candles in my palm. I'm spinning and warm, tingly. Mute, I sink my fingers into his hair and tip his head back, then lower my mouth to his. Welcoming my kiss, he softly caresses my lips with his own, then cups the back of my neck to pull me closer.

With his hand stroking around my hip, he stands and pulls me flat against his chest. The power ebbs and flows between us, our connection growing. The spark within me begs for release. I can feel the heat catching in my throat, my skin coming alive with blue twisting veins of energy. His body is reacting in the same way, filling the room with light and warmth. I tug on his hair and force the kiss deeper, running my fingers along the nape of his neck. I wrap one leg around his—weightless, burning, totally in the moment.

"No." He stops and pulls away. I desperately want him to move in the opposite direction, to touch me in an intimate way. I'm ready to come out of my skin for want of him and there's nothing to stop us here. No rules or elders or expectations.

I grip his shirt to keep him close. "Please."

To seal my invitation, I grab the hem of his shirt and lift it over his head, placing my hands on his bare skin underneath. His eyes widen. With a shaky breath, he steps into me again, hands sliding over my ribs. I run my nails across his abs and along the muscles of his back.

"Lydia..." Korwin groans and shakes his head. "You don't have to do this." I trail kisses up his neck to his ear. "You shouldn't."

I suck his earlobe between my teeth. His eyes flutter closed and he pitches forward slightly, resting an elbow against the wall. One hand skims up my spine to my nape.

All at once, he unbuckles the collar at my throat and tosses it on the dresser, making a face like it sickens him. The overture makes me smile. Our lips meet and the familiar snap connects us once again. Hot energy pours down my throat and out of my fingertips into his skin, a complete circuit. Hotter we burn, until we glow like a star. I'm relieved that this room is made of concrete because I can't control the heat I'm putting off and I can't stop. I won't stop.

Korwin grabs my wrists, panting, and pushes me away, not roughly but with enough strength that I can't misinterpret his intentions. One step, then two, he retreats, his face contorting in pain.

"Kor—" He cuts me off by raising one hand.

"Get into bed," he says, pointing at the brown wool blanket beside him.

"Yes. Better." I do as I'm told, leaning back on my elbows.

He shakes his head and moves for the door.

"Where are you going?"

"To save us both from a huge mistake."

"It's not a mistake," I say, ignoring the slur of the S sound as I say it. "If things had gone as planned, we'd already be married."

Korwin places his hands on his hips and hangs his head. "We would be, but we're not. You deserve better than this. We both do."

"But—"

"Get some sleep," he whispers. The door rolls back, and then he's gone.

NINETEEN

When I wake, I have no recollection of what has occurred between Korwin's leaving and my eyelids fluttering open. Silver light washes over me from the window above the bed. Early morning. It's cold and I'm lying on top of the blankets. I shift to wrap the edge around me and a heavy arm rakes me against a wide chest. Korwin's arm. He's returned and slept beside me.

The events of the night before come back to me along with a thumping ache between my temples. My mouth is dry and pasty, as if I've been sucking on a wool sock all night. Ugh, if this is the effect of too much drink, I will not be partaking again anytime soon. Gently, I disentangle myself from Korwin's arm and crawl off the end of the bed, careful not to wake him. Aside from rolling to his other side, his breathing remains even.

I find the black backpack David gave me in the corner and dig in it for the dopp kit. Behind the folding screen, I wet my brush in the sink and scrub my teeth. The braid I fashion in my hair is tight and I scrub my face almost raw. When I'm finished, I take a long look in the mirror. Who have I become, drinking too much and throwing myself at Korwin? I'm a lucky woman to have an honorable man to save me from myself.

Only then does it occur to me that I need something to wear. The dress from last night can't be appropriate for day work. Even Sophie was wearing pants when I arrived. I come out from behind the folding screen and take a quick inventory of the room. The corner of a box pokes out from under the bed. I move toward it, but then notice a zippered bag just inside the door—a recent addition and the probable source of my new clothing. I squat down and unzip it. Sure enough, a few outfits, all brand new and the height of Republic fashion. Did Korwin steal these? Spend units on me that he won fighting?

I don a pair of stretchy leggings and an orange tunic with a deep vee neck. When I'm finished dressing, I want to help clean the tiny apartment, but Korwin is still sleeping. "The laundry," I say softly. I've left it hanging in the laundry room. It will need folding and by the sheer amount of wash, I doubt he has anything to wear if I don't get it. Not to mention, the reason Korwin and I slept on top of the blanket is likely because the sheets are still drying on the line.

Silently, I unlock the door and slide it open, just enough to slip through without too much of a rumble. With a last look at Korwin's sleeping form, I decide to try to find my hero breakfast. Something fitting to accompany the many apologies I owe him.

The kennel is empty as I cross the row of rooms that used to be prison cells and jog down the stairs to the laundry room. My headache is in full bloom and I rub my temples. It doesn't help. If I see Sophie, I might ask her for those painkillers she offered yesterday.

Thankfully, Korwin's clothes and sheets are still there. It occurs to me, I've been lucky. I'm sure most of the mutts would love to get their hands on these. I pull them down and fold them carefully into the basket. I've just finished the last shirt when footsteps bring my attention to the doorway.

"I thought I saw you pass my cell," Pit says. He glances over his shoulder and around the room before approaching me. The results of Korwin's beating are evident in the bruises that cover his exposed skin, his split lip and black eye, but he doesn't move like he's in pain. Still, his eyes are rimmed with red and his hands tremble. A muscle in his lip twitches.

I lift the basket in front of me, but I can't leave because he's blocking the only door. "Just finishing some laundry."

Pit approaches, picks up the T-shirt on top with two fingers. "You do good work. I'm sorry I lost you."

I shrug. "I'd better get going. Ace is expecting me." I try to shoulder around him, but he steps sideways, blocking my progress.

"You're not wearing your collar." He brushes a crooked finger across my exposed collarbone, grinning.

I jerk away from his touch, and his smile melts into a scowl. "Don't disrespect me, girlie." He grabs for me but I block his hands with the laundry basket. We engage in a tug of war. I don't let go. A chemical stench wafts off him. Not alcohol but he's intoxicated. Clearly, it's not the clothes he wants.

"Let go, please," I say. "Ace will be angry if I'm late."

"Bullshit." One solid tug and the basket and clothes scatter across the table of wash bins. Pit rushes me. I scramble backward until I hit the full-length mirror on the wall. His breath is foul in my face as he presses himself into my raised hands.

I'll fry him before I let him get any further. "Please no. Leave me alone."

"Pit," Bella says. She's standing in the doorway in nothing but a short, silky kimono and her red collar. "Alpha wants to see you."

Pit glances over his shoulder and backs off a quarter of an inch. "She's not wearing her collar," he says indignantly.

Bella shrugs. "Alpha wants to see you, *now*."

"Bullshit. You're trying to distract me from taking what's mine."

"I'll tell him you refused." Bella turns to leave, flipping the bangs of her silky black bob out of her eyes.

Pit slams his fist on the folding table and storms from the room, pushing Bella as he passes. Her body slaps the wall, the side of her head bouncing off the concrete bricks. "I'll ask him myself and you better pray you're telling the truth," Pit growls.

I run to her side. "Are you hurt?"

"No, but you'd better hustle and find your collar, New Girl. I doubt it's going to take long for Pit to figure out I made the whole thing up."

I run for the basket and start to gather the scattered clothing. Bella helps me. "It was hard for me too in the beginning," she says, ushering me into the hall with my basket of now wrinkled laundry. "When Sting took me, I was an Uppercrust." She scoffs. "I wanted to be a doctor one day."

"Took you? So you aren't here by choice?"

She snorts. "Not any more than you or any of the other women here. Except maybe Sophie and that's because she doesn't know anything else. I guess you could say it's our choice not to leave, one way or another." She draws a finger across her neck. "No one has ever made it out alive. If the mutts don't get you, the Greens will and they are much, much worse."

"You're running from the Greens too?"

She gives me a strange look. "Why else would I be here?"

"But you said you were an... Uppercrust." I've heard the term before and assumed it meant someone who was wealthy and influential in Green society.

We jog up the stairs and pause in front of Korwin's apartment. The look she gives me is positively deadly. "I'll forgive you for the faux pas because you're new, but we don't like to talk about the past around here. And we never, ever go out without our collars." She pushes back the door.

Korwin startles in bed at the rumble, rubbing his face and propping himself up on his arms. "What's going on?"

Bella shoves me into the room. "I found your woman in the laundry room without her collar."

"What?" Korwin's voice is reproachful. He bounds out of bed and snatches the red collar from the dresser, wrapping it around his fist.

"Good thing I found her too. Pit was about to stake his claim in a way you wouldn't have cared for."

Violently, Korwin tears the basket from my hands and throws it against the wall. It hits with a crack of plastic on concrete. I jump and give a high-pitched squeak as the clothes fly across the bed. I try to back out the door but he grabs my shoulder.

"Leave us," he growls at Bella.

"She's new, Ace. I talked to her."

"Bella, walk out and close the door *now*," Korwin says through his teeth.

She obeys. The door isn't fully closed before Korwin's fist flies toward my face.

TWENTY

I SCREAM, EXPECTING KORWIN'S PUNCH TO CONNECT with my jaw. Instead, it skims past my cheek and collides with his opposite palm with a resounding *crack*. Confused, I raise my eyes to his.

"You need to learn your place," he yells, and punches his palm again. He places one finger in front of his lips. On bare feet, he crosses the apartment to press his ear against the door. After a few seconds, he turns his face back toward me.

I'm shaking and tears have welled in my lower lids. No matter how much I sniff, I can't stop them from spilling.

"Lydia..." Korwin approaches and gently cradles my face in his hands. Wiping the tears from my cheeks, he pulls me into a firm embrace. "I'm sorry it's like this here. It's not the way you should be treated, I admit. It's just the way it is," he whispers. He kisses me on the forehead, then slips the collar around my neck and buckles it into place.

I recognize my own words, although I sense no malevolence in the way he says them. "I said almost exactly the same thing to you."

"You did? When?"

"In Hemlock Hollow. About the paintings."

"See how that turned out? I should have listened to you." He smiles sadly.

"As I should listen to you now. If we're going to stay here, I'll have to be smarter about things."

"If..." He turns away from me and reaches for the basket. I help him gather up the clothes. "Are you sure I can't convince you to go back?" He nudges the collar around my neck. "This place isn't for you, Lydia."

I shake my head. "I told you. I'm not going anywhere without you. Whatever we decide to do, we do it together."

"I can't go back to the Lapps," he mutters. "You don't know what it was like."

"I heard."

"What?"

"Jeremiah told me. Well, Jacob Bender overheard Abram's confession to Isaac. He was intentionally hard on you. He wanted to tempt you to leave. Abram started the fire to frame you."

"He admitted it?"

"Yes. In private confession."

"It was bad, Lydia. I was practically shunned in that house. No one spoke to me. If I wasn't at the table, they wouldn't call me to dinner." Korwin's face reddens as if the memories are both embarrassing and painful. "I can't do it for another year."

"But..."

"But what?"

I frown toward the floor. It's an intimate question I must ask him, but I have to know. "What about your baptism?"

Korwin's eyes shift away from me.

"Do you still believe in God, Korwin?"

He groans and runs a hand through his hair. "I don't know. Probably. Maybe."

All the air rushes from me like I've been punched in the gut. I take a few slow, deep breaths before I react, trying my best to rein in the emotions that threaten to explode from me. "When we first met, I could tell you thought I was silly for believing, but I thought... you were almost baptized, Korwin. Are you telling me, during all our time in Hemlock Hollow, you never believed in God?"

"I thought I did, for a while. But then I wondered why. Why were the Lapps so cruel to me? Why was the world so cruel to us? We don't even know if we can safely be together physically, Lydia. What kind of God does that to people? Makes us fall in love, makes us want only each other, and then makes being together this horrifically risky act. Why?"

"It's not our place to ask why."

He scoffs. "Or maybe there is no one to ask. Isn't it easier to believe that there is no mastermind in the sky? Maybe this is all chance." He pauses. My eyes are filled with tears and my chest is weighted. I take shallow breaths. "I don't know. I'm just saying... the circumstances... It's a difficult leap to make."

Nodding slowly, I bite my lower lip. My mind races with the implications. Am I willing to make this sacrifice for Korwin? Have I already made it? My head aches thinking about it. But deep inside, I refuse to accept Korwin's change of heart. If he believed once, maybe he'll believe again.

"Then we can't go back to Hemlock Hollow," I say.

"No."

"Where else can we go? We both hate the Liberty Party. David is on the council now."

"Wait, wait, wait," he says, extending his hand. "Are you saying that David, the traitor who turned my father in to the Greens and shot you full of Nanomem, is on the leadership council of the Liberty Party?"

"Yes."

"Why?" He shakes his head. "How?"

"It's like he said when he came to Hemlock Hollow, they think he was justified. Your dad made some choices the Liberty Party didn't support."

"The West Hub."

I nod.

"No way am I taking orders from my father's killer," he hisses. "The Outlands are not an option and everywhere else is on-grid."

"Maybe you could get us new ID's," I say.

"And the facial and vocal recognition software would still catch us." He frowns. " I know it's not ideal here, Lydia, but we are completely off-grid and you're safe."

"Yeah, when I'm not fighting off Pit."

"We both know you could have fried him if things went too far."

"Like a donut," I agree.

"It's better you didn't. There's still a huge reward offered for us. Most of the Red Dogs have their own reasons for avoiding the Greens, and most have been off-grid so long they couldn't care less about who is wanted for what. Even if they recognized us, most would be too lazy or too scared to do anything about it. But no sense bringing attention to our abilities."

"Korwin, there's something I need to tell you," I begin. "Something I've been worried about since Pit brought me here."

"What?"

"I've been here before."

He crinkles his brow at me.

"And last time, it didn't end well."

"What are you talking about?"

"Last year, when I left the manor through the sewer, a Red Dog named Hambone captured me. Another named Patchwork almost collared me. There were at least six men touching me when I sparked out. They all went down."

He rubs his chin. "Patchwork and Hambone? Never heard of them. They might have moved on to another clan."

I frown. I hope he's right. I didn't mean to hurt those men, just protect myself. It's crossed my mind during the last year that I might have killed one or all of them when my power lashed out.

"Try not to worry about it, Lydia. Even if one of them saw you, they might not recognize you. Try not to be alone in public areas. If we run into one of them, we'll... explain things to them."

"What's to explain?"

"Self-protecting scamping equipment." He shrugs. "We'll come up with something."

"Okay." I circle my fingers over my temples.

"What's wrong?"

"Please, can we get some water? My head."

He flashes a lopsided grin. "You're hungover."

I press my fingers against my temples. "It throbs, here."

"Yeah, that'll happen. Lucky for you, I have a cure."

He hooks his arm in mine and leads me from the room. The hallways and stairwells are conspicuously empty. "Red Dogs are usually late risers. I'm surprised Pit and Bella were up."

I shrug. "I don't think he'd been to bed yet. He smelled like chemicals and acted drunk."

"Probably smoking Slip."

"What's Slip?"

"It's an acid that's produced during the production of meat products. The meat makers coax a stem cell to become muscle in a vat of solution. The solution becomes acidic as the meat draws in certain minerals from the solution to grow and pumps out enzymes... byproducts of the manufacturing process. Slip is toxic to plants and animals, so NGA puts it into barrels and dumps it in the deadzone. The people here boil it down into a tar and smoke it to get high. It's addictive and deadly."

"If it's addictive and deadly, why do they smoke it?"

"It's free and causes an intense high. I've seen people go three days on the stuff without sleeping or eating. I've seen people die after taking it."

"Hmm."

"Everyone here has to earn their keep. Mutts' lives are hard. Brutal sometimes. It's a cheap escape."

I nod, although I don't truly understand why someone would risk his or her long-term health for a temporary high. I remember the chemical smell from my first run-in with the Red Dogs and form another theory of what happened to Hambone and Patchwork.

I'm relieved when we arrive at a door labeled *kitchen* and I can put thoughts of Slip and my prior escape from the Red Dogs behind me. The industrial-style galley is just around the corner from the laundry room.

"I call this recipe Old Reliable, and when I say old, I mean a couple of weeks, as that is the history of my drinking career," Korwin says.

"Since you came here?"

"Since I left you." From the back of a stainless steel cupboard, he slides out a pitcher with a blade at the bottom attached to a base with a plug.

"What is that?" I ask.

"A blender."

"I thought there was no electricity?"

"Oh, we have units here. They're just highly rationed. Anyway, I don't plan to use any."

Near the back, he opens a pantry and retrieves a few jars and boxes. "Bananas," he says, holding up a jar of yellow fruit slices. He opens the lid and dumps the contents in the blender. "Eggs." A box this time, full of powder.

"Those are not eggs," I say.

"As close as we come here." Rotating his hand over the stash, he selects a plastic bottle. "OJ." The entire bottle glugs into the mix. "And the secret ingredient." He plucks another box from the stack and adds a heaping scoop of black granules.

"What is that?"

"Instant coffee."

"Eww. Sounds hideous."

"Watch for nosey mutts," he says, pointing toward the door. I cross the room and look left and right down the hall. "It's clear."

Hand wrapped around the prongs at the end of the cord, Korwin concentrates until the blade at the bottom of the device spins with a low hum. In less than a minute, the ingredients are blended into a frothy orangish beverage. He releases the cord. The blades stop. A gesture of his chin has me checking the hall once more.

"Clear," I say.

"Good." He retrieves a set of glasses from the cupboard and fills one, then the other, before washing out the blender in the giant sink. "Go ahead. I need to clean this up before anyone asks questions."

I take a tentative sip. "It's not bad."

He scrubs and rinses the pitcher. "Give it a chance on

that headache. You'll come to appreciate it beyond the taste."

The throb between my temples has me tipping the glass once again. "Why isn't anyone up?"

"Most of the kennel sleeps well past ten. Red Dogs are thieves, and thieves' comfort comes with darkness. Plus, breakfast is a dish rarely served. They eat hot meals twice a day, although some might have a package of this or that in their room between times."

The last of the shake empties into my mouth, and I feel some relief. Korwin finishes drying the appliance and tucks it away again at the back of the cabinet.

"About last night," I begin. "I'm sorry I was inappropriate."

He frowns. "Not inappropriate, just premature. I know where you come from, Lydia. I know who you are. I refuse to be the source of your regret."

"Thank you. It's getting harder," I say, placing a hand on my cheek. "My self-control is waning. If we don't return to Hemlock Hollow, how will we ever be married?"

"The collar around your neck is the closest thing Red Dogs get to marriage," he says. "We might be able to find someone on the outside. With the right motivation, we could get it done, I think. Not an Amish wedding but a Christian one."

The idea of not being married the Amish way breaks my heart. I try to distract myself with focus on the practical. "What do you mean by motivation? Like units?"

He nods. "I've been saving up from my fights. If I win Friday night, my cut in the units will make anything possible."

"You fight the Knights' contender Friday." I purse my lips.

"You don't approve?"

"Proverbs 13 says the unfaithful have an appetite for violence."

"Yeah? Well, I have an appetite for keeping my head on my shoulders. It's not as though I have a choice here."

"No, I suppose not."

Korwin tips his glass and swallows the rest of his shake. "Here. Hand me your glass. I'll do the dishes."

"Let me," I say. I take the glass and turn on the water. "Can I ask you something?"

"I don't know. If you have to ask permission, it must be something I don't want to answer."

I roll my eyes. "How do you keep winning?"

"You mean, do I use the spark?" he whispers.

I nod.

"No, I don't. They'd assume I was scamping power from the pack and rip me apart."

"Great."

"But fists... fists you can use. And thankfully, I have a lifetime of training to put to use here."

"Not to mention the genetic advantages that come with being a Spark."

"As long as it doesn't make me glow, I use it. I'm faster and stronger."

"But not invincible."

"No. When I'm hit, I hurt. When I'm cut, I bleed."

"This opponent worries you. I could tell last night."

He rubs a hand over his mouth. "I don't know this guy. He's new. I've never seen him fight, but if the Knights are willing to bet five thousand units on the man, he's got to be good."

My stomach twists. "The thought of someone hurting you makes me sick."

"You and me both. Just do me a favor and stay away from Pit and the rest of the mutts, all right? I need to save it for the ring."

I finish with the glasses and put them away. "I can protect myself."

"I'm serious, Lydia. It's best if you don't use the spark."

"I'm not talking about the spark. The Nanomem worked. I have all of David's training here, in my head." I tap my temple. "I took down a Green Republic officer on my way here yesterday."

He freezes. "Did the Greens see? Do they know who you are?"

"I was wearing a motorcycle helmet. They saw someone, but they don't know it's me. Pit saved me from being arrested. That's why I didn't end him in the laundry room. I felt a certain obligation."

"Shit, Lydia." He stares at me in awe for a moment, then breaks a smile. "You drove a motorcycle?"

"A Tomahawk Infinity." I raise my eyebrows. "The grid was quite an experience."

He tosses an arm around my shoulders and ushers me from the kitchen. "You never fail to amaze me. Brave. Strong. You're going to save the world someday." Warm lips land on my forehead.

It's a sweet thought, but I'm not interested in saving the world. As I think about the fight to come, I'd settle for saving us.

TWENTY-ONE

"I HAVE TO MEET ALPHA TO FINALIZE DETAILS FOR Friday and then I better get a light workout in. You going to be okay here?" Korwin asks me. I look around his room, *our* room now, with reserve.

"Maybe I could pick up a bit?" I stare at the cluttered floor disapprovingly.

"I should help you with that," he says from the door.

"I can manage. Where are your cleaning supplies?"

"I...ah. I'll send Bella or Sophie up with some." He kisses me goodbye, a short, casual kiss that might be easy to take for granted in this world but would not have been acceptable in Hemlock Hollow. I close my eyes for a moment to appreciate it, and when I open them again, he's gone.

After turning a circle, I decide to start by making the bed. I strip back the wool blanket and spread the freshly laundered sheets across the mattress. The pillows and blanket come next. I'm tucking in the edges of the brown wool when I notice the box I saw this morning under the bed. I tug the corner and slide it out where I can see it better. Inside is a sketchbook and some colored pencils. Korwin's art. Out of curiosity, I take a seat on the edge of the bed and pull out the spiral-bound paper.

The cover and edges are worn from use. With a shaky hand, I open the book. The first drawing is of me in Hemlock Hollow. In full color, it depicts me standing in the summer wheat, the light illuminating my clean face, *kapp*, and plain dress. The next sketch is of me in the Lapps' buggy, a cup of hot chocolate in my hands. The third surprises me. As I turn the page, bright blue catches my eye. I'm in the ballgown at Stuart Manor and I have electricity flying from my hands. I turn the page and it's me again, standing by the tree in my front yard, looking toward the wall. My expression is wistful, almost vacant. Is that what I looked like to him? I cringe at the truth in it, at the reflection of the sunset in eyes that clearly want to see it with an unobstructed view. Was I a terrible cheat, a fake? Was my closeted desire for freedom so obvious to the ones who loved me?

"That's beautiful," Bella says from behind me.

I slam the sketchbook closed. "I didn't hear you come in."

"Ace said you needed these." She hands me a bucket with rubber gloves and powdered cleansers.

"Yes, thank you."

"What was that he drew on your head?" she asks. "Some kind of white scarf?"

I lick my lips and shrug. "I just found it. I'm not even sure it's supposed to be me." I'm a horrible liar. I have to look away just to say it.

"It looked exactly like you," she says. "Weird though.

When did he have time to do it? Come on. Let's take a longer look." She reaches for the pad, but I drop it in the box before she can grasp it.

"No," I say too sharply. "I'm not sure my keeper wants me to see this. I could get in trouble."

Bella's eyes narrow and she hands me the bucket. "You don't look as bad off as I expected after this morning, but then again it sure sounds like you've taken on a new appreciation of obedience."

I shrug. "Just because you can't see the bruises, doesn't mean they aren't there." Not a lie. A half-truth. Korwin did leave bruises, albeit emotional ones.

"It usually takes new girls a few light slams to fall in line with the way we do things around here. I had a black eye and a broken rib for almost a month before I stopped fighting it."

I stare into the bucket between my feet. "Thank you for helping me earlier with Pit. I didn't realize about the collar. I didn't think anyone would be awake, and I just forgot."

"You owe me one. Alpha was pissed that Pit woke him up. Sophie covered for me. Made some crap up about Pit helping Friday night and me being confused. Pit didn't buy it. He would've taken my head off in the hall if he thought Sting would let him live."

"Sting's protective of you?"

"All the pack leaders are protective of their mates. We are a status symbol. As long as you take care of your keeper, he'll be obligated to take care of you."

The warning in her voice makes me ask, "What if we don't take care of our keepers?"

She snorts. "Girls who cause trouble go missing." Her brow furrows. "Don't ever try to leave. You won't make it a mile. The mutt who catches you gets to own you and not like this." She points at my collar. "They get to sell you for units during the fights."

"I'm not going anywhere."

Bella sinks next to me on the bed. "No, you're not. It's almost like you want to be here."

"I'd rather avoid the black eye," I murmur.

She rubs her hands together, her eyes flicking toward the box under the bed. "It's more than that. It's the drawing and last night at dinner, the way he looks at you." She shakes her head. "It's almost as if..."

"As if what?" I ask, giggling a little to make light of her observations.

"As if he *loved* you." She rolls her lips together and pokes her tongue into her cheek, eyes narrowing as if she's trying to puzzle me out. "Ace appears out of nowhere. No history, no former clan. He's here for a few weeks and climbs the ranks like no one has ever seen. Never takes a woman, despite plenty of offers. Then you come along, and no offense, but you aren't exactly flashy. I mean, you show up smudged with grime, no makeup, hair a hot mess."

"No offense taken," I say softly.

"And Ace practically runs half the place over, pushing and shoving, to challenge Pit for you." She laughs. "How does that happen?"

I spread my hands. "I've never understood men." My heart picks up its pace and my stomach clenches in fear. Where is she going with this? What will happen if she suspects we knew each other before?

"Hmm."

"Thank you for the supplies," I say quickly. "I should probably get to work."

She stands and moves slowly toward the door but

doesn't leave. "Lydia, did you and Ace know each other before you came here?" Her eyes lock on to mine and I can feel her dissecting my every gesture, the way my hands fidget, and the sweat on my upper lip.

"That's a silly question," I say.

"That's not a denial."

I meet her eyes and lie. "No. We didn't know each other."

She looks down her nose at me. "It just seems odd, you both appearing out of nowhere."

"Life's odd, I guess." I can tell she's not buying it, so I give her something more, a full-truth to cover the lie. "I'm wanted by the Greens. I have to be... pleasant. If Ace kicks me out, I'm as good as dead."

"Hmm." Bella sweeps her bangs back from her forehead and snorts. "So that's it." She nods like she understands. "See you at dinner."

I decide to give her a taste of her own medicine. "Hey, Bella."

"Yeah?"

"Since we're sharing, what's an Uppercrust like you doing here anyway?"

She turns to meet my eyes. "If I'd stayed with the Greens, I'd have killed myself."

There isn't a hint of humor in her expression, and I swallow a lump that forms in my throat at the pain in her large, dark eyes.

"Thanks again for the supplies."

"Bring them down when you're through." She slips out the door without saying goodbye.

Once she's gone, I breathe a huge sigh of relief. No one can know about Hemlock Hollow. Not only would it put us at risk, but the community as well. Sophie said that coming from a competing pack in the deadzone without revealing your origins is a major taboo, something the Red Dogs kill over. Was Bella's interest in my roots a product of her suspicions that I was a spy or plant of the enemy?

The enemy. The true enemy is the Green Republic. Strange to think of clans from the deadzone warring over scraps while the Greens feast on the fruits of their corruption. Still, my gut tells me I should be more careful around Bella and Sophie, to act more Red Dog and less *other.*

* * *

By the time Korwin returns, it's late in the day. I've finished my work and am stretched out on top of the bed. The books are shelved in an old crate. All of the clothes are away in the drawers, the porcelain is washed as is the small window, and I've mopped the floor.

"It's time to get dressed for dinner," he says.

I groan. "Too tired."

"The place looks great. Did you break for lunch?"

"I had a meal bar from my pack," I say, pointing at the backpack from David.

"Why didn't you go down to the cafeteria to eat?"

I look at him in confusion. "You never came back, and you told me not to leave the room on my own."

"Yes, but I got distracted with preparations for Friday. After I met with Alpha in the commons, I asked him to have Sophie escort you down."

I shake my head. "Sophie never came to get me. The only person I saw all day was Bella, who brought me the cleaning supplies."

Korwin tilts his head and squints in my direction. "That's odd. I asked Sophie to bring up the supplies."

A chill runs the course of my body, and I sit bolt upright from the bed. "What if he hurt her?"

Korwin shakes his head. "I don't think he'd do that. Maybe she just got busy."

I hug myself, rubbing the outside of my arms. Bella said Alpha was angry about Pit. Did he take that anger out on Sophie? Worse, was it my fault? "We'll see her at dinner." I bound out of bed and head for the door.

"You can't go like that."

"Why not?"

He walks to the wardrobe and pulls out a slip with a meshy black sheath. It's backless and short, unbelievably short.

"You can't be serious."

"This is expected," he says apologetically.

"It's humiliating."

Korwin places the dress back in the wardrobe. "Maybe I can say you're sick."

"What? And stay in this room all night? No way."

"You decide, Lydia. Do you play this game or hide from it? It's not ideal but we're safe here. The dress, all the other stuff, it's just stuff. It's not that important."

"Easy for you to say." I glance woefully at the wardrobe.

He raises an eyebrow. "You haven't seen what I have to wear in the ring on Friday."

"Ack."

"Your choice."

I stare at him for a moment and then storm to the wardrobe to retrieve the dress. "The bath is ready for you. Don't forget the shoes."

Snatching the strappy heels from the floor of the wardrobe, I huff from the cell toward the bathroom. Korwin follows me. I stop. "What are you doing?"

"After what happened with Pit, there's no way I'm letting you go down there alone."

I lower my voice. "Too far," I whisper. He may get me in the dress, but I am not letting him watch me bathe.

"I'll wait outside the door." He smirks.

My head feels hot. By the time I reach the bath, I feel at war with myself, between my desire to be with Korwin and the deep-rooted faith that tells me everything about this place is wrong.

* * *

THIRTY MINUTES LATER, I EMERGE FROM THE BATH afraid to move. While the fabric is beautiful, I still can't figure out how the dress stays up. The mesh balances precariously on the tips of my shoulders. I've curled my hair and left it down to cover as much of my back and shoulders as possible.

"You look stunning," Korwin says.

"I look like a harlot."

He takes my hand and kisses my cheek. "Never."

The corners of my mouth sag, and a deep sadness comes over me. I've not felt this way before, not when I was being trained at CGEF or being chastised by the elders in Hemlock Hollow. In this dress, I feel like a thing, an ornament to be displayed and judged by my keeper.

"Something's wrong," Korwin says.

Tears prick at the corner of my eyes. "I don't like it," I say, running a finger under the collar. "It's dehumanizing."

He groans in frustration. "Come on, Lydia. I've told you, this is how it is. Everyone dresses like this here. We don't have a choice."

I nod and wipe under my eyes.

"We're late for dinner."

We turn the corner and arrive in the dining room. We are not the last to arrive. Alpha and Sophie's chairs are empty. As we sit down, Bella notices my eyes lingering on the vacant chairs.

"Domestic dispute," she says.

Bailey, who rarely speaks, nods her head and says softly, "Let's hope Sophie comes around."

Sophie? I've known this group for less than two full days and it's clear to me that Sophie isn't the problem. "Should we go get her? I'm sure it's a misunderstanding. Maybe we can help set things right."

Bella shoots me a sharp look and Jake rubs a knuckle under his nose. He sneers at me. "Ace, inform your woman."

Under the table, Korwin nudges my knee, hard. I clamp my lips closed. "Alpha is disciplining her," he says firmly. "In an argument with the alpha, the alpha is always right."

Sting hooks an arm over Bella's shoulders and runs his palm over the front of her dress. The movement makes me uncomfortable and I look away. "You're new here," he says to me. "Ace will teach you how things work, one way or another."

I stare down at my empty plate.

Alpha and Sophie arrive moments later and her appearance makes me cringe. The right side of her face is black and blue and she's walking with a limp. She sits down across the table from me but does not meet my eyes. Alpha takes the head of the table as usual, brushing my knee with his own as he lowers himself to his chair.

"Excuse me," I say, scooting my chair away to make more room.

His hand clamps around my thigh under the table, and his eyes lock on to me. "You're fine. Stay where you are."

His voice is a low growl and his meaty hand lingers. I glance at Korwin, but he can't see it and I dare not call it out at the table.

The alpha is always right.

Fortunately, a mutt arrives with the food and conversation turns to Friday's fight.

TWENTY-TWO

THIS TIME, AT DINNER, I'M CAREFUL NOT TO DRINK TOO much. I ask the mutt server for water, and she brings it immediately, without question. The others are deep in conversation about Friday's fight. As far as I can tell, the Red Dogs' entire economy revolves around fighting. They don't grow or build anything, but everyone steals. What they steal, they sell for units, which they store in portable devices. They gamble those units in the weekly fights and use them to buy the things they can't steal on the black market.

Before I came to the English world, I never knew the deadzone existed. I might've guessed there were others living off-grid. Bradford Adams, for example, is barely on the map. But organized clans that exist only through the propagation of crime? I never would have believed it.

"Would you like some more wine?" Alpha asks me. Never mind that my glass is more than half full and I could easily ask the mutt for more.

"No, thank you."

Korwin slows the pace of his eating beside me and looks

at Alpha out of the corner of his eye. "Lydia is only allowed one glass tonight," he says authoritatively.

Alpha laughs. "Nonsense. She can have as much as she wants. I insist."

"No, thank you," I repeat.

The giant of a man folds one meaty hand over the other. His eyes rake over me. "What do you think of your new home, Lydia?"

My eyes dart around the table. Sophie is contemplating her plate, Korwin has an utterly confused look on his face, and everyone else is staring at me like Alpha just asked a monkey to recite Shakespeare. I swallow what's in my mouth and try my best to be diplomatic. "I feel blessed to have a roof over my head and food to eat."

For a moment, no one says a word. They stare at the monkey, trying to decipher its jumping and armpit scratching. But then Alpha laughs. "You hear that, Sophie? This one knows her place. She knows how to show a little gratitude."

Sophie hunches into herself across the table.

"It was Sophie who taught me to think this way," I say. Korwin kicks me under the table.

Alpha snorts and drains his wine. He snaps his fingers repeatedly and the girl fills his glass again. "Let me see your dress." He motions with his knuckle for me to stand up. I glance at Korwin, who is statuesque in his chair next to me.

"Ex-excuse me?"

"Stand up and let me see your pretty dress," he says again.

Sophie gives a soft whimper and then clears her throat to cover it up, but Bella catches my gaze. Her eyes widen and she nods as if to say, "Go ahead."

But Korwin's hand falls on my thigh. "Why does she need to show you her dress?"

"I want to make sure you've dressed her appropriately for her station," Alpha says. The two men glare at each other, the tension at the table blooming to dangerous levels.

"It's okay," I say. "I'll do it."

"That's a good girl," Alpha says.

I push back my chair and stand, adjusting the dress on my shoulders to keep it from falling. Teetering on the heels Korwin provided me, I slowly pivot, feeling exposed, totally on display. A low whistle comes from behind me, and then Alpha's out of his chair and standing beside me. He sweeps my hair into one hand and traces a finger down my spine.

"You've seen the dress." Korwin's arm is around my shoulder, pulling me into his chest. "It goes perfectly with her collar."

Alpha's hand lingers on my lower back for a beat, and then he retreats to his seat, sweeping his goblet into his hand and draining it dry. "It's a good thing you're a prizefighter, Ace, or someone might snatch this little piece from your side."

Korwin says the next through his teeth. "But I am a fighter, and I never lose. I pity anyone who takes what's mine. I'll take his life in return."

With a snort, Alpha lifts his refilled glass over his head as if to toast us. "To Ace! Win tomorrow and I won't have to put that threat to the test."

We haven't finished eating, but Korwin turns me from the table by the shoulders and leads me back to his room.

* * *

IT'S LATE AND WE'VE HAD A FULL DAY, BUT WHEN I LAY down next to Korwin, I can't sleep. The memory of how Alpha touched me makes my skin crawl. "Why did he do it?" I finally ask. "Does he hate me? Is he trying to humiliate me in front of everyone?"

Korwin snorts. "Hate you? No, he doesn't hate you. On the contrary, I think Alpha is quite taken with you. I think Alpha would prefer that I lose this time."

I turn on my side and stare at him in the dark room. "Prefer that you lose ten thousand units?"

"I've seen the look in his eyes. He wants you for himself, and by the look of Sophie's face, I think he's willing to do just about anything to have you."

"Are you saying he might kill Sophie and challenge you for me?" I whisper. The thought is too horrific for me to take seriously, but Korwin doesn't laugh.

"I'm worried about you, Lydia. Maybe..."

"Maybe what?"

He clears his throat and whispers in my ear. "Make it through Friday night. I'll win my cut of the units and then we can discuss our next move."

I meet his eyes and my heart leaps. "Really."

"I have no idea where we'll go, but yes."

I throw my arms around his neck and squeeze.

"Okay, okay, don't get too excited. You need to be careful. Try your best to fly under the radar until I can figure something out. We don't want anyone to suspect we're leaving."

Tucked into his side, I finally drift to sleep, my soul hopeful about the future.

TWENTY-THREE

FRIDAY'S FIGHT PROMISES TO BE BOTH A CURSE AND A salvation. I'm not sure how I'll survive watching Korwin fight, but I'm anxious for the day to come and for us to move beyond it. I keep to myself, rarely leaving Korwin's room and never without him at my side. Bella comes to see me when I miss dinner, claiming to be ill. She probably thinks Korwin beat me like Alpha beat Sophie. I speak with her briefly and set her fears at ease. Without me saying so, she seems to understand my true goal is to avoid Alpha and she encourages me in that pursuit.

The day of the fight, the main floor of the kennel is transformed. A massive cage constructed of chain link, steel posts, and wire brackets is erected. I take dinner in our room, then dress in what Korwin brings for me.

"Wow," I say, holding up the emerald green dress. The bodice is a strapless and stiff fan of silky material. It has no discernable back. The cloth gathers over one hip and cascades on either side of a slit to the floor.

"I'm the incumbent champion. Everyone is going to be watching. You have to play the part."

"I'd like to play it with clothes on."

A whisper of a smile raises the corner of his mouth. "It covers all the important parts."

I lower the dress and look at him ruefully. "Korwin Stuart, I think you are enjoying this."

He shrugs slowly.

My mouth falls open. "You would have me parade around half-naked in front of strangers?"

"No. No. Not if I had a choice." He steps into me, wrapping his arms around me and sandwiching the dress between us. Lowering his chin, he presses his forehead to mine. "If I had my way, you'd only be half-naked in front of me." With a slight shift, I meet his lips for a kiss that forces me to hold the dress away from my body for fear of burning it. He pulls away slowly when things get dangerous. "Besides, wait 'til you see the humiliating thing I have to wear in the ring."

"Looking forward to it," I say, laughing.

"I've got to go. The other clans will arrive soon, and everyone wants to see the fighters before they place their bets."

I nod. "Good luck. I'll pray for an easy fight."

"Thanks, but I don't need the prayers. If there is a God, I doubt he's going to want to see this." He pecks me on the cheek and disappears out the door.

I stretch the emerald green material between my hands as my smile fades from my face. Bishop Kauffman's voice comes to me. I picture him sanding a porch rail, smiling at me, but what he says is from a reading he did once. My mind puts the two together, seamlessly, into an event that has never happened but seems ultimately real. "Do not yoke yourself to an unbeliever. For how can righteousness and lawlessness be partners? What fellowship does light have with darkness?" It's from Corinthians. The memory, like all of my memories from Hemlock Hollow, is a part of who I am. The Bible is stamped on my heart and the songs of my *Ordnung* hum in my soul. I cannot separate myself from it like I can separate my body from the physical place of my youth.

As I don the emerald dress, I do pray for Korwin, but not that he will win the fight. I pray that he will find God and in the deepest recesses of my soul, I pray for the strength to do what I'll have to do if he doesn't.

* * *

I JOIN THE OTHER PACK LEADERS FRONT AND CENTER IN a viewing area on the second floor, the same place where I'd watched Korwin fight Pit for me. This time, they've brought in a set of eight thrones with plush red velvet cushions and burnished copper studs. Bella, Sophie, Bailey, and I sit in four low-backed models at floor level, while the men are on a raised platform behind us in more ornate, high-backed versions.

To my right, Sophie shivers in her chair, looking like she could mentally come unhinged at any second. One of her eyes is swollen. Bruises pepper her arms and legs. She's layered makeup over the damage, an effort that might do the trick for the sea of people below us but does nothing to disguise the swelling and uneven appearance of her face. I'd like to reach out and take her hand as a sign of support, but Alpha is sitting directly behind me and I fear his reaction. To my left, Bella and Bailey sit straight backed and empty, like they forgot their souls in their rooms. Jake and Sting sit directly behind their partners—eyes not vacant but dark, souls not missing but ruined.

It occurs to me that Sting sits behind Bella and Jake sits behind Bailey but Alpha sits behind me. Shouldn't that spot be Korwin's? Left empty until he wins the fight? I stand and say to Sophie, "I think we chose the wrong chairs. Will you switch with me?"

Alpha shakes his head. "Sit down."

I lower myself back into the chair in front of him. Goosebumps break out across my skin. I am in the presence of evil, plain and simple. I stare into the cage and feel my mind blank, my soul recede to a protected place with concrete walls within me. Bella glances at me out of the corner of my eye, almost imperceptibly. I was wrong. She's in there. She's just learned to protect herself too.

People swarm the kennel around the cage, their voices an indistinguishable buzz. Flashes of color reach me through the crowd. Armbands. Each clan has its own color. On the wall behind the cage, the clan names hang above glass-paneled cylinders. Red Dogs, Knights, Shadows, Saints, Bears, Dragons. A giant chalkboard below the signs contains boxes and lines that must be used to track the order of fighting.

A man in a red jacket with black lapels enters the cage and strides to the center where a microphone dangles from the ceiling. He raises his arms in a vee above his head. "Welcome, ladies and gentlemen." His voice echoes across the kennel and every person halts to listen, the buzz of voices blending into silence. "Today, six clans come together to wager on the finest warriors of our communities. The stakes are high. Odds are listed at the counter in the back. You can place your bets up to five minutes before a given fight, but don't wait too long because once the window closes, there are no exceptions. All payouts will be in units to your mobile device. House cut goes directly to the battery behind me."

A metal cylinder on the wall in front of us has a bright green gauge, half lit, that bobs incrementally as people approach the window to place their bets. The men hold devices similar to the one the Green officer had when he pulled me over my first day here. The fights are truly gold to Red Dog. The host clan must make units regardless of the outcome. Then again, the floodlights glowing from each corner of the ring can't be cheap to run, and every member of the clan is at work below.

"Is the fight always here?" I ask. I don't direct the question at anyone in particular.

"As long as we keep winning," Alpha says.

"And now," the man below bellows over the murmur of the crowd, "allow me to introduce your champions. From Bear clan, Gustof!"

A pale giant enters the ring. Gustof must have some sort of abnormality because his skin is stark white, his eyes are red, and there is no hair on his entire body. I cringe at his odd appearance and Bella whispers, "He's albino." As if those two words explain everything.

"From Saints clan, Pope!" The man who waddles into the ring must be four hundred pounds of short, round jiggling flesh. He wears a white bathrobe tied at the waist.

"Don't be fooled by the excess weight," Bella whispers. "He was one of the last practitioners of the art of sumo wrestling before it was outlawed. I've seen him crush a man's ribs."

"Uselessly short arms," Sting says from behind us. "As long as Ace keeps his distance, Pope'll be on the mat in no time."

"From Shadow clan, Merciless!" A lanky but athletic

man flips into the ring, springing from hands to feet before rotating in the air and landing next to Gustof. His skin is bright purple, a striking contrast to his jet-black hair.

"He's purple," I say.

"They bathe in a type of genetically modified chili pepper that stains their skin. The Shadows become tolerant to it but their sweat is mildly toxic. You punch a Shadow with split knuckles and it's gonna sting for days," Jake says.

"From Dragon clan, Torch!" Applause erupts as a short but stocky man enters the ring, his brown skin covered in tribal tattoos. He motions for the crowd to clap in time with him and the roar of appreciation grows louder. When the din in the kennel reaches a fever pitch, he slaps his hands together and a plume of fire explodes from between his palms toward the ceiling. I can feel the heat.

"He's had flint surgically implanted in the skin of his hands. He can actually ignite his fists. Scary son of bitch, but all show. Ace can take him," Bella whispers.

"From Knight clan, a new fighter all the way from the heart of Crater City. Let me introduce you to Boulder!"

A giant of a man enters the ring with thinning brown hair and shifty eyes.

"No," I say, as recognition dawns.

"Relax. He's big but I'm sure Ace can take him," Bella assures me.

But it's not the size of Boulder that concerns me, even though the man is a walking muscle, face distorted by what I can only assume are medical alterations to his size and weight. Under it all, I recognize Brady, the firefighter Jonas introduced me to the night Korwin and I attempted to take down the transformer. What is he doing here? I bite my lip, worried for Korwin. Brady knows who Korwin is. He knows what Korwin can do. I clench my fists, praying that Brady wants to keep his anonymity as much as Korwin.

Bella grunts. "Guy's been hitting the juice. He might win the fight but he's going to lose his liver if he keeps that up."

"What's the juice?" I ask.

She doesn't answer but turns back to the ring. "And now, your reigning champion, from Red Dog clan, Ace!"

The crowd goes wild. The people stomp their feet and beat the chain link until my ears hurt. Korwin jogs into the ring wearing nothing but a pair of silky red boxing shorts. There's a Rottweiler face on his butt with an ace of hearts in its mouth. "I see what you mean about humiliating," I whisper to myself.

"What?" Bella asks, raising her voice over the din of the crowd.

"He's intimidating," I say louder. It's a lie. He's noticeably shorter than the competitors from Bear, Shadow, and the Knights, and lankier than the Dragon and Saints fighters. In fact, if I didn't know Korwin was a Spark, there would be no way I'd put my money on him. No way.

"The best there is," Bella says encouragingly.

"First bracket, Gustof vs. Boulder. All others, please evacuate the ring." The man in the red jacket follows the other competitors through the chain-link door. After they leave, an iron bar is lowered into place to block the exit.

"Square off," the announcer says. The albino man lowers into a crouch and Brady/Boulder takes a step back with his right foot.

"Begin!"

Gustof jabs at Brady's face. Brady blocks and counters. His fist connects but Gustof retaliates with a hook to Brady's head. Brady tackles the albino to the concrete. A punch to the nose sprays bright red blood across white skin. I have to look away.

Alpha leans forward into my field of vision. "Wine?" He hands me a glass.

I accept with a curt nod but don't drink it. Instead, I shift away from him in my chair. My body stiffens and I stare straight ahead, hoping he will lose interest in me.

He doesn't. "You know, I meant it when I said I'd take care of you if something happens to Ace," he whispers in my ear. He runs a knuckle down the length of my neck and I grind my teeth to keep from jerking away. "Even if Ace wins, I see a future for you and me, Lydia. Sophie and I have come to an agreement that someone in my position should have more than one woman at his disposal." His hand brushes down the outside of my arm, making my skin crawl. Thankfully, at that moment the crowd roars and I jump to my feet, breaking contact. I clap, spilling wine over the back of my hand. A mutt dabs at it with a moist towel until I tell her to stop.

My eyes drift to the ring below where six men are removing Gustof, the albino, on a stretcher. Brady roars in victory. I'm fairly certain the only blood on the man is Gustof's. Horrified for Korwin, I sip the wine despite myself.

"Next bracket, Merciless and Torch!" the announcer says.

The purple man and the one with all the tattoos enter the ring while a mutt scrambles to mop up layers of sticky blood. He leaves a bright red stain on the concrete, obviously terrified of being caught in the ring with the fighters. I wait until the last possible moment to sit back down.

"You have an appetite for sport," Alpha whispers in my

ear. He has the wine bottle and tops off my wineglass. "I like that about you."

Fists and feet fly below us, and I focus my attention on the fight. I am a possum playing dead. My body language sends a clear message: *I'm not interesting. Turn your attention elsewhere.* Inside the ring, Merciless uses his superior height to his advantage, landing kicks to Torch's head and abdomen. Torch retaliates by slapping his hands together and sending plumes of fire toward his opponent.

A meaty hand grips my shoulder like a vise and turns me in my chair. Wine spills across my bare knee. "I don't like to be ignored," Alpha growls.

My eyes flick to Bella for help, but she is statuesque, obviously trying her best to avoid scrutiny. I clear my throat. Survival instinct kicks in and I lie. I lie like I was born to it. "I wasn't ignoring you," I say softly. My eyes flick to his and then dart away quickly. "Your attention is overwhelming. I'm completely unworthy of it." I brush the wine off my skin. It leaves a sticky residue on my hand. I fidget with the slit of my dress, holding the sides together to cover my knees. "I am a simple woman with few words at my disposal. You, Alpha, deserve someone much more sophisticated who can respond more appropriately."

A roar rises from the crowd and my attention darts to the ring. Merciless has pinned Torch and is dragging the man's hand across his tattooed abdomen. Torch screams as the flint embedded in his palms shreds his skin. The purple man then spits in the wound. Seconds later, Torch begins to seize, shaking violently and foaming at the mouth. Poisoned.

The man in the red coat proclaims Merciless the victor. The six men return with the stretcher for Torch. I use the opportunity to again stand and clap with the others. Bella glances in my direction, her eyes widening before shifting back toward Alpha. Under the guise of taking another sip of wine, I glance at Sophie. But she doesn't acknowledge me. In fact, her eyes are glazed over. Dead inside. I can't say I blame her. If I was bound to a man like Alpha, I might become a shell too.

I'm still on my feet when the announcer booms, "Place your bets for the next event, Pope of Saints clan vs. Ace of the Red Dogs."

The crowd goes wild as Korwin and the overweight fighter slip into the ring.

A large body presses into my back and hot breath on my ear makes my skin crawl. "I think you're worthy of my attention. I think you're rather beautiful and you seem very good at following directions."

I press myself against the railing. My fear ignites the connection between Korwin and me. I don't mean to do it, but like clockwork, he raises his eyes to me. In an instant, he knows. His eyes narrow at Alpha, and I'll be damned if the man doesn't back off a quarter of an inch. I would too if Korwin was looking at me like that.

"Ace is a jealous man," I say to Alpha. "I have to be careful."

He laughs through his nose, flipping his long black braid behind his shoulder, and returns to his seat, verbally assaulting some unsuspecting mutt to fill his wineglass.

"Begin!" the announcer yells, and Pope moves in with his arms spread. His strategy seems obvious, even to me. He's going to try to get in close and pin or crush Korwin under his significant weight. He almost succeeds in backing Korwin up against a wall, but Korwin bobs under Pope's flabby arm and uses his superior speed to avoid a crushing grip.

My fingernails bite into the palms of my hand, tension

tightening the fists in my lap. But Korwin doesn't need my help or my worry. He darts behind the big man, grabs the Pope's chin and forehead, and twists—fast.

Pope collapses, head and feet rebounding slightly from the impact. There's a murmur in the crowd.

"Ace wins," Red Coat says. "In record time. A personal best."

Korwin holds up one hand and turns in a circle, pausing to meet Alpha's eyes with a menacing stare. The message in that look seems to say, *You touch her and you're next.* But when I glance at Alpha, his response isn't fear. Instead, his silence speaks, *Challenge accepted.*

TWENTY-FOUR

The match between Brady/Boulder and Merciless gives new meaning to the term brutal. The purple giant rises to an early advantage, his long limbs landing kicks to Brady's head, side, and crotch. There's blood as noses crack and knuckles split. But like his namesake, the rogue firefighter seems to feel no pain, even when Merciless's purple skin strikes an open wound on Brady's cheek. Likewise, several attempts of the purple man to spit his poison into the larger man's wounds fall short.

Eventually, Merciless slows, exhausted from the constant attack of the stone man in front of him. He jabs, and Brady entraps his arm with a circular block. The larger man steps back, using the weight of his hips to yank Merciless off balance, drives a knee into his abdomen and delivers a blow with the heel of his palm to the man's throat.

The combination move floods my head with images. David stands in front of me. "This is mixed martial arts, Lydia. A favorite of the Green Republic militia. Aim for the elbow with your block. Over the top. Lock your opponent's arm under yours and pull. You want his weight to work to your advantage." I can feel my limbs going through the motions, my palm pressing into David's throat for practice. Brady definitely trained with the Greens. Why is he here? Did they kick him out, or did he leave?

In the ring, the men are not practicing. Merciless lies twitching on the concrete and then stops moving, eyes staring into the distance. He's dead, I'm sure of it. Red Coat pronounces Brady the winner as a swarm of Shadow clan members remove the body of their fallen comrade. There is no cheering this time, and a woman with purple skin and a white dress weeps by the fighter's side. It takes forever for them to usher her and the man's body from the kennel, and by that time, I'm a mess from crying for her loss.

"Don't waste your tears," Sting says, handing a handkerchief to Bella and another one to me. "I met the man. He was intolerable."

I wipe under my eyes and brace myself as Korwin enters the ring with Brady. "Here we go," Jake says.

Alpha steeples his fingers.

"With fifteen thousand units riding on this, Ace better win or we are all in for a cold winter." Sting glances toward Alpha before grabbing the bottle of wine and pouring another glass.

Fifteen thousand. Last I'd heard, it was only ten thousand. A small fortune. My stomach clenches.

When Alpha offers me more wine, I decline, but turning allows me to see that Alpha is still staring at me and the look on his face is possessive. Just the feel of his eyes on my skin makes me pray for a quick fight. His predatory manner makes me want to flee. I have to get out of here.

Red Coat garners the attention of the crowd with three loud claps into the microphone. The kennel plunges into silence. "Our final match. New contender, Boulder of the

Knights vs. reigning champion, Ace of the Red Dogs. Fighters square off!"

Korwin faces Brady and again I am distraught at my love's relatively small size. The bar is lowered into place. "Begin!"

Once again, Brady holds back. Korwin is faster and no doubt the massive man's strategy will be to wear him out. But Korwin doesn't take the bait. He circles the big man, fists raised.

"Lydia, speak with me privately," Alpha says in a low, gravelly voice.

Brady throws the first punch and Korwin easily avoids it. I turn halfway around to glance at Alpha. "Of course," I say softly. "After the fight." I turn back in time to see both of Korwin's feet land on Brady's chest. The big man doesn't even flinch and lands a blow to Korwin's jaw before he can regain his fighting stance.

"Now," Alpha says.

Even Sting and Jake seem disturbed. "The woman should be able to watch the outcome of her keeper," Jake says.

"More importantly, Ace ain't gonna fight as well if she ain't here cheerin' him on," Sting says.

Bella and Bailey glance with frantic eyes in my direction. They're worried, but I don't fully understand why. There's something going on, a feeling in the air that is beyond my social experience. While Sting and Jake argue with Alpha behind me, Sophie turns her head and whispers in my ear, "He means to take you while Ace is distracted with the fight."

"Take me." The realization comes like a splash of cold water. He means to rape me, while Korwin isn't here to defend me. My eyes widen.

"Don't let him get you alone."

I straighten in my chair and turn back to the fight. The two men are pounding on each other, bodies close and fists flying. There's sweat and blood and a tooth that sprays from Brady's mouth into the crowd.

"Lydia, come with me. Now!" Alpha demands.

I don't move.

And then his hand is in my hair and the chair topples as my body falls to the floor. I yelp in pain, but no one does anything as he drags me from the platform. I have to crawl to keep him from pulling my hair out. His thick arm catches me around the waist and he throws my struggling form over his shoulder.

"Please," I mouth to Sting, but he simply frowns and turns away.

Alpha takes me to a cell down the hall from the viewing area and closes the door. When he drops me on my feet, I scramble against the wall.

"Let me go, Alpha. Ace won't fight as well without me there. You don't want him to lose with that many units on the line."

"Humph." Alpha paces in front of me, a wild animal toying with its prey. "Stop with the sweet-and-innocent act. I know who you are."

"What are you talking about?"

"You may not recognize me, but I recognize you, girlie. I remember the day Hambone brought you here, about a year ago, and I remember what you did to those six men."

I tremble against the wall, shaking my head.

"Oh, I wasn't touching you. I was watching, just beyond the circle. Funny, when you electrocuted those guys, they couldn't remember a thing. But I remember. You're a scamper and you've been in the deadzone before."

"No. You've confused me with someone else," I insist.

"I don't think I have." He steps in closer, close enough for me to smell the alcohol on his breath. "I did some research, *Lydia Lane*. You and your boyfriend, Korwin—oh, I know his name, too—have secrets. Secrets worth a hell of a lot more than fifteen thousand units."

My heart leaps into my throat. All I can do is shake my head.

"Here's the deal, sweetheart. I'll keep your secret and I'll protect you." He traces my collarbone with the pads of his fingers. "But I want something in return." His hands go to his waist and he unfastens his belt. He moves to kiss me, and I turn my face away. An iron hand clamps around my jaw and throat and he slams my head into the concrete wall.

I raise my hands between us, placing them over his heart. I'm not strong enough to push him away. The feel of his lower body pressing into mine through my dress makes my stomach turn.

"Are you the only one who knows?" I rasp through his grip.

"Yeah. And as long as you perform, it will stay that way." He grinds into me.

He's too close. Thirteen ways to kill him flash through my brain—David's ways. The level of hatred I feel for Alpha is all consuming. Not just because of what he's trying to do to me, but because of what he's done to Sophie. I can't take a moment more of this. I snap.

"Do you know what it says about this in the Bible?" I say in a low and even voice.

"The Bible? No." He snorts and buries his lips in the side of my neck.

"It says the wages of sin is death." I ignite the tingle at the back of my brain and send my power into his body. It's easy, a muscle that has ached to be used. He stiffens and trembles, tries to pull away, but the electricity binds us together. I grip his throat. Blue lightning reflects in his eyes. His tongue extends from his mouth and his pupils roll back in his head. His arms smoke, filling the room with the scent of burning hair.

Fueled by my anger, it's difficult to cut my power off, but my desire is to disable, not kill. I'm not a killer. With a shove, I knock his body to the floor and store the tingle back where it belongs. Two black circles are burnt into the flesh of his chest where my hands had been. I push him with my foot, then check that his heart is still beating. Just barely.

I brush my hand off on my dress, and for some reason, I picture the wolf from the woods. It's as if she's standing beside me, hunched over Alpha's body. This ghost wolf feels no remorse. She walks with a swagger. She does not downplay that her teeth are sharp and her claws could slice through bone. A wolf is not apologetic about being a wolf.

The door opens and the angry din of a worked-up crowd filters into the room around me.

"Lydia!" Bella gasps, gaze darting between Alpha and me. "Holy crap. Did you kill him?" Her words aren't accusatory but full of hope. She does not rush to his aid.

I stand from my squat. "No. He's alive." The wolf is gone, dissolved to wherever ghosts go. "What's going on?" I ask when another wave of hollering comes from below.

"Ace. He's down and not getting up." Bella's eyes search mine. "I thought you'd want to know."

I sprint back to the viewing area. Sure enough, Korwin is flat on the concrete, bloody and bruised. Brady is working the crowd. Half of the patrons are cheering his name, the other half pleading with Ace to get up. The man in the red coat is open mouthed. He seems reluctant to pronounce Brady the winner.

"Ace saw when Alpha took you. He got distracted and Boulder got the upper hand." Bella shakes her head.

Brady approaches Korwin's body. Is he still breathing? I grip the railing, a loud buzz growing between my ears.

"Lydia?" Sophie asks.

I turn to her and catch a glimpse of my arm. I'm glowing, bright as a star. "I'm sorry," I say. *Sorry for making your lives more complicated. Sorry, that after this, things will change for you. Just sorry.* I kick off my shoes and launch myself over the railing.

It's a fifteen-foot drop, but the spark protects me. I land on my feet between Brady and Korwin. Brady recoils and then grins smugly. I lower my hand to Korwin's throat while the crowd watches silently. As soon as I make contact, I know he's alive because power is drawn from me. Korwin's body knows what it needs. The juice flows until he stirs beneath my hand.

"Lydia?" he mumbles.

Brady pulls a small metal device from the material of his shorts and plugs it into his ear. He recites a string of numbers, pauses, then recites them again.

"We've got to get out of here," Korwin says.

"I'll protect you," I say.

He scrambles to his feet and drags me toward the cage door. "They're coordinates. He's transmitting our coordinates." With a solid kick to the chain lock, he breaks the door open. We rush from the cage.

Brady calls from behind us, "Stop. Don't make this harder than it needs to be."

TWENTY-FIVE

"So that's what happened to Brady," Korwin says, as we push our way through the crowd. "Do you think he was the Liberty Party mole?"

"Who else could it be? Looks like he's still working for the Greens."

Mobs of people block every exit. "Which way?" Korwin shakes his head.

"I need my pack," I say. "I have something that can help us."

"No time. They'll be here in minutes."

I drop his hand. "Then I'll be faster. It could be our only hope." I bolt up the stairs to Korwin's apartment and grab the backpack David gave me. The sound of approaching sirens makes my hands shake.

"I hope whatever is in there is worth it," Korwin says. He gathers his own pack from under the bed.

"How long have you been packed?"

"Since I promised we would run."

We break from the room and run for the stairs. Green officers charge the front doors and the crowd panics.

Bella spots us from the second floor landing and rushes to my side. "You can't let them find me," she begs. Her eyes are wild with fear. "You don't understand. My father—"

"Over," Korwin yells, motioning to the stair rail.

A sea of people bustle below. "You take Bella," I call. I plant my hand and kick over the top. A woman screams as I barely miss her and knock aside a man in the wrong place at the wrong time.

"Sorry," I say. He swears and lunges toward me, but Korwin lands by my side with Bella in his arms. He drops her, wide eyed, onto her feet and pushes the stunned man aside. "Come on!" He drags me toward the tunnel to the slaughterhouse.

"Not that way," Bella says. "The passageway is completely congested. I tried."

"We need another way," I say.

He pauses. "A window. Is there one in the kitchen?"

Bella shakes her head. "Bars. This was a prison. You won't be able to get out that way." She turns a circle, the crowd flowing around us.

I can see Green officers at every entrance. The masses are slowing them down but they're close, too close. "I have an idea. Come on." I grab Korwin's hand and we weave in the opposite direction of the crowd, deeper into the prison and away from the exits. My bare feet slap the floor as we break out into the empty hallway and I lead Bella and Korwin to the pack leaders' bathroom. I duck inside to the din of screams and gunfire and lock the door behind us.

"Strange timing for a bath," Korwin says.

"We're trapped," Bella says. "If they search the place. We're doomed."

"Sophie told me this room was added on by Alpha," I say. "Recently." I point to the fireplace. "That wasn't there before. It's wood burning. It has to vent outside." I knock on the wall next to the bricks. "Drywall. Not concrete."

"Move," Korwin commands.

I'm barely out of the way before a blast of electricity blows a two-foot hole in the wall.

"He... he just..." Bella points at Korwin, face pale. "Who the hell are you?"

I leave her side to help kick out the space below the hole and realize I'm still barefoot. Quickly, I grab the boots from the backpack, the ones I was wearing the day I arrived, and slip them on my feet, not even bothering to untie them first.

"Nice look," Korwin says as he pounds on the drywall.

I smile. "Some girls just have a knack for fashion."

"How did you do that?" Bella asks. "Are you scampers? Are you hiding a device? I didn't even know a device existed that could do that."

"It's better you don't," I tell her.

She narrows her eyes at me and looks toward the door like she's deciding which is worse, us or the Greens.

Korwin climbs out the makeshift exit into an alley. "It's clear for now, but hurry."

I follow. Red swirling lights color the pavement at the end of the alley. I motion to Bella. "Come on! We don't have much time."

She hesitates.

"The Greens are coming. We can't wait for you." I leave her and jog toward Korwin, who is opening the circular grid in the pavement that leads to the sewer.

"Wait!" Bella whispers, following after me. She balks at the opening. Unlike Korwin and I, who have the benefit of proper shoes, she still wears the same stiletto heels she wore to watch the fight. Korwin climbs into the sewer and I pause on the ladder.

"It's the only way," I say to Bella.

She shakes her head and presses the back of her hand over her mouth. Backing away, she points toward another door across the alley. "No way. Sorry. Go ahead. Good luck to you."

I close the hatch above my head and skim down the ladder into the darkness below.

TWENTY-SIX

I HOLD MY BREATH IN THE DARKNESS AND LISTEN. RED light passes over the grid. Footsteps. The clank of shoes on the manhole cover. Korwin places a finger over his lips and pulls me out of the light, deeper into the shadows.

"We've got trouble," a deep phlegmy voice says. "Hole blown in the wall on the east alley... No... Not a trace." The feet shift. The man coughs. "Wait. There's someone... I need backup." The shadow disappears. Shoes slap pavement. "Hold it right there!"

Korwin tugs me deeper into the stench and inky blackness that is the sewer. Poor Bella. If I had to guess, she is the one the officer is chasing. I pray she isn't caught, and if she is, that she won't give away our escape route.

Only when we have distanced ourselves from our entrance point do I snap my elbow and ignite my hand. The blue light illuminates the dripping, dark filth around us. Somehow it smells worse once I can see it.

"Looks about how it smells down here," Korwin whispers, eyeing the walls of the pipe.

"We always end up in the sewer." I frown.

"Question is, where should we go next?"

"We need to find Stuart Manor."

Korwin shakes his head and looks like he might cry. "The Greens took Stuart Manor months ago."

"Exactly. They won't expect us to go back there, and there should be a skeletal staff managing the property."

"A skeletal staff with guns and scramblers. We'll never get in. More importantly, why would we want to?"

"When I left Liberty Party headquarters, David thought you might be staying there. That's where I was heading when Pit found me. David said there were places in the basement compound that the Greens can't access, secret places where your father hid his research."

"Yes, there were, but we can't get in. My dad used a biological key to lock down the compound. His own blood. *I* can't even get in. Believe me. I tried. I thought maybe my father had given me access again, once you rescued me from CGEF, but no. That's how I ended up with the Red Dogs. Couldn't get in."

"David gave me the key."

"What?"

"I have a vial of Maxwell's blood. Your father gave it to the Liberty Party council as a backup, in case anything happened to him. David gave it to me."

"David," he says contemptuously. He scrubs his face with his hand, and I wince. He must be in pain. His knuckles are split open. His lip is swollen and he's sporting a black eye. By his stiff upper body, I can tell other injuries exist under the T-shirt he threw on over the red silk shorts.

"You're hurt. Do you need more juice?" I reach for his hand.

"No. Save it. We might need it later."

I don't like the thought of him walking around in this

cesspool with an open wound, but he's right. "Do you know the way?"

Korwin looks up and down the pipe we're standing in, then nods his head. "Yeah."

We start walking along the ridge of concrete beside the stream of sewage, but then Korwin stops abruptly.

"What's wrong?"

He turns and unfastens the collar around my neck, tossing it into the muck. "Just putting this where it belongs."

I nod my approval and we continue on our quest in silence. I'm not sure how long we walk. My mind goes somewhere else, replaying the events of the last several days. With the adrenaline waning, my strength ebbs and I become weepy, crossing my arms across my chest to try to physically keep myself together when I feel as though I may break apart at any moment. "Do you think a person can go through what we've been through and not be... damaged?"

For several moments, he doesn't answer me. I think, maybe, he hasn't heard me. I think to ask the question again, but he clears his throat.

"No," he says.

The simple answer makes the tears flow more freely down my cheeks. "I thought not."

"Damaged isn't ruined," he says. "We've survived. We've done the best we can do, given the circumstances."

"Sometimes I wonder what we did to deserve the lot we were handed." In Hemlock Hollow, when something bad happens, like a baby is stillborn or someone loses a leg in a farming accident, they call it God's will. But maybe not this. Considering I was accused of being a witch, I suppose this would be considered Satan's will. Sadly, as I think about the course of events, I believe Dr. Konrad's will is at fault. I doubt God had anything to do with it.

We reach a fork in the pipe and we turn left. "How are you doing?" He glances at my glowing hand, our only light. I've kept it lit for at least an hour.

"Okay. A little tired but not bad."

"Good. We're almost there." He continues on.

Maybe it's the fatigue, or the long stretch of silence, but the sewer takes on the contemplative quality of a confessional. "I almost killed Alpha tonight."

He pauses to glance back at me. "I'm sure he had it coming."

"He knew who we were."

Korwin's eyes widen. "How?"

"He remembered me from a year ago and did his research."

Brow furrowed, Korwin starts moving again—slowly, absently. "Do you think he knew who Brady was? Were they working together for the reward?"

"I don't think so. He was trying to use what he knew to have his way with me. He could have been lying, but he said he was the only one who knew."

"Bastard."

"Yeah. Hurting him though, on purpose, it was... strange."

"Believe me, the guilt you're feeling will fade with time. It was him or you. You were generous to keep him alive."

"But that's just it; I don't feel guilty."

He flashes me a confused look. "Then what's the problem?"

"Something happened in the forest on my way to you," I say. "Something that changed me."

"The forest outside the reactor?"

I nod. "A flasher went off and I tried to destroy it. There were too many." I shake my head, remembering the tip and skid of the motorcycle. "Afterward, there was a wolf."

"A wolf, like the animal?"

I laugh. "What other wolf would there be?"

"I thought they were dangerous. Did it attack you?"

"We stared at each other for a long time and, yes, the wolf attacked."

Korwin looks over his shoulder at me, confused.

"I covered my face when it leapt at me, but it never... It felt as though it landed inside of me. It felt like... like the wolf became part of me."

He squints at me. "Do you mean, like the wolf wasn't real? A projection of your imagination?"

I think about that, while I take a deep breath of thick air. "No. I'd been praying just before. Asking God to show me his will for my life. I think the wolf was a vision. Maybe God's answer? But I'm not sure what it means."

"And you say the wolf jumped into you?"

"Yeah."

"And there was only one?"

"Mmmmhmmm."

"Don't you think that's weird? Wolves usually travel in packs."

"This one was alone."

"A lone wolf is the leader of its own pack. Maybe it was a sign, encouragement that you were headed in the right direction by breaking out on your own."

"The wolf appeared to me after I almost killed Alpha. She seemed happy about it."

Korwin snorts. "The imaginary wolf was happy you defended yourself?"

"I think so."

He sighs. "I'm not sure what the wolf means. Maybe she

is a vision or a figment of your imagination, but if she helps you do what you have to do to survive, I like her."

We make a hard right and Korwin reaches one hand forward. Although it appears that the pipe continues into the distance, his hand bounces off the air. "We're here."

I run my hand along the invisible pressure blocking our path. "How do we use Maxwell's blood to get through this?" I dig in my pack for the vial.

Korwin traces the curve of the pipe with his gaze. "Dad always had three levels of security. First, a deterrent to finding the lock. We are in the sewer, which you would think would be deterrent enough, but I'm guessing no. He wouldn't settle for easy." He points at the center of the stream of sewage. "There's a slight break in the flow, like something is under the surface."

I wince.

"I take by your expression that you want me to do this part."

Biting my lip, I hold up the vial. "Someone has to hold the blood."

He reaches for the vial, and I pull it away with a chuckle. It amazes me that I can laugh about anything at the moment, but the connection between us, the love we share, works as a buffer against the reality of our situation. As long as we're together and breathing, there will always be laughter and always be home.

"Here goes nothing." He plunges his hand into the filthy muck and feels around the bottom. "Ah." With a twist of his arm, he opens a panel. The lid is designed to break the flow of sewage, with barriers on the sides to keep the access point clean and dry. Inside, there's a keyboard and a red glass square with a picture of a fingerprint etched in the glass. A small rectangular screen blinks *Enter Access Code*.

"Do you know the code?" I ask Korwin.

With his clean hand, he types a series of letters and numbers. "Hopefully, it's the same one as before."

Place finger on reader.

"Is it asking for Maxwell's fingerprint? I thought it needed blood?"

Korwin frowns, his finger poised over the red glass. "Fingerprint recognition is an archaic technology. I think it's a trick. Hand me the blood."

I take the cap off the vial and hand it to him. It's a dumb thing to do. I release too soon and the vial falls through his fingers. He catches the top between his pinky and the heel of his palm, but not before blood splashes into the sewage. Our collective inhale echoes through the giant tube.

I wade in, thankful for my motorcycle boots, and grab it by the bottom.

"Is there any left?" His voice cracks.

"I think so. A little."

"Don't risk handing it to me again." He points. "A drop on the red panel. Only, a drop. If I'm wrong, we'll need the rest."

I don't tell him that I think there is only a drop left. Gingerly, I lower the vial and tilt it a little at a time until the cylinder is almost upside down. One fat red drop rolls out and splatters on the red glass. Nothing happens.

Korwin reaches a shaky hand down and taps the enter key. There's a buzz and then the red glass lights up.

Snap. We both jump back as the lid to the panel closes abruptly and sinks back into the muck. Korwin curses.

I screw the cap back on the vial and return it to the side pocket of my backpack.

"Jackpot," Korwin says.

I turn to see what he's smiling at. Behind us is a circular

entrance to a pristine white room. I take a step, and before my foot hits the floor a strong spray of liquid and air pummel me from all directions. I grip my backpack to keep it from flying off my shoulders from the pressure. Holding my breath, I squeeze my eyes shut against the onslaught. When I'm almost out of air, the spray dies down and a vacuum suction drives me forward. Only then do I dare open my eyes.

Korwin is right next to me, panting and running a hand through his wet hair. The membrane has closed behind us. We are in a room with no doors and no windows.

He looks at his hands and checks the bottoms of his soaking wet shoes, now clean. "The good news is, we don't smell like crap anymore," he says.

I turn a circle looking for any imperfection in the walls that might indicate a way out. I find none. "When do you want to start talking about the bad news?"

TWENTY-SEVEN

KORWIN SMILES. HE HOLDS UP A FINGER AND PRESSES an ear to the wall. Tipping his face toward the ceiling, he says, "Freedom." The wall in front of us slides away. "Voice activated," he explains as he steps through.

"Convenient."

We enter another room with a Biolock door. If this is the room I escaped through a year ago, it will lead into the back hall of the compound. "We should be careful. We have no idea how deep the Greens have infiltrated."

He nods and places his palm on the Biolock. A pulse later and we slip into a stuffy hall. "It's familiar but I'm disoriented. What side of the garden are we on?"

An abstract painting of a man with an umbrella surrounded by bouncing red balls hangs on the wall beside us. "Northeast, unless David changed these after we were arrested." He leads the way down the corridor silently, each of us vigilant for any signs of the Greens. If the compound has been occupied, there is no evidence. Dust collects on the artwork and the air hangs heavy and undisturbed.

Korwin laughs through his nose as we pass the glass doors to the gardens. Everything is overgrown but alive.

"Has someone been caring for it?" I ask.

"No. It's on a timer." He looks up at the recessed lighting above us. "They've left the water and electricity on. The backup wouldn't have lasted this long."

"Why would they do that?"

He shrugs, frowning. With shifty eyes and quick steps, we continue past the library and the art studio. We touch nothing and speak rarely, and then only in whispers. Korwin stops in front of his bedroom, listens a moment, then carefully opens the door. The room hasn't changed at all. The same artificial window, dark now because it's night outside, hangs next to the same bed, made up under the same wool blanket. The room is neat, although I can make out a thin white film of dust on the floor.

Korwin closes the door behind us and turns a lever to engage the Biolock. He places a finger to his lips before rounding the room to the bath. A few moments later, he emerges, running his fingers along every lamp, every piece of furniture. Inside each drawer.

"What are you looking for?" I whisper.

"Cameras, microphones. It's clean. For now, it appears we are alone." He places his hands on his hips and takes a deep breath.

"So, we stay... here?"

Korwin rubs his eyes with his hands. "It's four a.m. The only thing holding us up is adrenaline, and I'm fairly sure you want to change out of that."

I look down at my green dress. The material is puckered and torn. If it was revealing before, it is now completely inappropriate. I cross my arms over my chest and hold what little fabric remains in place.

"You go first." He points to the bathroom. "It's still fully stocked from before I was taken. I'd shower if I were you. That liquid we were sprayed with was probably a disinfectant. Best not to leave it on the skin."

I nod.

"Do you need something to wear?"

I shake my head. "I have a change of clothes in my pack."

He motions toward the door to the bathroom. I stand there for a minute, just breathing. And then it comes. The waterworks. I sob as if I've been carrying a heavy weight behind my tear ducts and I can finally lay it all down.

Korwin crosses the room and puts his arms around me. "Shhh. It'll be okay," he says.

"Will this ever stop? Will we ever find a place where we can be safe?" I blurt.

His hand rubs my back and he pulls away slightly to make eye contact. "Lydia..."

"I beat a Green Republic officer until he couldn't get up. I wore a collar for a week and dressed like a whore. I was almost raped by a man and almost killed him." I swallow and hold my arms out. "Who am I, Korwin?"

"You're a survivor."

I shake my head. "I could feel Alpha's heart seize in his chest, and I didn't care. Not in that moment."

"But you stopped. You didn't kill him."

"Yes, I stopped, but don't you see? This isn't who I am. It's not who I'm supposed to be."

Korwin rubs the back of his neck. "The Red Dogs and the collars, it was wrong, but we had to do it to survive. And we didn't buy into it, Lydia. It was a disguise, nothing more."

I shake my head. "But surviving at what cost? And what now?"

"Now we go on surviving."

"Do you think a person can fight the way we do, kill and hurt other people, and still have a soul?"

He grabs me by the shoulders and shakes. "You have a soul, Lydia. A very good soul. A beautiful soul."

"But do you think God will forgive us for all of this?"

He gives a curt nod. His hands drop from my shoulders.

"You don't believe there is a God," I say bluntly.

"I'm not sure what I believe, Lydia, but if there is, after all we've been through, I'm not sure about who should be forgiving whom. After all, He got us into this mess."

* * *

An artificial progression of light wakes me. The fake window on the wall is supposed to simulate a sunrise, but it's a poor imitation. A multicolored butterfly flits across the glass and a lone white cloud floats in the distance. I wish I could believe the illusion.

"I'm sorry I upset you last night," Korwin says next to me.

"Sorry you upset me but not sorry for what you said. You don't believe in God anymore."

"We have to protect ourselves. I can't think about faith right now."

I roll over and look at him. With a deep sigh, I say, "When's the right time to think about faith?" My stomach growls, loud enough that he can hear it.

"I'm hungry too," he says. "Can we talk about this another time?"

"I have some rations in my pack." I sit up and grab the

pack from against the wall. All the way on the bottom are two perfectly flat silver packets. One is labeled *curried lentil* and the other *chicken noodle*.

"I call curried lentil," Korwin says. "Breakfast of champions."

"Fine by me. It says we're supposed to add hot water." I turn over the package. "There's a fork shrink-wrapped to the back."

He takes his packet and heads for the bathroom faucet, turning the water on as hot as it will go. Once the pack is opened, there's a line inside that shows us how much water to add. We stir the contents and try to wait the recommended three minutes.

"This smells scrumptious," I say. Truth be told, it smells like pig slop, but I am hungry enough to appreciate any food at all.

"These are military rations," he says. "You say David gave you these? Out of the goodness of his heart?" Korwin looks skeptically at his packet of food, as if it could be poisoned.

"Not exactly. He made me promise to bring something back with me, besides you."

"What?"

The alarm on Korwin's watch interrupts us. Our three minutes are up. Famished, we both pause to dig in. My chicken noodle is a mushy paste of meat and vegetable chunks. I can't get it down fast enough.

I speak around a mouthful. "David said your father has some specimens locked in a safe and it is imperative that I retrieve them so that they will not be misused by the Greens."

Korwin narrows his eyes. "Specimens?"

"He said there was a safe behind the blue palomino painting."

"What kind of specimens?"

I shrug. "I have no idea. The bottom of my backpack has a chemical refrigeration unit. I'm supposed to bring them back to the reactor in that."

"And then what?"

"And then David promised to leave us alone. I promised I'd retrieve the vials in exchange for him letting me go. I gave him my word."

"Hmm." He frowns into his lentils, then scrapes the bottom of the packet and eats the last bite. "What do you say we go find these vials?"

I finish my last bite of chicken paste and move to throw the empty packet in the garbage but Korwin shakes his head. "We can't leave anything behind. The garbage comes with us."

"Oh."

"The fork goes inside and the packet folds in on itself to seal away the mess." He shows me and we store everything in the backpack. Then I make the bed while he double-checks that everything is exactly how we found it.

"There's something I haven't told you about my time at the reactor," I say, thinking about the promise I made to David. "I met someone."

"What kind of someone?" A note of jealousy creeps into Korwin's voice.

"My mother."

He gags like he's choking on his tongue. "Your biological mother? I thought she was dead?"

"Me too. Turns out she survived. And one more of the Alpha Eight, Charlie Stone."

"Is that it? You're not going to tell me my parents are alive?"

"No. I'm sorry."

"Don't be. I've always assumed they were gone." He laughs but I can tell a tiny flicker of hope has faded for him and feel guilty to be talking about my mother being alive.

"So along with David, that makes three of the Alpha Eight alive and well. How are they surviving without the serum?"

"They've replicated it. They have a full medical lab in the reactor."

"Damn. So why don't you want to go back?"

I shake my head. "She's a stranger. She's been alive all this time and never sought me out. What type of *mother* does that?"

Korwin shrugs. He walks to the door and places his ear against the wood.

"I know what you're thinking," I say. "You're thinking she did it to protect me. She wanted to save me from this life for as long as possible. But look where it's gotten me."

He nods and unlocks the door, looking right, then left down the hall. He motions for me to follow.

"I know you think I should be forgiving. I should at least hear her side of it and give her a chance. Maybe. Someday. But is now the time? Is she just confusing my emotions to try to entice me to join the Liberty Party?"

The hallway twists and turns. I'd forgotten how maze-like it was down here. But somehow, Korwin finds the blue palomino painting. I look behind me, across the hall, to the place that should be the base of the stairs. There's only a wall.

"Dad and I sealed it off before Stuart Manor was taken.

They'd need a diamond-tipped drill to get in here without my father's blood."

"Then why have you been so cautious this entire time?"

"Because the Green Republic has access to a diamond-tipped drill and worse." He winks at me.

Together, we lift the painting off its hook. Behind it is a barely visible panel recessed into the wall. Korwin runs his finger along the edge.

"Ouch." He retracts his hand, shaking it. There's blood. The safe door opens slowly and makes a whooshing sound like it is vacuum-sealed. The air inside rolls out in a dense, icy fog that falls toward our feet.

"What is this?" I ask.

"A freezer with a taste for blood," he says, raising an eyebrow. "Looks like Dad had this one set up to use my blood as well as his."

I wrap my sleeve around my hand and reach inside. A metal crate holds six frosted vials. I rub the sleeve of my opposite arm across the labels. "They have your name and a date on the outside."

"Huh?" He tries to take a vial but the cold burns his fingers.

"My hoody is temperature controlled," I explain. Even so, my fingers are starting to feel the cold.

"What do you think they are?"

A loud hiss comes from behind us. We pivot to see the vault door opening. I try to react, but within a split second a scrambler is pointed at my face and a man I'd hoped to never see again steps out from between a circle of Green officers.

"I want to thank you for your assistance." Dr. Konrad dons a pair of black gloves and takes the vials from me. "I've been trying to find Maxwell's missing specimens for months. I had a hunch all I had to do was wait."

TWENTY-EIGHT

I DON'T REMEMBER THE SCRAMBLER. ONE SECOND I AM thinking about Dr. Konrad's face, how the lines around his eyes and mouth have grown deeper during the last year and his pasty white skin gives him a corpselike appearance, and the next I wake shivering. Everything aches. I try to curl on my side but can't. A sharp pinch at my wrists and ankles brings me further into consciousness but my eyes won't open. I shift my head from side to side in panic.

"Shhh. Lydia, shhh. Calm down." Korwin's voice is on my right. "Your eyes are taped shut."

"K-Korwin? Where are we?"

"Some type of operating room. Listen, you need to focus your power on burning the tape off your eyes. Do this now." His words are steady but urgent.

I dig for the tickle at the back of my brain. It's elusive and weak. It comes forward only with prodding and is not strong enough to free my eyelids. "It's not working," I croak. My throat is dry and it hurts when I talk.

"Try again. It's going to be hard. It's only going to get harder the longer you wait."

With a deep breath, I find the tickle again and this time I hold my breath. I pull energy from the rest of my body and direct the heat to my eyes. The smell of burning plastic fills my nostrils.

"Good. Good girl. Almost there."

"Aah," I yell as my eyelids wrench open. The pain is excruciating and my power retreats into its cave with a snap that rocks my body. Even open, my vision is blurry and I blink repeatedly to clear my eyes. "What's wrong with me? I can't move and everything hurts."

"Look at me," he says. I turn my head to the right and a Korwin-shaped blur comes into my field of vision. With each blink, my vision becomes sharper. "You're hooked up to a drainer," he says. "You're strapped to a table. Don't waste your energy on the bindings; they have draining technology. You can't burn them off."

My vision finally clears. I cry out as I see the sores on Korwin's exposed skin. He lies on a silver surgical table awash in bright light. The white ceiling and walls look sterile but the smell in the room is of blood. Our blood. I look down my body to the wires poking out of my skin and lose it. Whimpering, I struggle against the restraints and whip my head back and forth on the table.

"Lydia, listen to my voice. You have to calm down. If you panic it will drain you faster. You'll lose consciousness. We're alone but I'm not sure for how long. We need to try to make the most of it."

"What does it matter? Konrad has us. We'll never get out of here alive." I weep. My nose starts to run and I can't move to wipe it. This in itself is enough to make me panic again.

"I have a plan," he says. "But you have to conserve your strength. It's our only hope."

I force myself to take deep breaths and lie still. It doesn't help. My heart hammers in my chest, and my eyes dart to the machines against the wall that drain our energy.

"Here's what we have to do. We need to try to move the tables closer so that we can touch. If we can touch and complete the circuit, we might be able to overload the equipment. Shut down the drainers, even for a moment, and we're out of here.

"How?"

He moves his body as far away from me on his table as possible, pulling against the restraints, then surges, throwing his weight to the other side. There's a screeching sound that makes the hair on my arms stand on end, and Korwin pales like he might die from the pain. His table is a quarter of an inch closer. There's still a good three feet between us.

I follow his lead and try the method myself. The effort makes all my joints ache. Because of my lesser weight, the table only moves an eighth of an inch. Korwin goes again. A fraction closer. The space between us might as well be a mile.

Fatigue hits me fast and hard. I can't even fathom trying again. I don't get a chance anyway. The door opens and the devil walks in, dressed in the skin of Dr. Emile Konrad.

"Welcome to my laboratory," he says. "Or my kingdom, as I like to call it." He places a black bag on a steel rolling tray near the front of the room and pushes its squeaky wheels between us. "What a relief to have you back within the fold. You gave us quite a scare when you escaped last year. Chancellor Pierce thought you were dead. He wanted to drop the entire search. But I want you to know something: I always believed in you."

"Let her go," Korwin says. "I'll do anything you want. I'll help you, just let Lydia go."

Konrad shakes his head slowly. "That won't do at all, Korwin. I have a scientific hypothesis that must be tested. Do you know what a hypothesis is, Lydia?"

I shake my head.

"A hypothesis is an idea that a scientist thinks might be true but requires additional testing to prove. My hypothesis is that you two are much harder to kill than ordinary humans."

"What do you want from us?" I ask. It's futile to engage Konrad, but I can't help myself.

"You're not paying attention, young lady. I want you to lie on the table while I see how long it takes to kill you."

His words are ice water. Goosebumps break out across my arms and legs.

"We'll work with you," Korwin promises. "Wouldn't it be better to keep us alive? We could be powerful allies."

Konrad shakes his head and clucks his tongue. "Oh dear. That old tune. I think you've proven you can't be trusted. Not only are you a threat to the Republic, but thanks to recent events, we don't need you anymore." He exaggerates a patronizing grimace. I have no idea what recent events he's referring to, but I don't have the strength to ask. "You have two choices. You can meet your end quickly or, and I really hope you choose this one, slowly... painfully. Which way you choose will be determined by how quickly and honestly you answer my questions."

I stare at the ceiling and don't say a word. Korwin remains silent as well.

"Ah," Konrad says. "I bet you'd like to know more about how you will die." He paces back and forth near our feet. "Your physiology presented a special challenge for me. Usually when I have a guest here I have a number of tools I use to elicit information. Specialized tools for specific purposes." He chuckles. "I have a vise specifically designed to separate a patient's shoulder from the socket and a toothy clamp that could shred muscle from bone without tapping an artery. But I realized after we strapped you to the table that my entire toolbox was metal and, therefore, useless without great hazard to myself."

"Isn't it enough to drain us?" Korwin says. "If you kill us, you'll waste the energy."

"Sacrifices must be made," he says with a shrug. "But like I said, you have control over how this happens." Konrad holds up a white tube with a green light on the side. "I want to introduce you to a new addition to my toolbox. This instrument is called an Accunitt. Handy tool for mainstream doctors to do surgery without breaking the skin. This useful gadget can focus atoms to a point as thin as a fraction of a hair width. It can be used to destroy a tumor or solder a torn artery without an incision." He rolls it in his fingers. "All that power, right here in the palm of my hand. Allow me to demonstrate."

His eyes dart between Korwin and me, his thin lips curving as he decides between us. Accunitt raised, he focuses on me, and I squirm under his coarse gaze.

"No...No," Korwin begs. "Start with me."

Konrad ignores his pleas. His gloved hand strokes the bottom of my foot and up my leg, trailing his fingers over the thin white hospital tunic. "The inside of the arm, near the armpit, is an exceptional pain point, often overlooked by the amateur." He grips my bicep and touches the cylinder to the place he describes. When his finger presses the green light, fire shoots straight through my arm, straight to the bone. The muscle between his grip and my neck contracts, my body trying to protect itself. But I can't move. My eyes widen and my mouth opens, but the pain keeps me from drawing a full breath. Instead, my jaw gapes until some-where, somehow enough oxygen leaks into my lungs and I release a shrill scream.

Konrad smiles at me as my scream peters out. "That was a good one. You might be an easier nut to crack than I expected." He pulls the cylinder away. The pain ebbs but not fully. When I look down at my arm, the dull ache and the way my skin puckers tells me he's damaged me. Maybe the bone is broken or there's a hole in my muscle. Crippled. Broken. Irreparable. To my core I understand that he will take me apart piece by piece.

Soulless and evil, Konrad turns on Korwin and raises the Accunitt. My hopelessness is trumped by my desire to spare my love pain. "You said you had questions," I say to Konrad.

The doctor stops, cylinder hovering over Korwin's chest, and rolls his head back on his neck. The sigh he lets out is exasperated, as if I've ruined his fun. "Ready to talk so soon?"

"Yes," I whisper.

"Where have you been hiding these last months? Who helped you?" He snaps the words toward Korwin but I understand he's asking me.

I answer quickly. "Willow's Province. We lived in the woods on the edge of the Outlands."

"Tsk. Tsk. Tsk." Konrad turns a sadistic smile in my direction and shakes his head. "Don't lie to me." He drops the cylinder to Korwin's hip.

Korwin turns away so that I can't see his face but his leg twitches with the effects of Konrad's torture. The sadistic doctor carves his way from hip to opposite shoulder. It's a long time before Korwin screams, an awful, gurgling sound that makes me weep. Blood dribbles off his jaw and onto the table. He's covered in sweat and white as a ghost. Konrad is killing him.

"Stop!" I yell, between sobs. "I'll tell you the truth."

Konrad grunts with disappointment but raises the cylinder from Korwin's flesh.

"Where have you been hiding?" Konrad asks, and this time he focuses the full force of his dead gray eyes on me. The Accunitt hovers over my heart. His lips are peeled back and I can see his yellowed teeth.

"The deadzone," I whimper.

"Don't!" Korwin yells. "Lydia, don't say another word."

"I have to. I can't watch him hurt you."

"Touching," Konrad growls, "but we're not done here. We've had undercover officers in the deadzone for months. Tsk. Tsk. There is no possibility you were there the entire time. A lie means I get to do more of this." He raises the Accunitt.

The cylinder presses into my right hand. I hear my bones snap. I scream as my thumb pops from its socket. Below my wrist, there is nothing but limp, useless pain. I turn my head and vomit next to my shoulder.

"That was a good one," Konrad says again through his thin grin.

The ring of a phone comes from his pocket and the grin morphs into a frown when he glances at the screen. "I'm going to leave the room for a moment. You two think about what just happened here. When I come back, we'll talk." He places the phone to his ear and steps around his black bag to leave the room.

All I can do is whimper and cry as my body tries to deal with the pain. My throat is raw. I can't tell if it's from electroscurvy or screaming. I want to die.

"Lydia," Korwin rasps.

I turn my head to look at him and a tear cascades over my nose. All I can smell is my own vomit. I blink at him because I can't speak.

"Pray with me," he says. "The Lord is my shepherd, there is nothing I shall want."

He's praying Psalm 23. I know it by heart, but I can't bring myself to join him. I stare at Korwin with contempt, anger brewing within me. "Stop. What are you doing?"

He pauses. "Praying. Pray with me, Lydia."

"Why? You were right, Korwin," I say through the pain. I swallow and the result is excruciating. "There is no God. What God would let this happen to us?"

Korwin sobs, tears flooding his face. "Don't say that. I wasn't right. I don't know anything."

I turn my head to stare at the ceiling and my soul sinks. I am sucked into a black hole of despair. I am nothing. I have nothing. I will die and there will be nothing on the other side.

"...though I walk through the valley of the shadow of death..." Korwin begins to pray again.

I close my eyes and try to block everything out—the pain, Korwin's mumbling.

The door opens and Korwin goes silent. "Now then, are you ready to talk?"

I sniffle.

"Who helped you?" he demands, picking up the Accunitt from his black bag.

I don't hesitate. "David Snow," I say, closing my eyes as if giving up the information is painful.

"David and Natasha Snow are dead. We found their remains."

"Burnt badly enough to make DNA testing difficult," I say. "David planned it that way."

"Lydia, stop." Korwin sounds so disappointed.

Konrad shows his teeth again. "Do you know how I can tell if you are truthful?"

I am too tired to respond. The drainer and the torture have brought me to the point I can no longer keep my eyes open.

"The probes I have hooked to your body measure over thirty factors across multiple body systems proven to be associated with lying. You can control your voice and what you say, but you can't control your chemistry. If David helped you escape, where is he now?

"Outlands," I whisper.

"Outlands? How?"

I say nothing.

"Hmm. So, you hid in the Outlands with David. My machines say it is true, but there's something you're not telling me. More to the story. What are you hiding?"

My eyes flutter.

Konrad is shaking me. How did he get so close that fast? "Where did you stay?" he demands.

"A cabin in the woods," I whimper. This is perhaps the best lie I've ever told because it's true. I did live in a farmhouse beyond the woods.

I pull another breath. I'm vaguely aware that it has been too long since my last.

"Disappointing. I thought it would take longer to break you, but it appears our time together is coming to an end. As promised, your honesty will be rewarded."

My eyes flutter open when Konrad bumps into me. He leans across my body to reach a rubber mask on a hook near my head. It's attached to a tank labeled *oxygen*. I take a shaky breath. He lowers the mask over my mouth and nose and straps it to my head.

TWENTY-NINE

SHATTERING GLASS. THE CLANG OF METAL ON METAL. What is Konrad doing? I am locked in darkness, unable to open my eyes. I have a sense I've been asleep but can't say for how long. I'm holding my breath.

"Don't be stupid," Dr. Konrad says.

He sounds defensive. Who is he talking to? Korwin? I'm not strong enough to move my head or open my eyes. I'm not even strong enough to take another breath. Fingers of darkness are pawing me under, luring me back to the depths of unconsciousness with the promise of something more permanent.

The mask is torn from my face and a hand slaps my cheek.

"Breathe, Lydia!" David's voice. When did he get here? Stabs of pain pepper my arms and legs. He's ripping the wires out. I take a shallow breath. Everything hurts.

"Even you must know these two are too far gone," Konrad says. "You'll never get away with this. Every officer within a thirty-mile radius will be here in seconds."

"You mean because of the alarm?" Laura's voice. It's as

soft as the coo of a dove, but somehow deadly. "We disabled it, Emile. No one is coming."

Feet scuffle. Zap. The smell of ozone and blood. The weighted thud of a body hitting tile. The clank of raining metal objects.

"Save it, Laura," David says. "We need you to be sparky if we're to have any chance of making it out of here."

"The old-fashioned way then. This guy deserves to die," Laura says.

Laura and David came for me. I try to fight. Try to stay alive to make myself worth their risk. But it's hard. I can feel myself slipping away.

Sirens in the distance. "No time. We've got to hustle."

"Bullshit. He's seen me." There's a rustle and squeak. "There. He can breathe in the *oxygen* he seems so fond of."

"Laura... now!"

A zip and rustle, like an opening duffle bag near my head. "Be careful not to touch her skin to skin. Her body could drain you trying to heal itself."

"Right. Help me."

I groan as I'm lifted from the table. When did they remove my restraints? The most I can do is flutter my lids. Every breath is a struggle.

"She's dying, David. We've got to..." I lose what she's saying in a fog of scrambled words. I'm not exactly asleep. I can still hear David and Laura speak and feel my body bounce in one of their arms, but I can't make sense of anything. It's like I have one leg in this world and one in a dark place where no one feels anything at all.

I revive again when I am thrown forcefully into the back of a Green Republic Humvee.

Have I been captured again? My body rolls against a long and hard object before coming to a stop. A duffle bag?

"They're still coming, David!" Laura yells. "Go, go!"

The Humvee jerks and then turns abruptly, throwing me against the far wall and rolling the duffle bag into me. I open my eyes. Korwin's face pokes from the black bag, eyes closed and skin almost gray. It's not a duffle bag. It's a body bag. I glance down. I'm in one too. Do they think we're dead? Fighting the urge to sleep, I try to reach for him. One of my arms does not respond at all. The other is pinned under me. I can move it but the hand throbs when I do, clearly broken. As the engine rumbles and bumps beneath me, I work the dead fingers up and out the neck of the bag. I flop the broken hand onto his cheek and close my eyes again.

Pop. Pop-pop.

"They've opened fire!" Laura yells. The Humvee swerves, and Korwin rolls away from me, breaking contact.

"We can't lead them back to the reactor," David says. "Where should I go?"

"Deadzone. Maybe we can lose them on the backstreets."

The vehicle swerves. Korwin slams into me, and I position my broken hand again. I can't feel Korwin's pulse. I reposition my wrist where his artery should be. Nothing. A hot stroke of anger ignites within me. Korwin cannot die. I was supposed to die. I absolutely refuse to continue in this cruel, hateful world without him. I can't. My anger wakes the tickle at the back of my skull and I immediately send it into Korwin. His body jolts inside the bag.

I rest my head on the floor and let what little is left in me out, into his body. I am a raw sore. I am nothing but pain. The wounds on the arm between us start to ooze and then bleed. Still no pulse. I refuse to believe he's dead. I take one last breath and give him everything I have left, until darkness claims me again.

Bam! A door slams. We've stopped and I'm still breathing.

"David, to your left!"

Pop. Pop-pop. Pop. Plunk. A bullet pokes a hole in the side of the jeep and pings off the opposite wall before falling at our feet. I look over at Korwin. There's been no change. I press my cheek against his and feel a featherlight breath brush my face.

"Korwin?" my voice cracks. His skin is too cold, but this thing inside of me, the spark, seems to know he's alive. I feel it start to flip, feeding him, then me. My arm stops bleeding.

"Laura, NO!" An explosion rocks the vehicle onto two wheels and I snake my arm around Korwin's shoulders to keep us together. My broken hand throbs from the effort. I manage to squirm out of my body bag, then unzip his and lay across the top of him, my head tucked into the side of his neck. The engine that is us keeps burning. I fall asleep again.

I wake to Korwin's raspy breath in my ear. He's whimpering in pain. I shift so that my weight is not on his injured hip. Outside the windows of the Humvee, I see lightning. David and Laura have resorted to using their electrokinesis. They won't last long.

Korwin and I are wearing white hospital tunics. I shift mine then his so we are skin to skin. The exchange goes faster. I am able to move my dead arm, and I dig out Korwin's hand and thread my fingers into his. Palm to palm, heart to heart. The sores on my arms have crusted over.

"Lydia?" he says, and his eyes flip open.

"I'm here."

"I saw my parents." He looks away from me and his eyes start to tear.

"You were gone." I look from eye to eye and I know it's true. He was dead. "I brought you back."

"What's happening?"

"David and Laura are fighting to save us, but it doesn't look good. We need to help."

"I can hardly move."

"Kiss me." I lower my lips onto his and the familiar rush hits me hard. It isn't about lust or anything physical. In that moment, it's about connection. Fire pours in and out of me. We charge each other—skin to skin, heart to heart, lip to lip, palm to palm. The smell of burning plastic drives us apart. We've singed the interior.

"Better?" I ask. Laura's screams confirm we're out of time.

He nods. "Still not a hundred percent, but I think I can move."

"Yes."

"Don't let go of my hand."

We rise to a squat and straighten our tunics. Korwin unlocks the back gate but holds it closed. "Can you spark? They're not going to try to take us alive."

I lift my broken hand. I can move the thumb again but not the fingers. With a wince, I snap it out at the elbow, and the blue glow burns bright around us. As long as I hold his hand, I'm gaining strength, healing.

"I'm ready," I say. But I'm not ready. I feel like I've been run over by stampeding horses.

Korwin nods. He opens the gate and we leap into the war.

THIRTY

HAND IN HAND, WE WALK STRAIGHT TOWARD THE advancing Greens. There's no place else to go. I see now why David had to stop and fight. The road beyond the jeep is gone, as if construction ended with the loss of power. There's an orange-and-white roadblock and then nothing, the asphalt gives way to a deadly drop.

The Greens shower us with bullets, the ammunition melting in our mounting heat. We find Laura and David huddled in a shallow doorway, the telltale signs of electroscurvy spotting their faces. Their blue clothing is stained purple with blood, and working together, they can barely maintain an energy shield strong enough to repel the open fire. Together, Korwin and I cast our energy out, wrapping them in our protection.

"Get in the jeep!" I yell. They don't hesitate. Leaning on each other, they limp to the vehicle behind us.

Scrambler probes fly as we approach, but the officers can't get close enough for them to work due to the heat we're putting off. I turn up the power. My link with Korwin doesn't fail me; the spark takes on a life of its own.

We've done this before—created this engine that is our connection. Like before, the fire within takes over. It fills me and protects me. I do not analyze it or judge its source. I simply trust my instincts.

"They won't leave on their own," Korwin says. His voice takes on a resonant embouchure, hollow and tinny.

I roll my shoulder and throw my power forward, blasting one soldier and then another. The men I hit drop, twitching. The others scatter as we step over the fallen and into the street. The road is packed with military vehicles. "Your turn."

Korwin sends a blast of lightning into the nearest one. It pops into the air and then crumples into the pavement. I have the faintest concern for the driver as he goes tumbling, but the longer we stay like this, the further I feel from human. My remorse is limited. As jeeps fly and people scream, I experience it as a distant observer, even when it is my hand that causes the destruction.

David and Laura follow behind us in the Humvee as we break from the alley into the street. "Right or left?" I yell.

Korwin scans the block. "Nearest entrance to the grid is this way." He points left.

"They're coming from both sides!" I direct my shield of energy to protect the Humvee.

"We can't separate. I'm too weak to do this without you."

"Can we get hot enough to cover them?"

"We'll have to try."

I open up the channel and feel the current race between us. The circle of blue expands. We're able to contain Laura and David, but the globe of energy only reaches halfway across the backseat. David nods and pulls up closer to us. We advance.

Step by step we battle our way forward, lightning bolts branching to the buildings around us, then breaking apart. We make it through to the back of the formation, partly through brute force but mostly because the men start to cut and run.

"Lydia, behind us," David yells through the windshield. I glance over my shoulder. Heavy artillery pulls in behind the men.

"There's a tank," I say. "We're not strong enough."

"We need to get mobile. Come on."

Tugging my hand, he leads me to the side of the jeep. We prop ourselves on the running board, our hands coupled between us. Korwin slaps the roof, and I hold on with my free hand.

David takes off, just as a blast of fire erupts from the tank's cannon. The artillery misses us but the impact rocks the Humvee. I lose my grip and windmill my arm to keep from flying off the side of the jeep. Korwin grips my hand tighter and yanks me back up before I lose my footing.

The corner is our savior. After we turn, the tank isn't fast enough to follow within range. Korwin bangs on the back window. The glass lowers and he pushes my head in. I grunt as I force my body through the opening, then help Korwin inside.

"Get to the grid," Korwin yells to David.

"What does it look like I'm doing?" David growls. "Everyone pray we make it."

"We will. The tanks are too slow," I say hopefully.

"I wish that was our only issue. A bullet punctured the gas tank. We're running on fumes."

I chew my lip as David takes the next corner. I can see the ramp through the windshield and Laura starts keying coordinates into the dashboard. "We can't go there!" David shouts, looking at the numbers. "We won't have enough fuel to make it home."

"What would you suggest?" she hisses.

The engine sputters and David's foot hits the floor. The jeep slows in response. We can see the blinking lights of the grid just a few yards ahead but the jeep won't move. I glance behind us. "They're coming!"

Laura and David look at us in exasperation. The Humvee lurches forward, then stops, then lurches again. "We're on empty," David says, "but the grid is pulling us. We must be just beyond the range of the electromagnetic field."

"It's magnetic?" I ask.

"Sure. That's how the grid works. It connects with the bottom of the vehicle. Reduces friction and forces the vehicle forward."

I look at Korwin and he understands without me saying a word. He grabs my hand and forces it onto the floor of the jeep. *We* produce an electromagnetic field. I concentrate on the grid, my power asking the atoms to connect with us. I throw the spark, then pull it in. Korwin does the same. We lurch forward but barely.

"Oh hell," David says. "The tanks!"

A tug rips through me as Korwin sends our power out again. This time it works. The jeep gives one mighty lurch and catches on the grid. "Come on. Come on. Come on," David says as we slowly build speed.

A shell explodes behind us, knocking us forward. It's meant to hurt but it helps. We snap to the grid, accelerating to maximum speed. The Greens turn into a blur in our wake.

David swivels in his chair. "Neat trick."

"I wasn't sure if it would work. We've never used our power like that," Korwin says.

"I'm not talking about the grid, although you did just save our hides. No, I'm talking about the healing each other part. When did you learn to do that?"

Korwin drops my hand for the first time that night and pushes himself off the floor and into one of the seats against the wall of the vehicle. I do the same.

"My dad figured it out. When we're together, we can charge each other. We can pull the energy from the atoms around us to fuel our bodies in a way we can't separately."

Laura shakes her head. "Better together."

"You could say that."

"How did you find us?" I ask David.

"Tracker in the helmet. We recovered the bike days ago but didn't know where you were until the Greens showed up. You want to find Lydia Troyer, just wait for the explosions." He grins.

"The Greens are probably tracking us by now," Korwin says. "Shouldn't we do something to lead them off the trail?"

"We have a blocking device, specifically designed to keep them from tracking us. But even if we didn't, we don't have a choice. Jonas is meeting us at the off-ramp with a van. This baby isn't going to make it any farther than it rolls."

I feel all the blood rush from my head. "The Greens know where we're going," I blurt. "I told Konrad we were hiding in the Outlands."

"You were being tortured," Korwin pipes in. "It wasn't your fault."

"Not my fault? I was the one too weak to stand the pain. You were tortured too, but I was the one who cracked."

"I don't care if he extracted it from your brain," David

says. "It doesn't matter why Konrad knows, only that he does."

"Konrad is dead," Laura says. "I killed him myself."

"We don't know if he transmitted what Lydia said," David sputters. "We have to be prepared that when we leave the grid, there will be someone waiting for us."

I chew my lip at the familiar jerk-and-tilt signal of the jeep leaving the grid. Korwin reaches for my hand. "We'll handle it," he says.

The blur outside the window slows to a rush of trees and then gives way to a slow roll into Willow's Province. David steers the Humvee onto the side of the road. Sure enough, there's a large white van waiting for us. "It's ours. Jonas made it," David says.

"Quickly," Laura says. "Before the Greens have a chance to figure it out. We'll send cleaners back to sink the Humvee in the lake."

No one hesitates. We pile out and sprint for the van. As soon as we're within striking distance, the side door slides open of its own accord. I lunge inside with the others, moving from daylight into total darkness. It takes my eyes a second to adjust. It's a second too long. The door slides shut behind me, and I can hear the lock engage. There's a man, bound and unconscious on the floor. Jonas! My neck cranes toward the front seat and my breath catches in my throat. Behind the protective divider, Brady keys coordinates into the dash.

"At last," he says, rubbing the side of his face as if it still stings from Korwin's punch. "Dr. Konrad will be pleased."

THIRTY-ONE

"Brady, don't do this," Korwin says. "You're better than this."

"Seems the Greens are willing to make sacrifices to have you back," he says.

"What kind of sacrifices?" David asks.

"Bringing me back into the fold, for one. Do you know how long I worked to infiltrate Jonas's inner circle? And in one night, you two ruin everything. After your little stunt with the transformer, I was excommunicated to the deadzone. It's a small world, the deadzone. Just a matter of time before I found you."

"The Greens kicked you out once. They'll do it again. Help us and we'll show you a better option," David says.

"What? Camping in the Outlands?" He scoffs. "After landing you two and a bonus for delivering Jonas, the goddamned Liberty Party leader, I'll be living like an Uppercrust for the rest of my life."

"How did you know where to find us?" I ask.

"I've been doing odd jobs for Konrad since I left the fold. Stuff the Greens can't get their hands dirty doing. Guy has deep pockets. He called me as soon as you left the laboratory and told me you'd try for the Outlands."

"Impossible. Konrad's dead," Laura blurts.

"No, he's not. I talked to him minutes ago when I saw you exit the grid. You don't know anything about the doctor if you think he's easy to kill. Man has nine lives."

"You should know. You've kissed the ass of every one of them," David says.

Brady peers at David cynically. "You a-holes always underestimated me. *I* was the one with the technical know-how to hack into the Stuart Manor compound. I built the damn thing while I was working for the Liberty Party, for God's sake. I'm not just some kid with big muscles to carry the firehose. That's why I couldn't stomach you people. All for one and one for all? People aren't equal. I deserved more. Always taken for granted. Not this time. You are my key to the lifestyle I deserve." He points at me with venom in his voice.

I blast the divider, but the power spreads and fizzles harmlessly.

"Don't even try it, sweetheart. It's got drainer technology and the door won't open from anywhere but up here."

The spark within me does not like this. A dark, burning force awakens within me. I can't deny the urge to survive. It's an instinct, a force of nature.

Brady presses a button on the dash and the engine grinds to life. My heart pounds and my mind whirls like a swarm of angry bees. I cannot go back to Konrad. I envision him peeling my skin from my body, not letting me die until he extracts every ounce of suffering I am capable of. A bead of sweat gathers at my hairline. Someone is screaming. The low moan of a dying animal.

Korwin shakes me and I realize I am the source of the noise. Brady drives toward the grid. I can't go back. This isn't happening.

I grab Korwin's hand and slap the floor.

"Uh-oh," David says, retreating to the rear of the van and tugging Laura and Jonas along with him. Korwin follows my lead as I pour energy into the van. Only, instead of concentrating on propelling it forward, I command it to reverse. I ask the atoms of the grid to use their force to push us away. The axles grind as the engine battles with itself and the smell of burning oil fills my nostrils.

Korwin nods at me, his eyes filled with blue light. The inside of the divider peels from the heat coming off us.

"What are you doing?" Brady yells.

The van stops. The screeching sound of the tires spinning in their stationary ruts is an anthem to our freedom. I pour on the power, grunting with the effort. Ultimately the engine can't take the heat, and it stalls where we are.

"Stupid little..." Brady explodes out of the cab, face red, and walks around the front of the vehicle, pulling a scrambler from his hip. The side door slides open.

Without thought of consequence, I nail him with a blast of electricity, fully expecting to burn his heart from his chest. Instead, his muscled frame absorbs the blast, blue ribbons meshing over his over-pumped muscles before absorbing under his skin. I stare at him in disbelief.

"I told you I was working for Konrad, and the doctor doesn't take any chances."

Of course. Brady is as strong and fast as he is because he's had the serum too, just like the Alpha Eight. And just like David, he's immune to my firepower.

"Come on, chickee. I got a call in to Konrad to come pick us up. We might as well make good use of the time."

He beckons me with his right hand. Korwin pushes in front of me, ready to do whatever it takes to protect me. David and Laura are at our flank, but with their electroscurvy weakening them, I don't suspect they'll be much help. Still, David taught me all I need to know about Alpha sparks. Even more than Korwin knows. And this one is mine.

I grab Korwin by the bloodied shirt and yank him back. "He's mine," I say.

"Lydia..."

"No," I announce. "He. Is. Mine."

I step in front of Korwin and face off against Brady. The man finds the whole exchange amusing. He thinks I'm a joke.

"Are you going to fight me, Lydia?" he says, laughing.

I hold out my right hand and urge him to attack by beckoning him with my upturned fingers. He obliges, rushing me, with no consideration to my petite size or my gender. In a way, it is a blessing. His full-on assault gives me a reason to suspend my usually merciful disposition.

He hits me. I catch his wrist as it rebounds off my jaw. And then I pull, not with my weight but with my power. I draw the blue juice from his body mercilessly, gulping down hot dregs of energy. He groans and falls to his knees.

"You didn't know I could do that, did you? Alphas can't pull energy from other Alphas, but Betas can. I'm going to pull every drop from you until there is nothing left to charge your foul black heart."

Bloody sores break out across his arms and up his chin to his hairline. "No," he mumbles.

"Don't feel bad. Konrad never understood I could do this. He never tested this because, really, he never expected me to attack someone like me. David didn't expect it, but he never shared because he hated Konrad."

Brady's eyes roll back in his head and foamy saliva bubbles out of the corner of his mouth. I don't lay off. Instead, I draw harder on the tap of power at my fingertips. The wolf is beside me again, hunched over Brady, growling and showing teeth.

"Lydia," Korwin says. "You'll kill him."

But the wolf within stands beside me, raging and wild. It is louder than Korwin and it knows the truth. I can't let Brady live. He's a risk, a loose cannon that I can't trust the Liberty Party to contain. With one last draw, I pull the dregs of his energy from his body. The life leaves his eyes, and he flops to the dirt near my feet without even a twitch.

THIRTY-TWO

"Why?" Korwin's eyes drift from Brady's body to me as if he can't fathom why I killed him.

"He never would have stopped," I said, shaking my head. The wolf pants over Brady's body. She's in my head. No one else can see her. But she's there, celebrating the kill.

"We could have taken him hostage. Used him for questioning."

"He couldn't be trusted. No way could we risk taking him to the reactor. He might've had a tracker implanted."

"We could have bound and gagged him and left him somewhere."

"Why, so that the Greens could pick him up and regain a weapon? If he were a rifle, would you leave him on the side of the road?"

"No, but that's different."

"Different how?"

"Brady was a human being."

"Hardly." I narrow my eyes. There's a tightness in my chest I don't want to think about. I can't meet Korwin's eyes. I know I'll find disappointment and I just can't go there right now, not when I'm entirely sure I've done the right thing.

David hobbles up behind me and places a hand on my shoulder. "No. Lydia had to do it. Brady wouldn't have hesitated to kill every last one of us. It was kill or be killed."

I'm not sure if David's support of what I've done makes it better or worse. David is a trained killer. He is a liar. I don't want to make David proud or do what David would do. Still, in this case, he is right. I do believe Brady was a terminal threat. I had to do what I did.

"We're on borrowed time," I say. "Brady sent for backup. We've got to get out of here."

Korwin takes a step closer and points at Brady's body. "Don't act like this was easy for you."

"Easy is exactly what it was," I snap. "The hard thing will be facing Konrad again if we don't get out of here."

"If Brady was telling the truth and Konrad's still alive," Laura says, "the day will come when we have to face him. Considering he now knows we are in the Outlands, most likely sooner than later." The sores on her body have spread and every word she speaks makes her flinch.

A groan comes from the van. Jonas. Still bound and gagged within, he stirs in his fight for consciousness.

"Can we get the van running again?" I ask.

David strides toward the cab as he answers. "Probably overloaded the operator's app. I should be able to reboot the kernel and bring it back online."

"Whatever that is," I say. "Couldn't you have fed something about mechanics and computing into my head with the Nanomem?"

He laughs through the open window and raises an eyebrow. "I only had six weeks."

With a flip of his hand he pops open the dash. His

fingers fly across a keyboard under the touchscreen. There is still so much about this world I don't understand.

"Can you teach me? When we get back?" I yell.

David smiles without looking away from the screen. "Of course," he says. "Does that mean you're going to be around for a while?"

Korwin squints at me, his hands on his hips. The distance between us feels strange, and I'm taken back to the Red Dog kennel when I couldn't feel our connection because he was guarding against it, just like he is now. "You've decided to stay? On your own, without talking to me?"

The engine growls to life and Laura climbs into the van. "There's no place else to go," I say.

"We can return to Hemlock Hollow. We'll take our discipline from the *Ordnung*. We can go home," he says.

"Hemlock Hollow is no place for someone who doesn't believe in God."

"I do believe. I see that now—"

"I wasn't talking about you."

Korwin locks eyes with me over Brady's body.

"Now, you two. We've got to go!" Laura calls. I turn and bound into the van. I'm relieved when Korwin follows.

THIRTY-THREE

LIGHT TURNS TO DARK AS DAVID PULLS INTO THE garage at the back of the reactor. The big doors rumble closed and a sea of blue uniforms approaches the van. An alarm sounds and lights blink above us. *Code blue—garage,* a robotic voice repeats. When the van door slides back, Dr. Stone pushes his way to the front.

"I need two," he eyes David behind the dash, slumped in his seat, "three stretchers. Stat."

Laura is down too. In hindsight, we shouldn't have let David drive. We're lucky to be alive. David's electroscurvy could have sent us barreling into a tree.

Men and women in blue tunics rush from a set of double doors near the back, ushering white padded stretchers to Charlie's side. They carefully load Jonas first, then Laura before retrieving David from the cab.

"Can you walk?" Charlie asks us. He's climbed inside the van and has a hand on my back.

"Yes. We're fine."

"You're covered in blood," he says matter-of-factly.

"Yes—" My breath catches in my throat as I look down at myself. My face and hands go cold and my head swims.

"We've healed ourselves," Korwin says. "We're fine."

Charlie takes a moment to squeeze my fingers and rub my back. "You may be healed, but you most certainly are not fine." Turning to his helpers in blue, he says, "Help them to the infirmary and get them cleaned up. I want a scan on both for internal injuries." He gently coaxes me from the van and the hands of strangers guide me inside.

WASHED, DRESSED, AND SCANNED, I END UP IN A recovery room in the infirmary where a harried nurse tells me I need to wait for Dr. Stone. Moments later, they bring in Korwin and seat him next to me. It feels like a long time before he says anything.

"Why did you kill Brady?" he asks.

"To save our lives," I say incredulously.

"You could have incapacitated him. You didn't have to be cruel."

"No? I think that's exactly how I need to be. Were you even there? We almost died in Konrad's lab. Konrad won't stop. He will never stop until he's dead or we are."

"I was there, Lydia. I felt the pain, and may I remind you that it was my second visit to Konrad's lab? But a long time ago, a beautiful woman taught me that there were more important things than living forever. She taught me I had a soul and a God. She taught me that this world wasn't nearly as important as the next."

"A fact that didn't seem to occur to you when you were beating another man in the Red Dog ring," I say through my teeth. "Yes, it seems both of us have made compromises in our morality, doesn't it?"

He hangs his head.

"I am done playing the part of the victim. I am done turning the other cheek. I choose to stay and fight. What do you choose?"

For a long time, Korwin says nothing. "I saw my parents, Lydia. I was dead, and I saw them. This... life, this isn't all there is." He licks his bottom lip. "There was a time I chose to leave. Maybe that's what got us into this mess. Had I stayed in Hemlock Hollow and took my punishment, faced the bishop's decision, maybe we wouldn't be here now."

"Or maybe we would. That flasher wasn't going to destroy itself." I picture the doll burning in my yard again. Would it have mattered if there were two dolls, one in a dress and one in suspenders? No. The *Ordnung* would have never accepted who we are. Never.

"If we've learned anything," Korwin reaches for my hand, "it is that we have to stay together. We are safer and stronger together. I won't leave this time. Not without you."

I scoot my chair closer. "I'm not going anywhere."

He makes a throaty whimper of relief and closes the space between us to lean his forehead against mine. Our glow warms the room until a nurse comes to usher me away.

EPILOGUE

When Amish women marry, they don't wear white dresses. White is reserved for our deaths to symbolize the purity we hope to have when we come before our Maker. Wedding dresses are typically blue and in the normal style so that we can wear them again after marriage. Blue is plain and hard working. Blue is the color of the day-to-day struggle.

With this thought in mind, I don my new uniform. It is also blue. Hard-working blue. Long-term commitment blue. The jacket has silver buttons and a navy armband embroidered with a circle of five white stars. This is the Liberty Party's symbol. The uniform is stretchy and formfitting, and the material is temperature controlled, which is good because for some reason the rooms in the reactor are always kept cold. I've been issued another pair of heavy black boots, and I pull them on over navy socks that cover my calves.

Finished, I stand and turn from side to side in front of the mirror. My hair is long and loose, still slightly wet from my shower, and I push it behind my shoulders to get a good look at myself. I've lost weight since the last time I indulged myself with a long look in the mirror, and my muscles appear hard under the clingy material. It's my eyes that have changed the most. The green has closed off and dulled. They look hard, even to me.

A knock on the door demands my attention. I use my fingerprint to unlock the Biolock. "Korwi—"

David stares back at me. "Sorry. No." Three days of rest and extra injections have done him good. He almost looks healthy again.

I back up and welcome him into the room. "Your skin looks better," I say.

"Completely healed, although I'm still having phantom pain in my joints. Charlie isn't sure why."

"It's just a matter of time. You were pretty bad off."

"Speak for yourself. I heard you have some lasting damage."

I hold up my right hand. It's still bandaged. "The tool Konrad used didn't just cut, it burned. He broke all the bones in my hand. When Korwin healed me, the bones weren't aligned." I rub my thumb over my bandaged palm. "Charlie had to break them again to set them properly."

"Sounds painful."

"He offered morphine but..." I shake my head.

"You didn't want to risk the seizures."

I nod. "It'll be as good as new in a couple of days. Thank you for coming for us, for risking your life for me."

He sighs. "It was Laura's idea. The Liberty Party would have come for you eventually, but Laura wouldn't wait. Insisted we do the special op ourselves. Reminded me a lot of the day you went after Korwin. Like mother, like daughter."

I cringe at the mother/daughter description. I still

hardly know Laura. "I'm grateful she came when she did. Konrad would have killed us."

"Yes. Odd, don't you think, that Konrad would kill his favorite guinea pigs? Betas. Almost unbelievable that he would give up specimens like yourselves so easily."

"I thought the same thing. He said he couldn't trust us anymore and that we were useless to him."

"Hmm." David's brow furrows and he couples his hands behind his back. "I need to ask you something. It's important, and I'm afraid it can't wait."

I take a deep breath and blow it out slowly. David does not call something important without cause. "Go ahead."

"When we recovered the Tomahawk and helmet, the backpack I gave you wasn't with it."

"No. I kept it with me until the very end. Konrad took it."

"Had you visited Stuart Manor before your arrest?"

"Yes. We were caught inside the manor. He'd been waiting for us, like he knew we'd come."

David's face pales. "And Maxwell's experiments?"

"Konrad took those too. He said he'd been trying to get into the safe for weeks." I scrunch my forehead together as I think about the incident. "Strange that Brady was able to break into the manor but not into the safe."

"Brady used to work for the Liberty Party. He was able to hack compound security because he developed the program and built in a Liberty Party fail-safe. But Maxwell didn't trust anyone with his most prized experiments. He developed his own security for the safe. He was prepared for the contents to be lost forever if he died. Perhaps he hoped it would be."

"It wasn't lost. And we didn't have to use Maxwell's blood. We used Korwin's."

David's eyebrows shoot upward. "I had no idea."

"We had them in our hands."

He closes his eyes. "What did the specimens look like?"

"Six metal vials, like the blood you gave me. Frozen solid. They had Korwin's name on the side. Do you know what they were?"

"I do."

I stare at him expectantly. "Well?"

"What happened to the specimens?"

"Konrad took them before he scrambled and tortured us. What were they, David? You're ghost white. You're scaring me."

"The vials contained Korwin's genetic material," he says toward the wall, as if he can't stand to say it to my face.

I shake my head.

"His reproductive genetic material," David explains. "Enough to father several dozen children, I suspect."

"No." I sit down on the bed.

"Unfortunately, yes."

"But the specimens are useless to Konrad without my genetic material, right? Unless he makes another Alpha and then the children wouldn't be true Gammas."

"He won't need to." David's voice cracks.

I swallow hard and wrap my arms around myself. "Why?"

"He has yours."

"No," I say. "He doesn't. He was going to take it, but I escaped before he could do the procedure."

David shakes his head. The muscle in his jaw twitches with anger. "By the time he talked to you about it, he had already harvested your genetic material."

I recoil. "I would have known if someone took my genetic material," I say through a false smile.

"Not if your trainer slipped you a drug that knocked you out for a few hours while a needle was used to extract what Konrad needed. You were in and out of awareness anyway because of the Nanomem and so beat up you didn't even notice the pain of recovery. He had what he wanted the fourth day you were there."

"You did what?" I say through my teeth.

He closes his eyes. "I had to, Lydia. I didn't have a choice. You don't know how it was."

I hold up my hand. "I know exactly how it was."

"And you didn't fair much better than I did. Last I heard, it was your information that led Brady to us. Lord only knows why the Greens haven't attacked yet."

"I..." I can't find the words to defend myself. "Why did Konrad meet with me and tell me he was going to extract my cells if he already had them? Why tell me what he was going to do if he'd already done it?"

"You know why."

I roll my lips together and pace between the bed and the door. "He wanted me to know what he was doing for the purpose of getting his hooks into me. A child would cement my loyalty to his cause. He knew I wouldn't leave my child."

"Exactly."

"But he had Korwin too. If he took my genetic material, why did he need to get Korwin's from Maxwell's specimens?"

"Because I destroyed Korwin's genetic material before we escaped." He rubs his fingers together. "Electrocuted it, then placed it back in the freezer. I suspect Konrad had a rude awakening to find a vial full of dead cells after we left."

"And now he has both," I say. "Because of you."

He turns on me, his gaze digging in. "Do you think I wanted this? I sent you for the vials because I wanted to avoid this. It was only a matter of time before the Greens found it."

"You don't know that."

"The safe used power. Once the auxiliary power went out, they would have known the basement was drawing energy from the main breaker. And once they knew something was back there, they'd use any means necessary to get inside. They would have found the specimens eventually, Lydia. I was trying to intercept Konrad."

"Then why not tell me to destroy it?"

"Would you have destroyed something with Korwin's name on it based on my word? Honestly."

The answer is no, but I don't give him the satisfaction of a direct response. "You should have told me the truth." I rub my temples. "What now?

"Now we make a plan to break into CGEF and stop Konrad from using what he has. He has a limited supply. He could try to use a surrogate, but I doubt it. He'll want ultimate control of every detail."

"In his office at CGEF, he told me he didn't need a mother."

"He doesn't. Last year, the first human baby was born in an artificial womb. It's a complex process, but knowing Konrad, he'll want to tinker with the science. Who knows what he'll try."

"So our job is to destroy the vials before he can use them."

He nods. "As soon as we can assemble a team, we'll go. The sooner, the better."

At the thought of returning to Konrad's lab, my stomach turns and my knees shake. I sit down on the bed. "Does Korwin know?"

"I spoke with him first. He was going to come with me

but I asked him to let me tell you." He places a hand on his chest. "I never meant for this to happen."

I raise an eyebrow. "Is that your idea of an apology?"

He gives a small half smile. "The only one you're going to get."

"Where is he now?"

"In the chapel, waiting for you."

"This place has a chapel?"

I FIND KORWIN KNEELING IN FRONT OF A TABLE OF candles in a small dark room labeled *chapel*. There are rows of folding chairs and a statue of Jesus with his arms outstretched at the front. It's not a statue of the crucifixion; it's the resurrection. I've never been in a church like this before, but I find it quiet and comforting with its dim lighting and flickering candles. It seems a hopeful place.

"I didn't think they would have a chapel," I say as I walk down the aisle between the rows of folding chairs.

Korwin looks up from his prayerful pose. "I was surprised they allowed the room for it. Space is limited."

I stare at the candles, trying to find the words to say what I need to say. "David told me about your father's specimens. After the ceremony, we need to make a plan to destroy them."

He frowns. "Right. The induction ceremony. Are you sure about this, Lydia? We swore we'd never do this. If we go through with today, we are promising to join the war—to be part of the problem instead of the solution."

"War *is* the solution."

He widens his eyes at me. "I never thought I'd hear you say that. Have you changed your mind? We didn't want to be part of this. We swore this wasn't our war and that we'd keep ourselves out of it."

"But we were wrong."

"How so?"

"When Konrad took your cells from my hands at Stuart Manor, it became our war. He has the power and the technology to make our *children*. You know what he will do if he succeeds. He will use them as soldiers, as bait, as weapons against us, all to continue Chancellor Pierce's brutal reign. The Liberty Party is our only chance to stop him. Our only hope to survive."

"This wasn't what I wanted for us."

"I know. I asked you at the manor when we could stop, when we could have a home again."

"I remember."

"You can't imagine what I felt when Konrad was torturing you. I thought he'd killed you."

"I can imagine because I felt the same way."

"I realized as David and Laura were carrying us out of there in body bags that the only way we can ever stop fighting is if we help the Liberty Party win."

"Was that the same time that you decided to become an atheist?"

I cross my arms over my chest and look at the floor. "I don't know what I believe anymore."

"You know what I think? I think you don't want to believe in God anymore because you can't reconcile the horror of what we experienced with the existence of a greater good. You grew up in a bubble and now that bubble has burst."

"So what?" I say too loudly for the small space. "You're right, okay? Lying on Konrad's table...when I watched him torture you, it changed me. All I know is I can't believe the way I did before and protect the people I love. God wasn't there for us that day, Korwin."

"You're so angry with God, you never want to think about him again. You killed Brady to make the break permanent. You want to be so lost that God can't find you. And if he doesn't find you, he can't judge all the horrible things we've had to do to stay alive."

I shake my head. "You don't know everything."

"But I'm right about this. God didn't fail us, Lydia. He sent David and Laura. He saved us."

My heart softens slightly at his words—until I realize we are not saved. We've just lived to die another day. The Greens know where we are. They could attack at any time. "You know why I killed Brady? I killed him because I was sick of waiting for someone else to save me. I killed him because if I didn't, he would have killed both of us. And I killed him because I hated him. And you know what? I don't regret it."

He rubs his chin with two fingers.

I take a deep breath. "Can we talk about this later? I think the ceremony is about to start."

Blinking slowly, he says, "I don't mean to upset you." With a huff of breath, a violent shiver passes over him. "It wasn't just that you killed Brady, Lydia. It was that, at that moment, I saw it all melt away."

"Saw all what melt away?"

Korwin stands. "A house and a farm, a wife in long skirts, laughing children climbing a half-dead tree, the feel of wheat through my fingers, church on Sunday. I thought we'd get there. Even when I left, I thought somehow we'd get there."

I tangle my fingers in front of me and look at the floor. "I'm not the same person I was in Hemlock Hollow."

He crosses the chapel to me, gathering me in his arms and planting a kiss on my forehead. "Maybe not. But I love you, just as you are."

* * *

GOVERNANCE HALL IN THE REACTOR IS THE LARGEST room I've ever been in. The circular and towering white walls almost glow between the blue uniforms in rows and rows of tiered seats. The shape of the place means that everyone will be able to see Korwin and me as we progress up the ramp to the curved desk where the Grants, Laura, David, Charlie, and Jonas prepare at the head of the room.

With a few minutes before the ceremony, we wait in the shadows outside the entrance as blue uniforms pass me uttering congratulatory words. The soldiers scramble up the ramp to the stairs to find their seats amongst the crowd. Part of me is amazed at their sheer numbers. The Liberty Party is bigger and more organized than I'd expected, while another part of me bristles at the thought that the Greens are far better off. More men, more weapons. The only thing they don't have is Sparks. Those are all ours. For now.

"Excuse me." A man in blue steps between us and points one hand toward the ramp. "It's time to begin."

The music starts and we take our marks at the entrance to Governance Hall.

Korwin turns a nervous glance my way. "Here we go. No turning back now."

I bite my lip. At the urging of the man behind us, we begin progressing toward the table. When we get there, Jonas approaches us with a large leather tome in his hand.

"Place your right hands here and repeat after me."

I lower my fingers next to Korwin's on the leather cover and repeat the oath.

"I pledge this day
on my life and eternal soul
to uphold and protect
the ideals of the Liberty Party.
The freedom to live,
The right to liberty,
and autonomy to pursue fruitful aspirations
without undue burden of government.
I promise to serve the Liberty Party
and to advance its causes,
including obliteration of tyranny in all its forms,
reinstatement of democracy,
and promotion of justice
so help me God. Amen."

Jonas sets the Bible down and retrieves two silver pins from the table. He lifts the lapel of my blue jacket and affixes it. A circle of five silver stars shines against the blue, the same symbol that is on my armband. "In the tradition of nations past and rooted in the hope of a new tomorrow, I induct you into the Liberty Party with the symbol of five stars in a night sky."

He turns and pins Korwin. "The five stars represent the five true sovereign provinces. Their placement in the night sky, a new constellation, a revolution of mind and spirit."

With a firm grasp, he shakes Korwin's hand and then mine before turning us by the shoulders to face the crowd.

"Please join me in welcoming the two newest members of the Liberty Party, Korwin Stuart and Lydia Troyer."

Applause breaks out, and I face my future in the form of thousands of blue uniforms. Korwin's hand bumps into mine at my side, then folds around my fingers. He is right to think our future has melted away. Nothing will ever be like it was in Hemlock Hollow. We can't go back. There's only one way out of this inferno, and it's straight through the fire.

David told me once that Konrad and Pierce wanted to kill us when we were born. They were worried we'd be monsters. It wasn't our birth but our near-deaths that made us monstrous. As I face my future, side by side with Korwin, I can't wait to show both of them just how monstrous I can be.

* * *

Thank you for reading CHARGED. If you enjoyed this book, would you be so kind as to leave a review at your place of purchase? Reviews are the lifeblood of indie artists.

Please turn the page to enjoy an excerpt of Wired, book 3 in the Grounded Trilogy, Available Now .

WIRED (EXCERPT)

BOOK THREE IN THE GROUNDED TRILOGY

Trinity Pierce pushed her breakfast around her plate and smiled sweetly at her father. She hoped the happy act was convincing. It should be; she was an expert. If there was one thing she'd learned from living with the Red Dogs, it was how to fake a smile. Under the persona of Bella, she frequently feigned contentment among the pack, especially when the men in her life acted distressed. And at the moment, her father, Chancellor James Pierce, was clearly distressed. His upper lip curled and his bushy gray eyebrows plunged above his nose as he scrutinized her eating habits. Yep. Distressed. With a side of agitated.

"You've hardly touched your food," he said.

"Just not hungry this morning."

Her father's mouth twisted with disappointment. "You're too thin."

"The people who held me prisoner didn't feed me regularly. I don't think they had a lot of food." Straight-out lying was also something she learned from the Red Dogs. Actually, she ate well at the Kennel, as did everyone there, fresh food they killed or sometimes grew themselves. Even sewer rat tasted a hell of a lot better than this Crater City slop. She'd stayed thin in the Deadzone due to her workload, not the food.

"Thank goodness we saved you from those monsters. I shiver to think what you've been through these years."

"Thank goodness." She did her best not to sound sarcastic.

"I understand your condition is not your fault, but now that you're home, with a little effort, it should be easy enough to rectify the deficiency." He forked eggs into his clean-shaven maw.

"Deficiency?" Trinity was thin but not so much as to appear ill or weak. Her arms and legs still carried a healthy amount of muscle. The way her father talked it sounded like she was an embarrassment.

"You've been gone for some time. The current fashion is to carry a softer appearance. You don't want to look like a laborer." He chuckled. "The boys at the Ambassador's Club will think I'm abusing you. I'll make sure Cook knows you will require extra meals, and we'll send Esther out to get a padded shaper for under your dresses."

Trinity sighed over her uneaten breakfast. The dresses her father referred to were nothing like the ones she wore in the Deadzone. She didn't mind the extra material, but his choice of style made it clear he still thought she was a little girl. She was nineteen and had lived with the Red Dogs for two years, since the day she'd run away from home following her mother's death.

As rough as things could get with Sting, most of her time was spent doing as she pleased. She valued independence above all else. Now that she was found, or as the media called it—rescued, she had a schedule and social expectations, a chancellor father who was looking forward to introducing her to the Republic elite. Introductions that would occur at the Ambassador's Club, a swanky social destination for government leaders and their families. Just thinking about the sons of dignitaries sizing her up for marriage potential made her claustrophobic.

For the thousandth time, Trinity regretted the night she'd been found. She should have followed Lydia and Ace and taken her chances escaping through the sewer. Being eaten alive by rats would be a better fate than slowly suffocating within her father's tight grip. Not that she missed being owned by Sting. That part had always been an unfortunate side effect of her liberation. But in some ways it was more honest than this. Her relationship with her father was truthfully strained but outwardly affectionate. All about appearances.

"Eat, Trinity," her father said, clearly exasperated with her. The doorbell chimed. Trinity released a held breath as her father's scrutiny ebbed with the distraction of the bell and he turned his face toward the foyer. "Who in the name of the Republic?"

Trinity used the interruption to hide some of the rubbery eggs in her napkin.

"Esther!" her father boomed, calling for the housekeeper.

Esther emerged from one of the bedrooms, dusting cloth in hand. She was undoubtedly cleaning an already clean room. Trinity's father had an unnatural obsession with cleanliness and organization. Everything must be kept in its place. Everything and everyone. He could have answered the door himself or asked Trinity to do it. But he didn't. Instead he used the opportunity to reinforce Esther's lower rank and position. Trinity hated that about him. Undoubtedly, he thought about her in the same way. Daughter or not, she had her place too.

Esther waved her hands in the air. "I will get it, Mr. Pierce." She jogged down the main hall to answer the door.

"Good morning, Dr. Konrad." Esther cleared her throat. "Chancellor Pierce is not currently receiving guests. Can I give the chancellor a message for you? Or perhaps make an appointment for later in the week?"

Trinity wasn't sure whom Dr. Konrad was, but Esther was right to put him off. Her father hated to be disturbed during meals. In fact, he looked quite peeved at the arrival of this visitor as he returned to eating his eggs.

"He must see me," came a gruff voice. The shuffle of feet echoed from the foyer.

"Dr. Konrad, please!" Esther was a ninety-pound Asian woman with a dust rag. Not exactly high security.

The man charged into the room from the foyer, Esther trailing behind as if she could somehow retract him by force of will. So this was Dr. Konrad. He was stern, with a yellowing, sickly complexion. He didn't look like a doctor. He looked like a patient, one with an unsuccessful treatment. The last time Trinity saw someone as thin and yellow, they were smoking Slip, the addictive byproduct of artificial meat production. She'd met plenty of Deadzoners addicted to smoking the stuff. All of them yellow like Konrad. All of them with one foot in the grave.

"Konrad," Chancellor Pierce said by way of greeting. He dismissed Esther, his thick lips descending into a scowl. The skin around his eyes wrinkled in annoyance. "Is there a reason you are intruding on our family meal?"

"I need a military unit to apprehend the four criminals who terrorized my lab. The commander is telling me I have to get special permission from you."

"He's right. You do."

Konrad's eyes widened incredulously. "They forced me to inhale toxic gas. I only survived because I've worked with the chemical before and built up a tolerance. I'm sure you've been briefed on the attack and escape!"

"Yes. Lydia Lane and Korwin Stuart. I was briefed. Unfortunately, I was not briefed about their original capture. Nor was I informed of the purported torture you inflicted on them and others in that lab of yours."

Trinity's stomach kicked when she heard the name Lydia. It was an unusual name, and her mind went immediately to the Lydia and Ace who'd evaded the Green Republic raid on the Red Dog Kennel. They'd escaped into the sewer. Of course, none of the Red Dogs used their real names. Still, the coincidence unsettled her. She chewed a bit of toast to disguise her intrigue.

"About that," Konrad said. "I planned to inform you as soon as I dealt with the immediate threat."

"Don't be absurd. According to my sources, we spoke on the phone while Lydia and Korwin were in your detainment. Not only did you conveniently forget to tell me of their presence but you mobilized troops upon their escape without permission or funding."

"It is my right to do so as the director of military science and technology. They are byproducts of the Operation Source Code experiment and are absolutely lethal. They cannot be underestimated."

Pierce bared his teeth. "Yes. We learned that, didn't we, when we had to bury six of the men involved in the skirmish. Talk about a political black eye." He pointed a finger at Konrad's face. "You didn't follow procedure, Emile. Frankly, I'm concerned you are abusing your power and circumventing the system. You don't respect my authority."

"Of course I do, sir," Konrad said in an insincere and condescending tone. "I simply wish to avoid any embarrassment to you. By taking responsibility, I merely sought to insulate you from the brutal and dangerous realities of my position."

"Cut the bullshit, Konrad. I was fighting in the Great Rebellion while you were pushing a writing utensil at that university of yours. I've made my decision; your position has been temporarily revoked, and there will be an inquiry into your office."

"I received no notice of this!" Konrad said through thin, drawn lips. "You can't do this. I know where the fugitives are hiding. Now is the time to strike! You must authorize my use of force to hunt down and apprehend Lydia and Korwin."

Chancellor Pierce held up one finger. "First, I'm notifying you now. It's all the notice you deserve after the stunt you pulled. Second, if you know where the fugitives are, why didn't you mention it before now? It's been weeks since the incident."

"I was recovering," Konrad squeaked. "I wasn't strong enough."

"Well? Now that you are strong enough, where do you believe they are hiding?"

"The Outlands."

Her father scoffed. "We've had people stationed in Willow's Province for months. They would have detected any rebel activity in that sector."

"I didn't say Willow's Province. I said the Outlands."

Pierce chuckled. "If you're right, I hardly see the problem. The radiation levels in the area will kill them off eventually. They might already be dead."

Konrad's eyes shifted from side to side. "I have reason to

believe that Korwin's and Lydia's electrokenisis makes them immune to radiation."

"Reasons to believe... What reasons?" Pierce asked skeptically.

Konrad fidgeted and licked his lips. "The girl said as much. I don't think she was lying. Other members of the Liberty Party are helping her. David Snow and Laura Fawn are responsible for their escape. They're still alive, and I believe they've done something to counteract the radiation in the Outlands. They've been hiding there. The Liberty Party was behind the attempt to steal the specimens from Stuart Manor. I'm sure of it."

Pierce shook his head. "You are even sicker than you look. David Snow is dead. We found his remains in the explosion at CGEF. DNA evidence, Konrad. The poison you inhaled is playing tricks with your brain."

Konrad huffed. He held up one hand. "I am fully in control of my faculties. I can prove I'm right. Give me a small military contingent to investigate the area and I will show you David Snow is still alive."

One of Pierce's meaty fists landed on the table, rattling the dishes. Trinity sat up straighter, her stomach clenching at the violent outburst. "Am I speaking to myself?" Pierce asked. "What evidence do you have that could possibly be strong enough to induce me to put more human lives at risk to search an area where we already have flasher drones safely doing the exact same thing?"

Konrad thrust his hands into the pockets of his lab coat and shook his head. "The flashers are useless. They relay too much information. Every time the wind blows it sets them off. The analysts are weeks behind—"

Face red, Pierce pointed a finger at the doctor. "The evidence, Konrad."

"The girl told me as much when I interrogated her!"

"Did you drug her to tell the truth?"

"The drugs don't work on her composition."

"Obviously a lie then. She chose the one place we can't thoroughly search without injuring our troops. That was her intention. It was a poison pill, Emile. We both know there's nothing alive out there."

Trinity cleared her throat and put on her sweetest, most curious expression. "Excuse me, Daddy, do you have a picture of the girl, Lydia? The name is familiar to me."

Her father did a double take, his face softening. Reaching into his pocket, he retrieved his phone and tapped the screen. Holding it up, he showed her a security photo. "Have you heard of them, sweetheart?"

Trinity stared at the picture. It was Lydia and Ace, real name Korwin. Was it possible they'd escaped to the Outlands? Images of the sketchpad she'd seen Lydia holding in Ace's room came back to her. The drawing depicted strange clothing and surroundings. For a long time she'd suspected the two had known each other before the Kennel. Not to mention, she'd seen both of them exhibit electrokinetic powers, although she'd assumed they were simple scampers. Ace was Korwin. Lydia was Lydia. Her friends were the products of Dr. Konrad's experiment.

"I knew them," Trinity said.

Pierce adjusted himself in his chair. "What's that, honey?"

"I knew Korwin and Lydia. They lived in the Deadzone with me. They were Red Dogs. I didn't know their history at the time."

Konrad lurched forward and grabbed her by the shoulders. "How did they get there? Where are they now?"

"Unhand my daughter!" Pierce said, standing.

Konrad lowered his arms but held her within the grasp of his intense stare.

She looked him in the eye and lied like a pro. "Lydia's been a Red Dog forever, since she was a baby. She never lived in the Outlands as far as I know. She left for a while to be part of some political movement and came back with Korwin. They said something about the group they were part of being eliminated. They called the Red Dogs home after that."

Konrad's mouth dropped open. "You must be mistaken. It can't be the same girl. A different Lydia."

"No. That's the one," she said, pointing to the picture. "She could shoot lightning from her hands. Everybody got used to it after a while. She's probably returned there. The Deadzone was home for her."

Pierce grinned. "There you have it, Konrad. We will search the Deadzone."

"With all due respect, Officer Reynolds and his team have scoured the Deadzone for weeks. She's not there." Konrad pressed the tips of his bony fingers together. "My assistant pursued Lydia and Korwin after they escaped my lab. He was found dead just a few miles from the border of the Outlands. He was"—Konrad's eyes shifted to the side—"electrocuted. It had to be them."

"Your assistant?" Pierce raised his eyebrows. "What type of assistant attempts to apprehend dangerous fugitives on his own?"

Konrad took a step back. "One who is familiar with Operation Source Code."

Pierce rubbed the bridge of his nose. "I did not approve a special assistant for that purpose."

"Give me a few men. I'll prove I'm right."

Pierce groaned. "Listen to me carefully. If Lydia was

living in the Deadzone until recently as my daughter suggests, that means the Liberty Party is scattered."

"Not necessarily—"

"Shh." Pierce held up one finger. "The Green Republic has never been stronger. Aside from the escape, the Liberty Party hasn't presented an organized attack since the night we assassinated Maxwell. They're weak. Let the girl rot from radiation poisoning in the Outlands or go on with her life in the Deadzone. I don't care. She's nothing to us. The boy is less than nothing."

"She's everything!" Konrad ran his fingers through his hair, leaving it wild and uneven. "It's too dangerous to allow her to live. If the rebellion has hold of her blood, they can reproduce the serum to make more alphas. Or worse, with both her and the boy, they could make an army of gammas."

Trinity laughed. There was nothing funny about Konrad's red face or his temper. The laugh was meant to deceive. If she was right about Lydia, it was imperative that her father believe what she was about to say. "I am positive that Lydia said the rebel group she'd fought with had disbanded. That's why she came back home to the Deadzone." She shrugged. "It's over. We've won. Whatever Lydia and Korwin were doing when you arrested them, I'm sure it was just an effort to survive after their home in the Deadzone was raided. They weren't working for anyone."

"You're a liar," Konrad barked.

Her father's hand slapped Konrad's chest, pushing him toward the door. "You will not talk to my daughter in that tone. Go back to your hole, Konrad. I'll be in touch about the official inquiry into your conduct. Until then, you are suspended on forced medical leave and Operation Source Code is on permanent hiatus."

Esther held the door open and Pierce pushed Konrad through it.

"You're going to regret this, Pierce," Konrad yelled. "If you turn your back on this, they'll do to your daughter what they did to your wife."

Trinity gasped. It was a low blow. Her mother had died of a massive stroke at a Republic dinner. Due to the circumstances, there was speculation she may have been poisoned. She'd been campaigning for peace and a more democratic government, the exact opposite of the Republic's current position with her father at the helm. There was never any proof of assassination. It was gossip. Hurtful gossip after all this time.

There was a pause as if her father was registering what Konrad said. The door slammed. "Esther, do not let that man back into this house." Pierce stormed from the foyer, giving Trinity a small nod before heading for his bedroom.

Trinity smiled, authentically this time. Success. She wasn't sure what Lydia and Korwin were up to, but she hoped they were safe. With any luck, she'd just witnessed the end of Dr. Emile Konrad.

Continue reading Wired...

BOOKS BY G.P. CHING

The Soulkeepers Series

The Soulkeepers, Book 1

Weaving Destiny, Book 2

Return to Eden, Book 3

Soul Catcher, Book 4

Lost Eden, Book 5

The Last Soulkeeper, Book 6

The Grounded Trilogy

Grounded, Book 1

Charged, Book 2

Wired, Book 3

Soulkeepers Reborn

Wager's Price

Hope's Promise

Lucifer's Pride

ABOUT THE AUTHOR

G.P. Ching is a USA Today bestselling author of science fiction and fantasy novels for young adults and not-so-young adults. She bakes wicked cookies, is commonly believed to be raised by wolves, and thinks both the ocean and the North Woods hold magical healing powers. G.P.'s idea of the perfect day involves several cups of coffee and a heavy dose of nature. She splits her time between central Illinois and Hilton Head Island with her husband, two children, and a Brittany spaniel named Jack, who is always ready for the next adventure.

www.gpching.com
genevieve@gpching.com

Made in United States
Troutdale, OR
12/22/2024

27195721R00181